AL CAPONE AT THE BLANCHE HOTEL

LINDA BENNETT PENNELL

SOUL MATE PUBLISHING

New York

AI CAPONE AT THE BLANCHE HOTEL

LINDA BENNETT PENNELL

Cover Design by Fiona Jayde.

Grateful acknowledgement is made to Bill Danoff of Starland Vocal Band for permission to use excerpt from the copy-righted song "Gonna find my baby, gonna hold her tight..."

Published in the United States of America by
Soul Mate Publishing
P.O. Box 24
Macedon, New York, 14502

ISBN: 978-1-61935-315-2
eBook ISBN: 978-1-61935-255-1

www.SoulMatePublishing.com

With love and gratitude

to my husband John

and our wonderful sons

Jake and Frank.

Acknowledgements

Most writers do not get to the publication stage without a lot of help and I am certainly no exception. Educational opportunities offered by the Writers League of Texas in Austin, Inprint in Houston, and Rice University's Glasscock School have enriched my understanding of craft and creativity. Specifically, best-selling authors Karleen Koen and Suzy Spencer have been very supportive in their instruction and guidance. In addition, Greg Oaks of the University of Houston's Creative Writing School was instrumental in my writing journey. And last but certainly not least, I want to thank my most important and staunchest supporters from the bottom of my heart. Ronelda and Carol, my very dear critique partners, I couldn't have done this without you. You two kept me on the right path with your comments and suggestions.

Chapter 1

Saturday
June 14, 1930
O'Leno, Florida

Jack jammed a finger into each ear and swallowed hard. Any other time, he wouldn't even notice the stupid sound. The river always sorta slurped just before it pulled stuff underground.

His stomach heaved again. Maybe he shouldn't look either, but he couldn't tear his eyes away from the circling current. When the head slipped under the water, the toe end lifted up. Slowly the tarpaulin wrapped body, at least that's what it sure looked like, went completely vertical. It bobbed around a few times and finally gurgled its way down the sinkhole. Then everything went quiet . . . peaceful . . . crazily normal. Crickets sawed away again. An ole granddaddy bullfrog croaked his lonesomeness into the sultry midnight air.

Crouched in the shelter of a large palmetto clump, Jack's muscles quivered and sweat rolled into his eyes, but he remained stock-still. His heart hammered like he had just finished the fifty yard dash, but that was nothing to what Zeke was probably feeling. He was still just a little kid in lots of ways.

When creeping damp warmed the soles of Jack's bare feet, he grimaced and glanced sideways. Zeke looked back with eyes the size of saucers and mouthed the words *I'm sorry*. Jack shook his head then wrinkled his nose as the odor of ammonia and damp earth drifted up. He'd always heard that fear produced its own peculiar odor, but nobody ever said how close you had to be to actually smell it. He prayed you had to be real close; otherwise, he and Zeke were in big trouble.

The stranger standing on the riverbank stared out over the water for so long Jack wondered if the man thought the body might suddenly come flying up out of the sinkhole and float back upriver against the current. Funny, the things that popped into your head when you were scared witless.

The man removed a rag from his pocket and mopped his face. He paused, looked upstream, then turned and stared into the surrounding forest. As his gaze swept over their hiding place, Jack held his breath and prayed, but he could feel Zeke's chest rising and falling in ragged jerks so he slipped his hand onto Zeke's arm. Under the gentle pressure of Jack's fingers, Zeke's muscles trembled and jumped beneath his soft ebony skin. When Zeke licked his lips and parted them like he was about to yell out, Jack clapped a hand over the open mouth and wrapped his other arm around Zeke's upper body, pulling him close and holding him tight. Zeke's heart pounded against the bib of his overalls like it might jump clean out of his chest.

With one final look 'round at the river and forest, the stranger strode to the hand crank of a Model T. The engine caught momentarily, then spluttered and died. A stream of profanity split the quiet night. The crank handle jerked from its shaft and slammed back into place. More grinding and more swearing followed until the thing finally coughed to life for good and a car door slammed. Only then did Jack relax his hold on Zeke.

"I want outta here. I wanna go home," Zeke whispered hoarsely.

Lucky Zeke. Before Meg left home to move into town, Jack would have felt the same way. Now he didn't care if he ever went home.

Jack cocked an ear in the Ford's direction. "Hush so I can listen. I think he's gone, but we're gonna belly crawl in the opposite direction just to be sure we ain't seen."

"Through that briar patch? I ain't got on no shoes or shirt."

"Me neither. Come on. Don't be such a baby."

"I ain't no baby," Zeke hissed as he scrambled after Jack.

When the pine forest thinned out, Jack raised up on his knees for a look around. Without a word, Zeke jumped to his feet and started toward the road. Jack grabbed a strap on Zeke's overalls and snatched him back onto his bottom.

"You taken complete leave of your senses?" Wiping sweat out of his eyes, Jack pushed his shaggy blonde hair to one side. "Check it out before you go bustin' into the open."

"Why you so bossy all the time? I ain't stupid, ya know. Just cause you turned twelve don't make you all growed up."

Zeke's lower lip stuck out, trembling a little. Whether it was from fear or anger, Jack wasn't sure. Probably both. Peering into the night, he strained for the flash of headlights. Nothing but bright moonlight illuminated the road's deep white sand. Finally confident that no vehicles were abroad, he grabbed Zeke's hand and pulled him to his feet. With one final glance left, then right, they leapt onto the single lane track and ran like the devil was on their tails.

Chapter 2

August 15, 2011
Gainesville, Florida

Liz Reams glanced at the caller ID and grimaced. She didn't have time for this, but guilt wouldn't let her put the conversation off any longer. Sighing, she pressed the talk button and prepared to listen with forbearance and humility.

"Hello, Roberta. I'm so glad to hear your voice. I was beginning to think we were going to play phone tag forever." Internally, Liz squirmed. Her conscience yelled, *liar, you returned calls when you figured you'd get her voicemail.*

Roberta's reply made Liz cringe. While she endured the diatribe pouring through her cell phone, Liz eyed her purse, book bag, and laptop case huddled together on the sofa. She couldn't afford to be late today of all days. Her eyes narrowed as her gaze paused on her laptop. She had paid more than a month's rent for the thing, but as much as she loved its power and speed, it was also a constant reminder of her dereliction. It only compounded her guilt that everything Roberta said was true.

"I'm really, really sorry. I know I said you would have it by now, but I've been in the process of moving. You know what that's like."

Several expletives burned through Liz's earpiece and then there was ominous silence.

"Look, I know how lucky I am to have a career practically dropped into my lap. You've been wonderfully patient and I've let you down. I feel so bad. I promise, no later than

October . . ." Glancing at the calendar, Liz paused. "I mean November 1st. I just need to get the first couple months of teaching behind me, then I can focus on the novel."

An angry question barked through the ether.

Liz tried to keep her voice cheerful and her tone even. "Of course I'm still seeing Jonathan. You know he's the reason I moved to Florida. You'll have something by November 1st. I promise. I've really got to go."

The call ended with Roberta's appeal to conscience ringing in Liz's ears, leaving her feeling like an ungrateful, spoiled child. Poor Roberta. She deserved better. Several years ago while on semester break and bored out of her mind, Liz dashed off a few ideas and half a manuscript. On a whim, she sent Roberta, a friend of a friend, a query letter for a series of mystery novels and the sample chapters. She'd been amazed by the response. Roberta had been more than enthusiastic. She believed Liz could be the next Mary Higgins Clark. Liz was thrilled and flattered, but alas, her attention to her fiction had been stop-start at best. Now with the move to Florida, she had a terrible inkling her new situation wouldn't allow time to finish her long overdue first novel.

While her first allegiance had to be to her professional responsibilities, after one of Roberta's talks, Liz would be unsettled for days. She feared her editor might be right: that a lucrative career was hers for the taking, that academia paid squat, and that Liz would live to regret neglecting her fiction for dusty research libraries, unwashed college students, and writing articles for esoteric journals that nobody read. As to the new deadline, Liz snatched November 1st out of thin air, but crossing that bridge could wait. Giving herself a last once over in the living room mirror, she slammed her apartment door and dashed to her Prius for the twenty-minute trip to campus. This job was a fabulous last minute save and Liz had no intention of blowing it.

The security guard in the building's reception area checked his list and gave Liz a set of keys, two of fairly recent vintage, one battered and old fashioned. He then directed her to the third floor wing, which housed the University of Florida history department's administrative suite. According to Maria, the departmental secretary, Liz's office was finally cleared of the previous occupant's possessions. After winding through the old building's maze of hallways, she stood before a door that could have used a fresh coat of varnish. She considered the set of keys and selected the one that looked as old and tarnished as the door's heavy Yale lock. Inserting and turning it, she heard the click of the lock's tumblers. She flung the door wide and peered into the sanctum from which she would now conduct her professional life.

My lord, girl, what you're willing to do for love.

She took three steps, dropped her things on the desk's scarred top, and took inventory: two metal folding chairs, a worn faux leather desk chair, and a bookshelf that listed slightly to the left—a converted storage closet just like the departmental secretary had described it. At least the AC was top notch. After Seattle's mild summers, north Florida's swelter was a physical blow, one that took her breath away. Inhaled air felt positively liquid, making her wonder if drowning would feel any different. But Jonathan was worth all of it, decidedly worth the inconvenience, the climate, the life altering disruptions, the difficult career choices.

She glanced at the wall clock. *Damn. Five 'til nine.*

She hurried down the hall to an old-fashioned wood panel door with Conference Room stenciled in gold leaf on its frosted window. Hoping to slip in without drawing too much attention, she opened the door as quietly as possible and stepped inside. Her heart sank to the soles of her feet. She crossed the entire length of the room to the only remaining chair, her new colleagues' eyes following her progress to the last moment, including observing her tucking her skirt under her knees before descending onto the hard wooden seat. She could feel a red flush crawling up from her throat and over her jawline until the apples of her cheeks felt like two glowing coals.

Sheesh, girl. You'd think after orals, defending a dissertation, and teaching college juniors and seniors, you would be immune to stage fright.

"Good morning, Dr. Reams. Glad you could join us." Hugh Raymond, head of the department, smiled before continuing. "Everyone, this is our newest addition. She's taking the spot vacated when Dr. Hargreaves left us so unexpectedly. For those who haven't heard, Dr. Reams's specialization is American crime, but all of you will want to make her feel especially welcome. For this year, she's keeping you from having to take on sections of the odious freshman survey courses."

Dr. Raymond was a youngish forty something, made distinguished in appearance by a few strands of gray at the temples of an otherwise dark, wavy head of hair. His prodigious scholarship made him a rock star among his colleagues. Liz felt very fortunate to be working with him, but a little anxious as well. Although he was only twelve or so years older, from their first meeting he had unsettled her. The man was just so very intense.

After a few minutes of departmental housekeeping, Dr. Raymond stopped speaking and let his gaze drop to the table. When he looked up, his expression was deadly serious and Liz sensed her colleagues' attention becoming much more focused.

"I suspect you're wondering why this meeting couldn't wait until after student advisement has ended, but this news is best served fresh. As some of you already know, the university is looking for ways to economize, as are most brick and mortars. Welcome to the brave new world of online degrees."

An undercurrent of grim laughter and muttered sarcasm filled the room. He allowed it to subside before he continued. "Personal feelings aside, people, we are in a fight for funding and I, for one, do not intend to see our department shredded in the financial meat grinder. So, what does that mean?" He paused and let his eyes drift from face to face. "Each of us must find new ways to market studying history to technology obsessed undergraduates. We've got to create a wow factor for a subject that so many of them learned to hate in high school. I expect each of you to find a way to improve our appeal. No exceptions. No excuses. Got it?"

Amid groans and snorts, every head eventually nodded.

"Good. Now, go forth and be creative."

As chairs scraped back from the table, Liz exchanged greetings and shook hands, but her attention wasn't totally on the brief conversations. Her head swam with the long list of things she needed to do before classes started next week.

She was easing her way toward the door when she heard Dr. Raymond say, "Dr. Reams, could you come to my office for a minute? There's something I need to discuss with you."

Several heads swiveled in her direction. Liz felt the red creeping up from her throat again. She hated being an object of envy, pity, or curiosity and she sensed that all of those emotions were prompting the speculation in her colleagues' eyes. Liz's smile tightened as she glanced toward her boss and nodded. She couldn't imagine what he wanted to discuss. She hadn't been there long enough to commit some grievous error and they had pretty well covered all-important topics during the hiring process.

When she and Dr. Raymond were seated in his spacious corner office, he leaned back in his chair and folded his hands loosely over his midsection. To keep from squirming like a kid in the principal's office, Liz concentrated her attention on their surroundings—lovely large windows overlooking the quad, crown molding on the ceiling, framed photographs, diplomas, and awards on the wall space not covered by books. Liz's nose twitched at the slightly musty smell wafting from the bookcases. Scattered among ancient tomes, volumes with glossy dust jackets popped out by contrast. Several of them bore Dr. Raymond's name as author. Liz dragged her attention back to the desk and met his gaze. Smile lines crinkled the skin around his eyes.

"Are you ever called Liz?"

Trying to keep the surprise from her voice, she replied, "Actually, it's what my friends and family have called me all of my life."

"It suits you." Dr. Raymond propped his elbows on the chair arms and made a bridge of his fingertips. "Liz, I'm expecting big things from you. Your references are outstanding. The department head in Seattle sounded rather peeved when I told him I was offering you a job. Something about losing the best draw they ever had."

"He's a great guy, but occasionally given to hyperbole."

"I hope not because you were hired based on his recommendation." Dr. Raymond raised an eyebrow and waited for her reply.

The muscles at the base of Liz's skull tightened. He might be regretting hiring her for some reason she couldn't fathom, but that was ridiculous. She hadn't yet taught a class or served on a committee. "I'll do my best to exceed expectations."

"I'm sure you will. And speaking of expectations," he paused and eyed Liz with an inscrutable expression. His gaze shifted to the wall behind her for a moment before he continued, "I have what may seem a surprising proposal for someone who's just joined us, but what I said about being in a fight for funding was actually understated. We have no choice. We've got to increase our undergraduate enrollment." He leaned forward slightly. "Liz, I want you particularly to work on the problem of attracting more students to our department. Kids today aren't interested in studying history beyond their basic degree requirements. They expect to be entertained. They want a wow factor. Apparently the history of the world in which they live isn't glamorous enough for them. Come up with something exceptional and you won't be teaching survey courses next year. And most importantly, it'll put you on the fast track to tenure. Think you're up to the challenge?"

Stunned and feeling somewhat slow witted, Liz could only stammer, "How . . . how wonderful. Of course. I'm . . . thrilled at the opportunity."

"Good." Dr. Raymond let out a long breath and then smiled broadly. "Crime is an unusual area of interest for a young woman. What's your favorite period?"

"Prohibition. Gangsters, Tommy guns, bathtub gin, speakeasies, G-men, the whole lot. Someday, I hope to produce a monograph on the psychological relationship between Al Capone and Elliot Ness." *Damn.* In her desire to make a good impression, her tone had quickly become vehement, didactic even.

Dr. Raymond chuckled softly. "I'm sure plumbing those depths will prove fascinating."

"Yes, well . . . I . . . I think so." Her voice actually trembled at the thought that her new boss might be finding humor in the objects of her professional passion. Liz wanted to slide onto the floor and crawl away. She had to get off on the right foot with him and her new colleagues. Since cutting her ties in Seattle, she needed this job and she desperately wanted to prove herself in this academic version of the big leagues. Now, she also needed to justify the confidence Dr. Raymond placed in her despite the humor he found in her choice of research topics. Of course, not everyone shared her passion for the likes of Capone, Baby Face Nelson, and the other bad boys of history.

Dr. Raymond tilted his head to one side, making Liz feel like a bug pinned to a laboratory specimen board. "You know, some in the department had reservations about hiring someone so young and with such a narrow specialty, but I think you're going to work out very well. By the way, tell me again who published your dissertation?"

Liz stared at the diplomas on the wall behind him. Perhaps it was her new colleagues' doubts filtering through Dr. Raymond's demeanor that she had sensed at the beginning of their conversation. Whatever it was, it sent her into a spasm of schoolgirl awkwardness, which did nothing for her self-image. She hadn't felt this flummoxed in a long time.

As she forced her gaze to meet his, she was surprised to see a fleeting emotion disappear from his eyes. If she hadn't known better, she would have said it was interest of a more personal nature. That was a complication she really didn't . . .

Good grief! You're really on a roll, girl.

Her imagination was in overdrive. It seemed determined to dwell on the ridiculous. All of the conflicting emotions that had accompanied her quick decision to leave her well-organized, planned-out life in Seattle must be catching up with her. Snapping herself back to the topic at hand, Liz gave him the name of a small northwestern historical journal. While he wrote, she became aware that her fingers were dancing on the chair's armrests. She forced them into the more subdued activity of picking at an imaginary piece of lint on her skirt.

Dr. Raymond put his pen down and looked up. Whatever it was she had seen in his eyes a second ago was gone. "Well, I'm sure you have a lot to do. I know I do."

"Yes. Of course. I didn't mean to keep you."

Liz fled down the hall to the safety of her office. She wasn't sure whether she liked her new boss or not on a personal level, but he was the least of her worries at the moment. With the door closed, she plopped behind her rickety desk and blew out the breath she had been unconsciously holding. The words "overwhelmed" and "drowning" came to mind. She leaned her head to one side and stretched her neck muscles, then repeated the action in the other direction. The tension eased and exhilaration took its place.

Welcome to big time academia, Lizzie girl. All your dreams are about to come true, ready or not.

Swiveling her chair toward her only window, her mind drifted to the choices she had made during the last few years and all that she had recently taken on. With a shiny new Ph.D., teaching in a small liberal arts college in Seattle had been a perfect fit. Drawing back the shades of the past for eager students and pursuing research for publication were her passions. In truth, the publication of her dissertation, albeit in an obscure journal, had been more satisfying than publishing fiction could ever be. She was completely sure of that, yet a small worm of doubt kept her attached to the idea of a fiction career. If she failed to achieve all she hoped in academia, success in fiction would make a nice consolation prize.

Of course, her decision to take the Florida position now made her fallback plan a lot more difficult, if not impossible. Instead of a light teaching load, she would be lecturing in auditoriums filled with seas of faceless students numbering upwards of 300 per section. The grading alone would consume her body and soul. Unlike her tenured colleagues, she hadn't been assigned a teaching assistant, that modern equivalent of slave clothed as graduate student. On top of everything else, there was now the edict to be amazingly creative so that the department could attract kids who hated history. No doubt it was unattractive self-importance, but she now felt like the department's survival virtually rested on her shoulders. *Shit!* Al and Elliot, along with her fiction, would have to wait for another year, maybe longer.

And then there was Jonathan.

Liz wistfully followed a Monarch butterfly as it danced over the pink and white powder puffs of an elderly mimosa hovering just below her windowsill. How simple its life must be. Butterflies surely didn't have to deal with the expectations and opinions of others. She loved Jonathan deeply. That should be enough for her family and friends, but they had been less than supportive when she followed her Navy pilot across the continent, saying no woman in her right mind would make that kind of move without a ring on her finger.

Well, too late now.

Liz turned and began pounding away on her laptop replying to frantic students who were just discovering that their academic advisor had changed. Mid-stroke of the umpteenth reply, her cell rang.

"Hey, Baby, coming to Jax for the weekend?" The very sound of Jonathan's Texas twang made her heart sing.

"How I wish I could, but I'm already eyebrows deep in work. How about dinner here Saturday night and stay over until Sunday as consolation?"

"Great, but not possible. Got a command performance at the Officer's Club. Captain's hosting a dinner. I was really hoping you'd be here. The guys think you're a figment of my imagination."

"Ooh, I really wish I could. You know how I love you in those dress whites. How about next weekend? Things should be a little less crazy around here by then."

"No can do. Got duty. How about I drive over next Monday afternoon? I'm off duty 'til Tuesday noon."

"It's a date. Love you and can't wait to see you."

"Me, too. Gotta go. See ya soon."

Liz slammed her phone back into her purse. *Damn it*! She'd done it again. She used the *L* word. For his part, Jonathan implied that he loved her, led her to believe that he loved her, had whooped with joy over the University of Florida job offer, but he never actually said the blasted word. *Me too* was as close as he ever got.

Chapter 3

"Jack Blevins, where have you been? It's after midnight." Meg grabbed her little brother's arm and pulled him through her bedroom window. "If Daddy finds out, he'll skin you alive."

"Well, he ain't gonna lests you tell him." Jack hit the floor with a thump. "Man, I'm glad to be home."

Meg's eyebrows rose. "That's sure new. Mama says you stay gone as much as you can get away with these days."

"Yeah, I guess." Jack kicked at the edge of the rag rug beside his sister's bed. "If I'd known you was coming home, I'd of stayed around."

"Nice to know you haven't gone completely wild."

Jack grinned at Meg and winked. "Not yet, but you never know. It could happen any day now. At least that's what Mama says." As he picked a thorn out of his elbow, he became quietly thoughtful. His words turned halting when he spoke again. "Meg, you ain't gonna believe what me and Zeke seen at the sinkhole."

"And just what were y'all doing down there?" Meg asked as she pulled the window screen tight and fastened the hook that held it shut.

"We was night fishin', but that ain't the important part. We seen a body go in the river. It went right down the sinkhole."

Meg fixed her brother with a maternal glare. "Jack, your imagination is getting out of hand. One of these days, your tales are going to get you in trouble."

"I'm not making this up. We really seen it."

"What you saw was probably a big log."

"It was a body, I tell you. For real."

"And just how do you know it was a body?" Meg asked. Jack really needed to grow up and stop this kind of nonsense.

"It was shaped like a full grown man, a great big one. The water sucked at him, kinda slurped him underground. It was real creepy. Made me sick to my stomach."

"Well, now. Did this body have help or was it obliging and jump into the river on its own?"

"Don't make fun of me! We seen a man throw a body in the Santa Fe River down at the sinkhole. It was wrapped in a canvas sheet like they use at the tobacco warehouse and it was all tied up with rope."

Meg studied him for a moment, trying to decide if he was telling the truth. "If you could see that much, did you recognize the man who dumped the body?"

"Naw, couldn't see his face. He had on a topcoat with the collar turned up and a big ole Panama hat. He was a funny lookin' sight, I can tell you." Jack giggled softly.

Of course. Ever the jokester. Jack was leading up to a big belly laugh at her expense. "What else did you and Zeke see this mystery man do?"

"Cuss and have a hard time starting his car. If we hadn't been so scared, we'd of laughed our heads off." Jack grinned up at Meg with a gleam in his eye. "Zeke wet himself he was so scared."

"Jack Blevins, you should be ashamed. Zeke's a year younger than you and gets scared real easy. You shouldn't play tricks on him."

Jack stopped grinning and his face flamed. "I ain't lying. We seen it. It ain't a trick and I can prove it. I'll know that car if I see it again. Beat up kinda yellow Model T with both passenger side fenders missing. I even got part of the tag number. BZ25 something."

Jack's tall tales didn't usually run to such particular details. Meg looked directly into his eyes and her heart skipped a beat.

"We seen it! Why won't you believe me?" His voice was louder with each syllable.

Meg clapped a hand over her brother's mouth and hissed, "You're gonna wake up Mama and Daddy."

When Jack squirmed free, Meg placed a hand on each shoulder and forced him to look at her. "Does anyone else know where you went tonight? Any of the other boys?"

"Nope. Me and Zeke didn't tell nobody. We slipped out after the folks was in bed."

"Good. You have no idea what you may have stumbled onto." She paused for a moment and then her eyes narrowed. "Did you bring everything back home . . . your poles, tackle, and all?"

Jack paled under his deep summer tan. "Oh crap! We left the rods and reels at the river. When we heard the car comin', we shoved them under some bushes and hid. I thought it might be Daddy."

"Would anybody recognize the things as belonging to you?"

"No. Zeke brung 'em. They was new. His grandpa bought the rods and reels just last week, but they wasn't all that special. Man, Zeke's gonna get a whuppin' for sure and it's all my fault. I talked him into sneaking 'em and slipping out tonight."

Meg was quiet while she thought about what they should do. Kids in regular families would tell their fathers, but that was out of the question. She squeezed Jack's shoulders and said, "You've got to promise me that you won't talk about this to anyone. Do you hear me?"

Jack looked up with huge eyes and nodded. His voice trembled slightly as he replied, "You're scaring the peewaddin' outta me. Me and Zeke already decided not to talk about it. I only told you 'cause I can tell you anything."

Meg sighed and dropped down onto the bed, pulling Jack down beside her. She slid a protective arm around his boney twelve-year-old shoulders and spoke in a calmer, more soothing tone. "Jack, I think we need to be very careful. I'm not sure exactly what you saw tonight, but whatever it was, it can't be good. Talking about it could bring that man after you. Understand?"

Jack nodded. "I ain't gonna talk and I'll make sure Zeke keeps his mouth shut."

"Good." Meg moved away so that she could look directly at Jack. She hated what she was about to say. "Daddy doesn't want you playing with Zeke. You know what he says about the races mixing. It's really unfair, but you know how he gets when he's mad. He means it, Jack. For both your sakes, you boys have got to stop."

"But Zeke's my best friend."

"I know. I like Zeke and his grandfather, too." She ruffled her brother's shaggy straw colored hair and hunched her shoulders. "I don't know what this world is coming to. Mr. Taylor and Daddy used to be friends."

The pair sat quietly for a few seconds, then Meg gave Jack a little hug. "Tell you what. We'll say we want to walk home after church tomorrow. We'll get the rods and hide them in the hollow log behind the hog lot. You can get them back to Zeke later."

Jack slipped his arms around his sister's middle. "Thanks. You're the best."

Meg's irritation faded away as she returned his hug. Not many twelve-year-old boys would be so openly affectionate with their sisters. Despite the six-year difference in their ages, she and Jack were extremely close, loving each other all the more for being the children who survived. When Jack was a first grader, scarlet fever descended on the rural community's two-room school and he came down with it almost immediately. Meg sat by his bedside for days. He was small for his age and looked so frail, his face under its red rash almost as white as the pillowcase on which his feverish head rested. When he finally recovered enough to regain his senses, it was Meg who told him that Jimmy, their two-year-old brother, had been buried the day before. It was twelve-year-old Meg, not their parents, who reassured the heartbroken Jack that he hadn't killed the baby. If she ever had children of her own, she wasn't sure that she could love them any more than she did the knobby-kneed little beanpole who was squeezing her in half at that moment.

As Meg thought about Jack's story, icy fingers closed around her heart. The world was a dangerous place. People got killed all the time. All you had to do was read the newspaper or listen to the radio to know that evil men did whatever they wanted without any fear of being brought to justice. Meg pulled Jack closer and rested her chin against his blonde mop. If something happened to this little brother too, she wasn't sure she could bear it.

Chapter 4

"I read your dissertation, Liz. Well written. Excellent scholarship." Hugh Raymond stood in the open door of her converted closet, arms crossed, leaning against the doorframe.

Liz glanced up from her laptop, fingers poised over the keys. She had no idea how long he had been standing there, but by the way he casually filled the space, she guessed it might have been longer than made her comfortable.

"Thank you. I may be one of the few people who actually enjoyed the dissertation process."

Dr. Raymond laughed. "Good for you. I'm afraid I can't make that claim. The department head at Tampa Southern was known to appropriate doctoral candidates' research topics from time to time. I had a devil of a time keeping him away from mine."

"I've heard of professors like that, but thank goodness I've never worked with one." Liz paused, hoping her boss would take the hint. She didn't want to seem rude, but she really had her hands full at the moment. When he made no effort to move, she said, "Dr. Raymond, please excuse me, but I've got a senior here who absolutely must graduate in December and it's going to be tricky. I think the kid's about to have a coronary right here on-line."

"I didn't mean to keep you. My apologies. I just wondered if you'd settled in enough to start on that special project we discussed."

Liz mentally kicked herself. In less than a minute, she had offended the man who had given her a job and had managed to be caught with her scholarly pants down around her ankles. She smiled up at her boss with what she hoped was visible sincerity. "You absolutely owe me no apologies. I've considered several ideas, but nothing particularly thrilling. Do you have any recommendations?"

"Actually I do. Two upper level courses would make a nice addition to next year's catalogue. I'd like for you to think about an American crime overview course and one covering crime in Florida from 1492 forward. If they do well, we may add another course or two at some point. What do you think? Ready to lead the charge?"

Liz swallowed and smiled. "It's what I've always wanted. Thank you so much for the opportunity and your confidence."

Liz hoped her voice hadn't betrayed her trepidation. The possibility of teaching upper college courses of her own design was something she thought wouldn't be possible for years. Taking on so much after just starting a new position was a bit daunting. She needed to talk to Jonathan.

As soon as Dr. Raymond disappeared down the hall, she grabbed her phone and pressed the one key, Jonathan's speed dial number. She knew there was a small chance of getting him during the middle of the day, so she wasn't surprised when she had to leave a message. The remainder of the afternoon passed uneventfully and Liz went home to a salad and glass of wine. That was all she seemed to want much of the time. The heat and her heavier workload were taking a toll.

She carried her supper on a tray to the living room and plopped down on the sofa. Television was a poor substitute for companionship, but she turned it on anyway so the apartment wouldn't be so deadly quiet. When the ten o'clock news ended and Liz still hadn't heard from Jonathan, she went to bed, but she tossed and turned while the bedside clock's glowing numbers taunted her like a neon sign advertising her loneliness. At some point, sleep finally blotted out consciousness.

Deep into the night, her cell rang.

"Liz, sorry to wake you, but I wanted to talk to you before we ship out." Jonathan's west Texas twang shocked her out of a deep sleep.

"Ship out! But we've just gotten here. Where are they sending you?" She couldn't keep the dismay and disappointment from her voice.

"Can't tell you anything except that it's supposed to be a short deployment, just an exercise really. May be home by the end of September. At least that's the rumor."

"When do you leave?"

"In about an hour. Baby, I can't talk any longer. Got to report for a briefing in fifteen minutes. Don't be mad."

"How can I be mad at you? It's the Navy."

But she wasn't sure how much he heard. He was gone and she had no idea where or for how long. This was clearly one of the covert missions he flew fairly frequently, the ones that kept her jumpy and worried the entire time of the deployment, especially when he went weeks without communication. A single tear trickled down her cheek and onto the pillow. Maybe her parents were right. Maybe she had been crazy to follow Jonathan across the continent and into a life she had never dreamt she wanted.

They weren't even engaged for crying out loud.

She rolled onto her back and kicked at the sheet. The one truly impulsive act in her whole life and it was a doozy. She flopped onto her side and punched her pillow. If she kept this up, large chunks were going to be torn from her confidence and craters dug in her happiness.

Liz looked at the clock and groaned. In three hours the alarm would go off. Lying there worrying and feeling sorry for herself weren't going to help get tomorrow's mountain of work done. After another fifteen minutes of tossing and turning, she got up and shuffled to the bathroom where she gulped down a couple of Advils.

Two weeks later and still no word from Jonathan, Liz wandered among the stacks of the Yonge Library of Florida History. She pulled a volume, scanned the table of contents, and shoved it back in place. She was supposed to be selecting bibliography titles for the Florida crime course. Working nights and weekends usually kept her sane when Jonathan and his P3–Orion crew were spying and gathering electronic data on America's enemies, but these days nothing seemed to work.

Writing the general crime course syllabus would be time consuming, but wasn't new territory. The Florida course was another matter and the specificity of the subject was getting her down. Her dissertation focused on the 1920's and 30's and Liz itched to delve into the psychological relationship between Al Capone and Elliot Ness. She dreamed of writing a book with popular as well as scholarly appeal. Ole Scarface had fascinated her since a paper she had written during her Masters course work. But between organizing the new courses and her current teaching load, she couldn't even think about starting research for the Capone/Ness project. Bored with the bibliography search, she wandered over to the microfiche cabinet and scanned the index. The Florida Times Union, Jacksonville's main print news outlet, caught her eye. Maybe reading a primary source would rekindle her interest and give her a feel for the area. She selected the film for the years 1928-1930 at random and loaded it into the closest microfiche reader.

After an hour of reading, she pushed her chair back and rubbed her eyes. Early twentieth century north Florida had certainly been a hotbed of criminal activity, but she was becoming weary with local robberies and moonshine still busting. She was about to call it a night, when an accidental tap on the forward button sent the film flying. When it stopped, a small headline came into focus.

Mr. Alfonse Capone visits Lake City's Blanche Hotel

Liz was certainly acquainted with Al's affinity for the Sunshine State. He bought his Miami property not long before the Feds nailed him for income tax evasion, but she had given no thought to his possible connection with other Florida locations. She did a quick Internet search on her laptop. No articles or books popped up that even mentioned this aspect of the Chicago crime boss's life.

She returned to the microfiche and read the brief newspaper article dated Friday, August 29, 1930. It gave little more than his arrival/departure dates and the number in his party. It piqued her interest that the editor waited until several weeks after Al's departure to write the article. But the thing that she found down right puzzling was the length of Al's visit—twelve days in a place of which she was barely aware. Capone had been a man who loved both luxury and the limelight, and by 1930, he had become accustomed to both. He had owned a grand palace on Miami's exclusive Palm Island.

Liz doubted that a small town hotel would meet his standards, especially not for a period of nearly two weeks. She searched the paper for three months before and after his stay, but could find no other mention of Al Capone or of his movements within the state during the summer of 1930.

Intrigued, she refused to allow herself to become excited just yet. Finding heretofore unknown, reputation creating information on twentieth century figures was rare, even for experienced researchers. Some historians searched in vain all of their lives for such a find. Surely she couldn't be that lucky so soon. She ran a new search and turned up the name of the local Lake City newspaper, but absolutely no copies existed in the university collection, microfiche or otherwise. Finally, she looked up the town itself. After reading what little there was, her heart skipped a beat. Twelve days was an unbelievably long stay in a place like Lake City for a man like Al Capone.

Chapter 5

"Keep up, Jack. I don't want to miss dinner," Meg called over her shoulder.

"Your legs are longer than mine. I'm coming as fast as I can." But he increased his speed to match his sister's strides. Their parents had agreed to allow them to walk home from church only after Meg begged that she needed to relax before returning to the grind of working as a chambermaid and waitress at the hotel in town.

Despite the shade of a tunnel of live oaks, the day was hot and sultry. Meg dabbed at her face and neck with her handkerchief as they walked along the lane of deep white sand leading to the Santa Fe River and its sinkhole. At the end of the lane, she knelt and splashed water on her face.

The river looked like a ribbon of rich dark coffee, stained as it was with acid leached from the bald cypress trees lining its banks. On brilliant days like this, sun diamonds danced on its surface, giving the appearance of jewels laid out on black velvet. In its own dark way, Meg thought the river was beautiful.

Jack pointed toward the base of an ancient live oak. Bottom limbs dipped down, almost touching the earth, before they stretched out in supplication for all available sunlight. Jogging to the brush on the tree's riverside, he squatted down and then looked up at his sister with wide eyes.

"The rods ain't here."

"You sure this is where you left them? It was dark and y'all were scared. Let's look around before we get into a dither."

Jack dropped onto his hands and knees. He lifted low hanging branches and pushed back brush. Sweat rolled from his face and soaked his shirt. After circling the tree, he looked up at Meg with troubled eyes.

"Oh man, Zeke's grandpa's gonna kill him."

"Do you think Zeke might have come back and gotten them already?"

"Maybe, but I doubt it. Their church goes 'til late afternoon."

"Could they have fallen into the river?"

"Naw, the bushes would of held 'em tight. I think somebody stole 'em. They was brand new." A crooked grin replaced his frown. "If I'd of found brand new fishing stuff just laying on the ground, I'da taken 'em."

"Yes and that would have been wrong. I swear, Jack, sometimes I wonder where you get such notions."

Jack's gaze dropped and his voice cracked when he replied, "I was just kiddin'. I know that's stealin'."

"I'm glad to hear it." Meg put her hands on her hips and bit her lower lip. "We've got to get home. You know how Daddy gets when folks are late." What Meg didn't mention was the little worm of fear slithering around the dark corners of her mind.

As they walked beside the section of road bordered by a neighbor's pasture, Meg glanced over her shoulder at Jack trudging along behind. He hadn't said a word in quite a while and his gaze was glued to his feet. An old bull leaned against the pasture fence with his head between the wires, nipping at seed heads and eyeing them suspiciously. No doubt he anticipated the flash of a red bandana from his customary antagonist. Jack passed the pasture without a glance. He must be really worried, but certainly no more than Meg was. She looked at her wristwatch and increased her pace.

When they finally reached their own farm, they took the field path in order to avoid using the front door. After taking the back steps two at a time, they went straight to the dining room. The round oak table's hand crocheted doily and dime store candlesticks stood guard over an otherwise bare surface. Jack glanced up at Meg and rolled his eyes.

She shrugged as she ran a hand over his blonde mop. "Guess we'd better go apologize to Daddy. Let me do the talking."

Jack nodded, his expression one of relief. She would be able to escape to town this afternoon, but he was stuck here all the time.

They found their father in the parlor.

"Daddy, I'm sorry we're late. My heel got caught in deep sand and I twisted my ankle some. It slowed us down."

Mr. Blevins looked up from the Bible in his lap and frowned. "Must have slowed you more than a little to make you this late. Your mother's already cleared the table and put the food away."

"I'm really sorry, Daddy. It was my fault."

"Jack could have come on without you. You're not a child that needs tending. Don't expect your mother to set out dinner all over again just because y'all cain't get to the table on time." Mr. Blevins's down-turned mouth matched the grim crescents of his bushy eyebrows. "Maybe missing a meal will help you remember how to keep time. Now find something quiet to do."

Meg nudged her brother and jerked her head toward the kitchen. They found their mother drying the last of the dinner dishes.

Mrs. Blevins craned her neck and peered down the hall for a moment, then whispered, "Don't pay him no mind. I saved you children's plates. They're in the oven. Take 'em out to the back porch."

As she ate, Meg wondered for the thousandth time why her mother had married their father. An old photograph of Mama showed a beautiful girl with long sausage curls and huge eyes. Grandma said that Mama could have had any boy for three counties around, but she took Arnold Blevins. It had been a mystery then and remained such to all who knew them. Meg thought it must have had something to do with Daddy's piety. As a girl, Mama was convinced that she was destined to marry a missionary or a preacher. Daddy was as close as she got. Pondering her mother's example convinced Meg that piety was a poor predictor of marital bliss. She felt lucky that DeWitt, her fiancé, went to church with her, but he was far from being a Bible thumper like her father.

Thinking of DeWitt brought both joy and a touch of anxiety. Their recent argument about setting a wedding date played in her mind like a movie reel going round and round. The issue wasn't if they would marry, but when and it was the only flaw in their otherwise perfect happiness. Her heart told her to give in to DeWitt's pleas and marry him now, but her common sense said wait until things regained some balance. Last year's Wall Street crash had pushed the world completely off its axis.

Chapter 6

Liz unlocked her office door and then turned back to face the departmental secretary. “Maria, how far is Lake City?”

The secretary didn’t even pause in her work. She looked up at Liz from under slightly lifted brows and replied, “About forty-five miles north on 75.” Her gaze dropped immediately back to the handwritten script from which she was typing.

“Have you ever been there?”

“Where?” Maria muttered as her fingers flew over the keyboard.

“Lake City.”

“Nope.”

“Know anything about it?”

“Not much. It’s not very big. They have a Civil War Battle site somewhere. Osceola. Olustee. Something like that.” Maria’s voice had an impatient edge. “You might ask Dr. Raymond. I think he goes up for reenactments sometimes.”

“Oh . . . Okay. Thanks. Sorry to interrupt.”

Liz went into her office and plopped down behind her desk. She couldn’t say exactly why, but she found herself dreading talking to her boss without others present. He hadn’t done or said anything unprofessional and she certainly owed him a debt of gratitude for her job and his interest in her career.

Liz chided herself for feeling so cool toward her benefactor, but it didn’t change anything. She felt uncomfortable around Dr. Raymond. It was simply a fact. One that she was going to have to deal with and conceal. She opened her laptop to renew her efforts to find other Capone north-Florida connections, but when a half hour of Internet searches produced nothing, she gave in to frustration and reluctantly walked to the big office at the end of the hall.

Hugh Raymond's rich baritone responded to her knock. "Come."

She opened the door and paused. Dr. Raymond sat hunched over his desktop computer keyboard, his back to the door. She could read the screen from where she stood: *Spring Semester Courses: Instructor Assignments.*

"I can see you're busy. I'll come back later."

Dr. Raymond's head snapped around. "No, no, come on in." Wearing a big smile, he rose and came around to the other side of the desk. "Have a seat and tell me what I can do for you."

That was it. He was just a little too happy to stop what he was doing whenever she appeared, too accommodating, too ingratiating, almost smarmy. It set her teeth on edge. When they were settled side-by-side in matching leather armchairs, she got straight to the point.

"I've come across an unusual detail and thought you might know something about it."

Dr. Raymond's expression brightened even more, but instead of making him look like a colleague happy to be of assistance, he appeared pathetically interested. Liz was beginning to regret the impulse that brought her to his office.

When she failed to speak, he tilted his head slightly and raised his eyebrows. "And?"

"Do you have any idea why Al Capone and his cronies visited Lake City for almost two weeks in 1930?" Liz inwardly winced at her abruptness. She knew she sounded rude, but she couldn't seem to control herself. One minute the man made her feel like a sadistic child who wanted to pull the wings off of butterflies, and the next, he made her feel like a silly undergraduate seeking her professor's attention.

"Two weeks? Can't imagine. Didn't know he'd ever been there except to pass through." Dr. Raymond's expression became thoughtful. "Back then, Lake City was just a little hole in the road on the way to other places."

"So I've heard. I've probably read everything ever written about Capone, but this isn't mentioned in any of his biographies."

Dr. Raymond's eyes narrowed. "Why the interest at this particular time?"

"I was researching Florida and accidentally ran across an article. I found the info puzzling. Maybe it could lead to something new about him."

A speculative frown creased Dr. Raymond's forehead. "I see. How are the plans for the new courses coming?"

"Just fine. Making lots of progress." Liz again winced inwardly, this time at the fabrication.

Dr. Raymond's eyes brightened. "My goodness, you're certainly a fast worker, but that matches your reputation. When do you think you'll have something for me to see?"

Liz cast about for a reasonable date, one that she felt she could meet and that wouldn't put the lie to her outwardly cheery optimism. "Would after Thanksgiving work?"

"Sure. That'll give you the long weekend to polish your proposal." He stopped speaking and looked at her with concern. "But you probably have plans for Thanksgiving. I really don't need it until after semester break. Just keep me posted on your progress."

"I will. Thank you for being so understanding."

His lips twitched with a rueful smile. "You may be the only member of the department who thinks that."

When she didn't respond, his smile faded and let his direct gaze linger before asking, "Are you planning to pursue the Capone thing?"

"I'm really intrigued."

Dr. Raymond nodded. "I agree it's puzzling. Perhaps it's worth looking into when you have the time." His word stress made his meaning unmistakable, but he hurriedly added, "If you ever write an article, you might submit it to *The Florida Historical Quarterly*. Editor's an old fraternity brother. I'd put in a good word." He leaned forward and patted her hand.

Before she could stop herself, Liz snatched her hand away as though a glowing coal touched it. Her boss looked startled and sat back. It appeared he was only now aware of the contact. His mouth lifted slightly into a tight smile.

Heat rose from Liz's throat until her face felt fiery red. "Thank you. I'm sure your support will be most valuable."

Dr. Raymond's smile faded and his gaze drifted toward the door. Rising quickly from her chair, Liz angrily thought, *Geez, girl, could you sound anymore stiff or awkward?*

She left the office with as much dignity as she could muster. She had always gotten on well with classmates and colleagues of both genders, so she couldn't understand why she reacted the way she did to the esteemed Dr. Raymond.

For the next month, Liz dealt with the logistics of settling into her new life and the loneliness of Jonathan's absence. She had office hours on Monday and Friday mornings and she taught classes Tuesdays through Thursdays. That left Friday afternoons for designing the new courses, but only the barest outlines existed. As she predicted, her student load and the grading were sucking up most of her free time not involved with eating or sleeping. It was all fine during the daytime, but her weekend nights were depressingly lonely.

Those nights when she couldn't abide reading another student essay, she wandered over to the Yonge and searched available sources for any mention of Lake City in reference to its infamous visitor, but found nothing. When Jonathan failed to return to Naval Air Station (NAS) Jacksonville as promised, she decided to distract herself with a short jaunt up I-75. She deserved to do something for herself to make up for being left alone for so long. If she couldn't have Jonathan, at least she might have Ole Scarface, her favorite bad boy.

The last Friday in September found her crawling north in rain so heavy that other drivers pulled onto the shoulder to wait it out. When a big rig's wake nearly washed her off the road, Liz's hands shook jerkily on the steering wheel. She thought about pulling off too, but she was already behind schedule. The US 90 exit appeared before she realized it was near and she swerved hard right, bumping over those little reflective guide markers that the DOT puts out to alert inattentive or sleeping drivers. They did the trick. Her heart pounded a mile a minute as she pulled up to the red light and then turned onto the four lane surface road. Ten minutes later, she pulled into a metered parking space. The rain had stopped as suddenly as it started. She climbed out of the car and looked around.

Downtown Lake City, like many of its contemporaries across small town America, was anchored by an old fashioned square with manicured lawn, trees, and flowers. Watery sunshine reflected off the gleaming white gingerbread of a Victorian bandstand in its center and commercial buildings of varying ages surrounded it on three sides. The county court house complex dominated the fourth side of the square. Across the side street from the courthouse was a building with United States Post Office inscribed on the pediment above its stone columns. When she looked down that side street, sunlight flashed dazzlingly off a small lake bordered by vintage homes. It was a peaceful, pretty place with a real hometown feel.

Liz turned to the newspaper storefront and entered the reception area, glad to be greeted by a blast of chilled air.

The woman sitting behind the reception desk glanced up from behind her computer monitor.

"May I help you, Miss?"

"I have an appointment with your editor. I spoke with him last week."

"Oh dear, he has a habit of not putting things like that on his calendar, then he forgets to tell me to do it. He's gone to Tallahassee and won't be back until Monday. Maybe I can help you?"

The pretty little town was losing some of its luster.

"Perhaps. I'm hoping to search your archives for 1930. I teach in Gainesville and the university's microfiche collection doesn't have any copies of your paper. Would it be possible for me to look through what you have?"

"If you wanted something after 1990, it wouldn't be a problem. All of that's digital. Unfortunately, the warehouse where the old paper copies were kept burned down last year, so whatever the museum has is all that's left."

Liz mentally sighed. "I'm so sorry to hear that. It must have been quite a loss. Can you direct me to the museum?"

Research was never intended to be easy, but she hoped that she wasn't on a wild goose chase. She hated wasting time. Still, she wouldn't know whether she was onto something worthwhile until she dug a little deeper. Having now seen the town and surrounding countryside, she was even more perplexed by Capone's stay.

Liz reached the home of the local historical society before the car had a chance to cool off. Pulling up to the curb in front of the lovely restored Victorian, she grabbed her keys and dashed to the door. Renewed rain splashed on the sidewalk and dripped from the Spanish moss hanging from every branch of the massive live oaks surrounding the house.

"Dear, we aren't giving tours today, but if you'll come back Sunday, we'll be having a wonderful presentation on historic farming methods." The woman behind the reception desk looked like the grandmother every kid dreamed of.

After Liz explained what she needed, the carefully coifed head of snow-white hair moved in the negative. "I'm sorry, but we just didn't have room for all of the old newspapers that people pulled out of their attics and barns. You just can't imagine how much came in when we put out the call for historic items. I think that the most intact documents were given to the library out at the junior college. You might check there."

A few more questions, more directions, and another run through the rain found Liz back in the car mopping ineffectually at the moisture clinging to her face and hair. A glance in the visor mirror showed her a woman who looked younger than her thirty years due to a mass of wildly curling auburn hair and huge blue eyes. She had a love-hate relationship with her crowning glory, which did only what it wanted no matter how much she paid stylists or how many miracle products she bought. During the dissertation marathon, she gave up and let it grow until it fell below her shoulders in a tumble of red spirals that she then pulled back with a large clip. She got tired of other women telling her how lucky she was to never have to do more than wash and wear. They had options of which she could only dream.

Options. That was what she had now. Return to Gainesville empty handed, admit defeat, and confine her efforts to the new courses or continue on with Scarface and the Blanche, as the perfect grandmother had called the hotel.

She slapped the wheel with her palm. She had come this far. What were a few more miles?

At the far edge of town, she turned in at the local community college's main driveway and followed it through an avenue of towering pines until she found the library and a parking spot. She glanced at her watch. It was a quarter 'til six on Friday afternoon and the library closed at 8:00.

Sidestepping puddles on the pavement leading to the building's entrance, Liz was determined to accomplish what she could that evening and to make the same trip the next morning, if needed.

Mechanically chilled air enveloped her as she passed through the front door sending a shiver down her spine, damp again from the intermittent drizzle. Giving herself a little shake, she approached the reference desk. Another round of explanations was followed by, "Ma'am, do you have inter-university privileges? Nobody gets into the rare documents collection without it."

"I'm not sure. I'm a professor at the University of Florida. Does that count?"

"Sorry. You'll have to get that set up through your library in Gainesville. Once you're entered into the system, they'll give you a picture ID."

Great. Just fantastic. Perfect ending to a completely unproductive afternoon. She hadn't been in Florida long enough to know that she needed a lousy inter-university ID.

Chapter 7

Meg's brow furrowed. "What do you think?"

Her fiancé, Sheriff's Deputy DeWitt Williams, sucked on his lower lip for a moment before answering, "That Jack better not be making up tales and that I'll tan his hide if he is."

"I really think he saw or thinks he saw what he said. He seemed really shaken up."

"Then you were right to tell me." DeWitt became thoughtful. "Whatever the boys saw, the man didn't seem to want any witnesses. Do you think they'll tell anybody else?"

Meg thought about her answer as DeWitt's ancient truck rattled over the rutted county road. They were headed north toward Lake City. Ferrying Meg between farm and town allowed them an uninterrupted hour together.

"Jack's scared enough not to talk about it, but I didn't get a chance to see Zeke. Daddy tries to keep those two apart."

"Do you think Zeke'll talk?"

"Probably, unless Jack gets to see him soon. Zeke's eleven. What boy that age could keep such a secret?" Meg's voice quivered.

DeWitt kept his eyes on the road as he lifted Meg's hand to his lips and pulled her closer. "Don't worry, Sweetheart. I'll find an excuse to get out to the Taylor farm and warn Zeke."

"That's why I love you. You're one of the good guys."

DeWitt cocked his head and gave Meg a sidelong glance. "Tell your old man that every chance you get. Maybe he'll start to believe you."

"Oh, don't mind Daddy. Now that I'm earning my own money, I don't need his permission about who I see or who I marry."

"And speaking of that, when we get married, you're going to quit that damned job. I hate you cleaning up after strangers and waiting on them like you're some kind of servant."

"Yeah, but think about all the lovely money I'm saving. And where else am I going to find a job? They aren't exactly falling off trees, in case you haven't noticed."

"I know, but when you're my wife, you aren't going to work for somebody else. Let's go ahead and set the date, Baby. Please. I can't take much more of this waiting."

"You know the goal. When we've saved enough for a place of our own, then we'll set the date."

"Lord, save me from a practical minded woman."

"I'll be the making of you and you know it. Even your mother says so."

"And she'd be right. Well, we're here." DeWitt pulled up next to the curb and put it in neutral. "When's your next day off?"

"Half-day Wednesday."

"So soon?"

"Yeah, I have to work next weekend. Take me for a picnic at Ichetucknee?"

DeWitt nodded and put his arms around her, but Meg drew back. "What if I get reported?"

"I don't care who's watching. The old biddy on the second floor can just run to the manager again. Maybe it'll get you to set a date."

Meg couldn't help but smile. DeWitt wasn't always as practical as she would have liked, but he had far more important traits, the greatest being the depth of his love for her. For her part, Meg could have stayed in his arms forever. She prayed that in the not too distant future, they wouldn't have to settle for quick kisses and hurried embraces. She wasn't sure how much longer she could resist his pleas. The one thing she didn't want, however, was a life like those she saw all around her. No money, no future—only a hand-to-mouth existence. She lingered in his embrace for a moment more then pulled back gently.

"I've really got to go or I'll be docked for the whole hour. See you at breakfast?"

"Wouldn't miss it. It gives me a chance to see what you look like in the morning. My daddy always said that was when you get to see the real woman." DeWitt winked and grinned.

Meg laughed and hugged him one more time, then stepped onto the sidewalk. At the hotel's entrance, she turned back for one final glimpse of his handsome profile. While she watched the truck disappear around a corner, the hotel's double doors opened behind her and male voices floated her way.

The men advancing toward her clearly weren't locals. Nobody from the South talked like that. Curious, she glanced as they passed, taking in their expensive, loudly stripped suits. Had she not heard their voices first, their clothes alone would have marked them as travelers. One of the four turned and tipped his hat. Meg would have nodded in acknowledgement, but the face that looked into hers was one that she felt sure she recognized. She stared, frozen at the sight of three scars, often described in the press, running across the man's left cheek and jawline from ear to chin.

Chapter 8

"Maria told me you made a foray north. Find anything worthwhile?"

Dr. Raymond had done it again. He appeared in her doorway without making a sound. Liz decided he had feline genes somewhere in the ancestral woodpile. She plastered a smile on her face and looked up from her laptop.

"Not yet. When my inter-university privileges are established, I'll go back to the junior college. That's the only place that has any archives for the local newspaper."

"How long did they say your ID would take?"

"They're pretty backed up right now. Could be as long as a month."

"I'll make a call. You'll have it sooner than that."

"Thank you. You've really made my transition here easy."

"It's my pleasure." An expression of discomfort entered his eyes before he continued. "Liz, I don't want to press too hard, but I hope your Capone research isn't distracting you from the course proposals. I really will have to have them by day one next semester."

"They'll be ready. I promise. And thank you again for your confidence and the opportunity."

Liz sat with her hands poised over her keyboard hoping he would take the hint. She needed to get ahead in her workload before she left today because she had finally heard from Jonathan. He was due back in Jacksonville on Thursday and they planned to spend the weekend at the beach. She'd found a charming little cottage rental and she couldn't wait to wake up beside him to the sound of the Atlantic kissing the sands.

"You're more than welcome." Hugh shuffled his feet as though about to walk away and then stopped. "Are you free for dinner?"

Liz mentally sighed. Here it was, the question she had sensed might come. She hesitated for a heartbeat. Perhaps this was just a collegial offer without personal strings or expectations.

"Nothing on the calendar."

"Good. How about a working meal? I'd like to discuss the Florida crime course."

"That would be great." Her enthusiasm was genuine. She wanted his input and guidance in that area since it was completely new territory for her. She just hoped her voice didn't betray a note of relief, as well.

"Ever been to Cross Creek?"

Liz shook her head. "Isn't that the place where Marjorie Rawlings wrote *The Yearling*?"

"That's the one. It's not far, but it feels like a different world. The drive's pretty and it'll give you a feel for the real Florida, the one I grew up in, before Disney and tourists invaded the hinterland. There's a good restaurant down there. How about we leave from here around 6:00?"

When Liz agreed, Dr. Raymond smiled and turned back toward his office. Deep in thought, Liz stared at the empty space where he had stood the moment before. He made it sound as though Liz seeing Florida through his eyes was personally important to him. She felt uncomfortable, but why she couldn't really say. He hadn't done anything but be nice to her. Irritated with herself, she shook her head and turned back to her keyboard. She was just being hypersensitive. In fact, sensitivity seemed to be the order of the day right now and Liz was beginning to dislike what she viewed as a new, unattractive trait in herself. If she felt more secure in her relationship with Jonathan, perhaps she wouldn't be reading so much into her boss's kindness and offers of help. But then, her boss did seem unusually attentive.

Oh, Lord! She was becoming the type of woman she'd always dismissed as egotistical, vacuous, and silly. In the past, she made fun of girls who focused solely on their relationships with men, the ones who read something sexual into every encounter no matter how minor. Now, she found herself doing just that. Man, her radar must be seriously out of whack.

The forty-minute trip to Cross Creek began on a lesser state road leading south out of Gainesville. Once the city was behind them, Dr. Raymond steered his elderly Land Rover through lush wetlands where tall cypresses stood knee deep in waving grass and past placid lakes where long legged herons waded among lily pads. When he turned onto a two lane county road, they seemed to step back in time. The land looked as though it hadn't known human presence since Ponce de Leon searched for the Fountain of Youth. Nothing but Spanish moss, pines, oaks, and palmettos stretched as far as the eye could see. The farther they went into the nature conservation area, the more civilization ebbed until they entered a tunnel of ancient moss draped live oaks.

Within minutes of emerging from the dimness of the trees, an old farmhouse appeared. It was surrounded by a rickety mostly white picket fence that enclosed a front yard made up of emerald grass interspersed with patches of startlingly white sand. The sun reflected dully off the metal gable roof that covered a screened in the front porch running the entire width of the house. The structure's raised foundation was partially concealed behind masses of azaleas. Huge live oaks completed the picture, casting deep shade over both yard and house. Liz felt the SUV slow and she wondered if Dr. Raymond was going to turn in at the mailbox. Looking at the house, she knew this couldn't possibly be the restaurant.

"This was my grandparents' farm. There's a lake behind the house where my grandfather taught me to swim and fish. My sister and I inherited it when our folks died. Carlene lives in Miami, so she only gets up here for holidays and maybe a week in the summer, but I come every chance I get. It's my little piece of heaven."

Liz caught the sparkle of late afternoon sun on water. "It's lovely. How wonderful that your family home's been preserved. You're lucky to have it, Dr. Raymond."

"I know. And it's Hugh."

"I beg your pardon?"

"Hugh, my name. It's what my friends call me." He wiggled his eyebrows and grinned.

Liz nodded and then turned to look out the passenger window as the Rover picked up speed again. She felt embarrassed and confused. In any other situation, she would have moved into an easy first name relationship with all of her colleagues, including her boss, without so much as batting an eye.

When they reached Cross Creek, they drove two short blocks and their destination appeared. The ramshackle building squatted beside a clear aqua tinted creek from which the town took its name. The restaurant's Cracker architectural style, complemented by a blinking neon sign and oyster shell parking area, guaranteed patrons an old Florida dining experience. A simple painted plywood sign standing beside the front door announced home cooking prepared with local produce and Gulf seafood.

Over fried shrimp and hushpuppies, Hugh outlined his thoughts on the new crime courses, but Liz didn't have the courage to admit how little work she had done on the proposals. Eventually the conversation turned to more mundane topics with Hugh dropping a few personal details along the way. His divorce was final a year ago this month. His ex had gone from signing the divorce decree in her attorney's office straight to a justice of the peace where she married her lover.

"I should have seen it coming, but I was too much in love to see that she was drifting away. Too many hours spent at conferences, doing research, writing, you name it. I was happy, so I assumed she was. Well, you know the old saw about the word assume." When Liz looked puzzled, he chuckled and said ruefully, "It makes an *ass* out of *u* and *me*? I know, I know. It's terrible, but it's also true."

Liz didn't want to encourage more confidences, so she simply replied, "I'm so sorry."

"Yes, well, they say that time heals. I'm sure it will eventually." Hugh stopped speaking and flushed as he looked into Liz's eyes. "I'm the one who's sorry. I ask you to supper to discuss professional matters and I end up embarrassing us both by pouring my heart out. I apologize. It won't happen again."

On the return trip to Gainesville, Hugh seemed lost in thought, which suited Liz's mood. His revelations had depressed her, but she couldn't put her finger on the exact reason. They hadn't known one another long enough for her to be so invested in his personal life. Then it occurred to her. The story hit a little too close to home. As she watched the last rays of sunlight fade from the lakes and forests, painful scenes with a former fiancé replayed on a continuous loop.

Angry words accusing her of caring more about dusty tomes and dead people than her lover echoed. Her dissertation chase had propelled the man she adored straight into the arms of another girl, one less career driven and far too available. The night she walked in on them in her bed, the one she shared with her fiancé, her heart shattered. That night, the only man she had ever wanted to spend a lifetime with dumped her for another woman because that other woman put his desires ahead of everything else. In their final argument, he had made it abundantly clear just how well the new girl met his needs and how short Liz had fallen in that area, both emotionally and physically.

After the door slammed on his retreating form for the last time, Liz's world tilted crazily off its axis. She knew she would never be the same. The experience changed the way she perceived herself. Her confidence to determine her own fate felt altered forever. Shaken to her core, Liz spent months in melancholy introspection. At the end of a year, she accepted that she bore the responsibility for the failure of the most important relationship in her life. Work was the one sure thing that remained and she threw herself into it with even greater fervor. It kept her sane. In time, she met Jonathan and the world righted itself once again. She never admitted it to others, but she sometimes feared her failed engagement was the primary motivation for abandoning common sense and following Jonathan across the country. However true that might be, Jonathan filled a chasm in her life and glued together the pieces of her broken heart. She was determined to prevent history from repeating itself.

The silence must have been weighing on Hugh because he suddenly turned on the radio without comment or request for Liz's preference. It didn't matter. She was relieved to simply listen. The university NPR station's classical music pushed the past back where it belonged and she hummed along with familiar passages of Borodin's *Polovstian Dances*. She smiled as she wondered how many people knew this piece was the origin of the Broadway song *Stranger in Paradise* from *Kismet*. Jonathan, rather unusually, was a fan of musical theater and sometimes sang the song to her. She leaned back against the headrest and let the beautiful melodies and alternating pounding rhythms wash over her until Hugh pulled up behind her car. She thanked him for dinner and made a quick exit.

She was half way into her driver's seat when he leaned out of his window and called, "Liz, wait. I almost forgot. The library sent your inter-university ID after I called them this afternoon. I meant to give it to you at the restaurant, but I guess someone distracted me."

Someone distracted me? What an odd thing to say. Feeling perplexed, Liz watched until Hugh's taillights disappeared in her rearview mirror. Was he implying that she had been the distraction or was it merely a slip of the tongue? Lord, she was doing it again. Seeing sexual innuendo where there was only collegiality. She put her car in reverse and surprised herself by squealing tires as she accelerated toward the street.

Chapter 9

"Hey, little girl, you still going around with that semi-Seminole?"

Hotel manager Albert Menzies's pink face grinned at Meg from behind the reception desk when she glanced up from the employee time sheet. Her eyes narrowed with the downturn of her mouth. *It's a good thing you can take as good as you give*, she thought, *otherwise I might punch you in the nose*. At his look of dismay, she relented and returned his smile. Albert was really just a clown who loved teasing everyone, especially pretty girls, most especially Meg regarding DeWitt's five-eighths Seminole heritage.

"If by that remark you mean Deputy Williams, I am. He's tall, dark, and handsome, and he's also a gentleman. Unlike present company, I might add."

"Ouch! That hurts. It really does." Albert placed his hand over his heart and adjusted his features to those of an orphaned puppy. "So I guess this means I don't stand a chance?"

Meg's eyebrows arched upward as she cocked her head to one side. "I think your wife, five children, and seven grandchildren might have something to say about that, don't you?"

"Well, if you're going to be like that, just go ahead and marry that ole boy. See if I care."

"I intend to marry when and whom I wish, with or without your approval." Meg's pursed lips twitched upward into a wry grin. Albert's feigned umbrage would have rivaled that of W. C. Fields. People often remarked that the hotel manager and the Hollywood funny man bore more than a passing resemblance, which only fed Albert's already bloated comedic streak.

Not wanting to encourage him in further ridiculous conversation, she stepped away from the desk, but then paused and turned back. "Albert, who were those men who just left the hotel?"

"Recognized him, did you? I figure most people will eventually realize that our Mr. George Phillips is known by a much more famous, or should I say infamous, name. Didn't fool me for a minute."

"What's he doing here?"

"Renting rooms. That's what most people do in hotels."

"Albert! You know what I mean."

"Not a clue. Didn't confide his business to me and I didn't ask. And if you know what's good for you, you won't ask either, young lady. And it would be best all round if you didn't talk about this either. No need attracting gawkers. Don't imagine he'd take kindly to that."

"How long is he staying?"

"Checked in on Friday after you left for the weekend. Didn't deem it necessary to share his travel plans with the likes of me." Albert's tone became managerial. "Don't you have work to do?"

Meg's mouth became a thin line of exasperation. It was Albert, after all, who had detained her with his silly conversation in the first place. As she turned toward the back hall, she wondered what they should expect from their infamous guest and his henchmen. Regardless of how long they stayed or what they did while in town, Meg decided it surely wouldn't have much of an effect on a nobody like her. She doubted they would even notice her existence.

Hearing the cook yelling in the restaurant kitchen about not having enough hands to cook the food and serve it too, Meg scurried down the hall to a dark little cubbyhole beside the delivery entrance. Taking a uniform dress, apron, and cap from her locker, she changed out of her street clothes. Meg rarely thought about whether she enjoyed her duties as waitress and chambermaid because she didn't believe in wasting time or energy, but she did sometimes find a little excitement in the restaurant. As she moved among the tables overhearing bits of customers' conversations, it gave her a peek at a life she could only imagine—travel, stylish clothes, luxuries, being from somewhere—anywhere—other than a backwater on the edge of the Okefenokee Swamp.

When she entered the restaurant, many of the tables were already filled. Laughter and conversation rose to the twenty-foot ceiling where it was tossed about by slowly turning fans and then ricocheted off the wide plank cypress floors, finally exiting through tall open windows. She noted local faces mixed in equal parts with those of travelers, but not the ones who had so intrigued her only a short time ago. Darting from table to table taking orders and carrying heavy trays pushed infamous strangers from her thoughts until the dinner rush ended. Just before closing time, a party of four strode in from the lobby and stood surveying the almost empty room. Albert followed close on their heels.

"Please allow me to show you to our best table." Albert indicated the center of the room with a sweep of his hand.

Mr. Phillips looked at one of his henchmen and shook his head. The second-in-command leaned over to Albert, who flushed and then led the men to a dark corner where a table was partially hidden in an alcove behind potted palms. Meg sighed. This was her table, which meant she wouldn't be getting off work at the usual time after all. When the quartet had been seated for a few minutes, she went over with her order pad in hand.

"Good evening. Welcome to the Blanche. What may I get for you gentlemen tonight?"

None of them looked up from the menus. She waited, shifting from one foot to the other. "Perhaps you need a few more minutes. If you have any questions or would like a recommendation, I'll be happy to help."

The second-in-command finally looked up and said, "What do people drink in this God forsaken hole?"

Though Meg might agree with the man, his description of her hometown rankled. She tamped down her irritation and faked a smile. "Most people order iced tea."

"Got any soda pop?"

"We've got Co'Cola, root beer, and ginger ale. Can I bring y'all any of those?"

"Yeah, bring four ginger ales in tall glasses with extra ice."

When the drinks were on their table, Meg was finally given the dinner order. As she turned to go, a hand grabbed her arm and asked, "Where would a guy find a friendly female in this town? You interested in a little fun after hours?"

Meg was accustomed to fending off the attentions of traveling salesmen and men who thought that any woman who worked for a living was fair game, but there was something unsettling in this man's eyes, as though no one ever said no to him, or if they did, they paid a high price. "I'm not that kind of girl. Now if you'll excuse—"

"Any girl's that kind for the right price. What's yours?" The man's grip tightened on Meg's arm.

"Please, sir. I need to get your orders to the kitchen before it closes."

"It'll wait for us. You got a husband? Don't see a ring on your finger."

"I'm engaged. We can't afford a ring."

The henchman's gaze ran up and down Meg's body as though he was removing her clothing one piece at a time. "Who's the lucky boy?"

"The sheriff's deputy. He'll be here any minute to pick me up." Meg wondered if the lie rang as clearly in her admirer's ears as it did in her own.

"Lawman, huh? Well, we don't want no trouble with the law. Of course, could be he'd never find out."

Suddenly *Mr. Phillips'* fist came down hard on the table, setting everything on it rocking. "Leave her go, Vito." He looked up at Meg. "Please accept my apologies, Miss. This bum forgets his manners sometimes. He won't bother you no more."

Heart pounding, Meg fled to the kitchen and handed the cook the dinner orders.

"You just go back and tell them customers of yore's they got to order something else like hamburgers. I ain't setting in to frying no chicken this time of night."

"Flossie, I'll do no such thing. You have no idea who those men are."

"I don't give a hoot who they is. It's closing time and I'm plumb wore out." The cook crossed her arms over her ample abdomen and fixed Meg with a determined glare.

"Please, Flossie. That's Al Capone out there. Surely you've heard of him."

Flossie's eyes grew large in her gleaming ebony face. With a stubborn expression, she replied, "Yeah, I heard of him."

"I don't think he takes orders from the likes of us. Do you?"

Flossie's dark eyes grew darker as she considered her answer. "Guess not. I suppose I can make an exception just this once. Mind I'm doing it for you, not for him."

Meg threw her arms around Flossie, who pretended to be offended by the gesture, but Meg saw the twinkle in the cook's eyes. "You're not just the best cook in town, you're the best friend a girl could have."

"Now you just go on, Missy. I ain't no such thing and you know it. But you can go on thinking it anyways if you wants to." Flossie groaned and rubbed her back as she yanked a large iron skillet from the drain board and shoved it onto the range. Soon lard melted in the pan while she floured chicken parts.

Meg bumped the kitchen's swing door with her hip and lugged her heavy tray into the dining room. With some trepidation, she noticed that her four customers were the only ones remaining. She placed a mounded-over plate before Capone and then glanced at the beverage glasses. Her eyes narrowed slightly as she looked again, the second time with more concentration. It seemed to her that the ginger ale wasn't any lower in the glasses, but the beverage was certainly darker in color.

As she bent across the table to place the last plate, she understood why. The distinctive odor of alcohol drifted up from an ice filled tumbler. When Meg first started waitressing, she'd been shocked by the amount of illegal alcohol consumed by the hotel's supposedly respectable clientele, but before long, nothing the public did gave her the slightest pause. Concealed hip flasks were the order of the day, the Volstead Act be damned.

While setting out slices of pecan pie for the blessedly final course of the meal, Meg heard footsteps echoing as someone crossed the room.

"How about bringing me a piece with vanilla ice cream?" Sheriff Ike Darnell's silky voice floated from the corner of the alcove. "Gentlemen, mind if I join you?"

The second-in-command gave the sheriff's uniform with its holstered pistol the once over and snarled, "Suit yourself."

The sheriff dragged a chair from a nearby table, and turning it backwards, straddled the seat. After delivering the additional slice of pie, Meg didn't hover, so she couldn't hear what the sheriff said to Capone, but when he finally rose to leave, his voice rang across the empty restaurant.

"It'd be best if you gents kept to yourselves during your stay. Decent folks in these parts don't take to the criminal element too well."

Capone's second jumped to his feet. "Why you goddamned uppity bastard. You can't talk to us like that. I ought to show you right here."

A fist drew back, but Capone's hand shot up and grabbed the man's arm, pulling him roughly down into his chair. "Whatever you say, sheriff. You're the boss."

Sheriff Darnell tipped his Stetson and strode from the room.

Chapter 10

Driving south along the coast highway, Liz sang with the radio, not caring that she was off key. Jonathan, with his pure clear tenor, teased her about being tone deaf, but it didn't stop her singing when he wasn't around. Once she arrived at her destination, she would happily not sing a note for the remainder of the weekend. It was no sacrifice at all.

A little shiver ran down her spine at the thought of having a whole two nights together. It felt like it had been years instead of months since she'd last seen Jonathan. She smiled dreamily as she envisioned strolling hand in hand with him beside the ocean and disappearing behind an obliging sand dune for a little romance *al fresco*. Glimpses of foamy breakers rolling in from an azure Atlantic drew her gaze like a magnet until the car's tires began spitting up gravel. She jerked the wheel, bringing the car back onto the road, and focused on her driving with renewed determination. Nothing was going to spoil this weekend.

The weather was certainly doing its part. The sun shone regally in a pure lapis sky. Not even a wisp of white marred the effect. Liz had loved Seattle's sunny days for their beauty, all the more for their infrequency, but she had discovered a secret about Florida. No sky in the world was quite as blue or nearly as clear. Perhaps it was because the peninsula was fairly narrow or that the trade winds blew in from both coasts. Whatever the reason, Florida skies surely were the origins of the term Chamber of Commerce days.

Internet searches for a rental that she and Jonathan could afford had been difficult on such short notice. Jacksonville

Beach proper had been out of the question, so she worked her way down the coast, finally settling on a little place far south of Ponte Vedra proper. It was a pleasant surprise that this stretch of US-1A was untouched by towering condominiums. Development was evident in the form of sprawling mini-mansions, but their blinding pastels felt somehow out of sync with the rough natural surroundings. They aggressively announced their owners' prosperity and their dogged determination to cling to the old Florida architectural style, but a style tweaked beyond all reason to include every possible modern convenience and technology. Interspersed among these Goliaths sat the real deals, their cypress or heart pine clapboard exteriors painted in gleaming white or simply left unadorned to weather to a silvery gray that withstood the test of time.

It was to the end of a line of these mixed structures that Liz steered her Prius. Her heart fluttered when she saw Jonathan's vintage red Corvette sitting askew on the oyster shell driveway of a cottage perched between the highway and mountainous dunes. The car and the house were perfect complements. Pulling to a stop beside the Vette, she slammed her driver's door and dashed up steps to the open front door.

Standing in the small foyer, she called, "Jonathan?"

Silence.

She could see straight through to the back of the house where a wall of windows looked onto a covered porch and a boardwalk leading to the beach. Ceiling fans revolved lazily and ladder-back rockers moved gently with the ocean breeze. Her lips curved upward in an indulgent smile when she spied a pair of long denim-clad legs protruding from the only stationary chair. She went through the house to the open French doors leading onto the porch and stopped. She just wanted to drink in the sight of him for a moment.

Jonathan's head slumped to one side, chin resting against his shoulder. Dark circles beneath his closed eyes testified to the riggers of the recent deployment. Feeling a mixture of something akin to maternal concern and a deep need to be near him, she moved forward. When a porch floorboard squeaked beneath her step, his thick lashes fluttered open, revealing the arresting emerald irises beneath. It was those eyes that had caused her breath to catch the first time he turned them on her.

"I didn't mean to wake you. I just wanted to sit here watching you and the waves."

Jonathan smiled sleepily and held out his hand. "Come here, you."

When she was beside him, he pulled her onto his lap and gazed into her eyes, brushing back an errant curl from her cheek. "Missed you. I love flying, but there's one thing I love even more."

He cupped a hand behind her head and pushed gently until her mouth met his. His lips were seriously chapped, but it didn't diminish his ardor. She could feel just how much he had missed her through the denim of his jeans.

"A little afternoon delight is what I need. How about you?"

"Always."

Jonathan sang the old Starland Vocal Band song softly as he lifted her and carried her to the house's master bedroom. "*Gonna find my baby, gonna hold her tight . . .*"

Long afterward, Liz rose quietly from the king sized bed. She left Jonathan undisturbed and padded to the small galley kitchen adjacent the front door. Her stomach growled loudly, reminding her she hadn't eaten since breakfast, but she wasn't really hungry. The glow that filled her echoed that of the setting sun pouring through the window over the sink. Its warmth painted the walls golden yellow and burnished the shadows a deep bronze. As she opened the fridge, she sighed happily. Golden and burnished was exactly how she felt.

Beer, wine, cheese, and salami. Liz laughed softly and shook her head. She should have known better. As usual, Jonathan heard only the parts of the grocery list that were important to him. Because his drive was thirty minutes verse the two hours it took from Gainesville, Liz had asked him to do enough shopping for Friday dinner. Oh well, she had passed several interesting looking restaurants on the way there. She retrieved her bag from the car and pulled out her laptop, placing it on the counter. Searching "eating out in Ponte Vedra" produced a long list. After writing down two places with great reviews, she moved the cursor to the mail icon. She didn't really want to check it, but her students often e-mailed on Fridays with frantic questions. Why the young couldn't plan ahead mystified her. Next semester, she wasn't going to give in to their pitiful last minute cries for help. College was about being independent and she feared she was being that most unattractive of adult figures, the well-meaning enabler.

Scrolling through the small avalanche of commercial communications and e-mails from friends with the telltale Fwd: in the subject line, she landed on two that had to be answered. Opening one from Roberta marked urgent, she sent a reply saying that pages would be on their way by Thanksgiving and prayed that it wasn't another lie. The other bore the tag line "your research." As much as she didn't want her job intruding on their weekend, she decided she'd better see what Hugh wanted.

Liz,

Talked to my friend at The Florida Historical Quarterly. More thoughts on the Florida course.

See me Monday. Enjoyed dinner. Do it again sometime?

Regards,

Hugh

"Who's Hugh and why did you have dinner with him?" Jonathan's voice murmured in her ear as his arms slipped around her waist.

"Dr. Raymond, head of the department, and we had a working dinner to discuss business as your snooping eyes should well be able to see." Liz laughed and turned to face him.

"I can understand why he enjoyed your company, but what makes him think he can have dinner again with my girl?"

His smile was broad, but behind it, Liz thought she saw something else. Jonathan always seemed so sure of their relationship, but perhaps that was bravado, perhaps he actually had a few insecurities of his own. It was a novel concept. Well, turn about was fair play. He knew how she felt because in moments of total happiness, she let her guard down and used the *L* word. Maybe a little imagined competition would be good for him.

"He's a nice man, divorced, lonely, and still in love with his ex-wife, if you ask me. Any dinner invitations are purely business. At least I'm pretty sure they are."

"That's a wicked smile you're wearing. I ask you, is this any way to treat one of America's fighting men?"

"You have nothing to worry about and you well know it." Liz gave him a peck on the lips, then cocked her head to one side, grinned, and twisted out of his embrace. "But it's nice to think that there's a fallback in case you don't work out."

"Why you little tease!"

Jonathan chased her into the living room where they collapsed on the sofa in a tangle of arms, kisses, and helpless laughter.

Jonathan caressed her bottom and murmured, "Baby, it'll be this good even when we're old and gray. When you've got what we've got, you never want to let it go."

Liz accepted the words as his way of saying he loved her. In some ways, it was better because he was talking about the future.

Jonathan sat up, held her at arm's length, and cocked his head to one side. "But seriously, does this guy think you're free?"

"No, I told him about you after he spent about an hour pouring his heart out. I felt I needed to."

"Good. I like a clear field when I'm coming in for a landing."

Now what did that mean? Jonathan had hinted around about their future for months. Liz's heart followed her hopes into the stratosphere.

"When do we eat?"

"What?"

"Eat. You know. Dinner?"

It took her a couple of seconds to process his meaning. Retrieving the restaurant list from the kitchen, she dropped it into his lap.

"Here. You choose. Either one is fine with me." The deflated quality in her voice seemed to go straight over Jonathan's head.

Dinner was excellent. As she dipped pieces of soft shell crab in a deliciously mild mustard sauce, Liz looked out over the lapping waves and wondered again where their relationship was headed. She had given up a job she loved to follow a man she loved even more. It had been her idea and her choice, but it was beginning to feel like she was doing all of the giving. *Hell, girl*, Liz mentally chided, *be satisfied with present happiness. Don't go ruining a perfect weekend.* But over key lime pie, ruminations about their relationship continued to intrude.

They had met quite by accident when Jonathan and his buddies crashed a beach party at Whidbey Island's Deception

Pass State Park. Liz and her friends had managed to commandeer the best picnic tables on a bluff overlooking the inlet and the Navy fliers had taken good-natured exception to what they viewed as an invasion of their private paradise. At the end of the day, Liz was already half in love with the handsome blonde, green-eyed Lieutenant Jonathan Lloyd. His west Texas cowboy charm turned out to be an added bonus.

For the next two years, they organized their lives around his deployments and her college teaching schedule. When they were sure he was assigned to Naval Air Station Jacksonville, she started applying for teaching posts within a reasonable distance of the base. It still amazed her that she had been offered a job at the state's premiere university. It amazed her even more that she had accepted it. A brief smile played across her lips as the words *grand passion* and *irresistible force* tumbled through her mind.

"Penny for your thoughts." Jonathan reached across the table and squeezed her hand.

"Sorry. Guess good food and excellent wine have put me into a very mellow mood."

"Well, call me conceited, but I thought this weekend was all about me and I don't want you thinking about anything else." Jonathan's mouth curved upward. The twinkle in his eyes and the disarming dimple in his right cheek made Liz's heart turn over. "Where were you just now? You were smiling like you have a secret."

"No secrets. Just thinking about you."

"That's what I like to hear. I'm a man of rather limited interests." A self-deprecating chuckle failed to hide the truth of his words.

It was Jonathan's looks and rugged cowboy mindset that had initially attracted Liz, but it was his ironic sense of humor that kept things interesting. She couldn't decide if he intentionally did it or if it was just part of his natural charm, but whatever the source, he kept her slightly off balance much of the time. Loving him required a spirit of adventure and considerable flexibility.

Chapter 11

Jack pushed out the window screen and he eased himself over the sill until his feet tapped against the house's clapboard. He paused, listened intently, and grinned. Daddy's snoring was so loud nobody inside the house or out could have heard the screen squealing on its rusty hinges. His grin disappeared quickly, though, when his father's most recent tirade began to replay in his mind. He didn't care. Daddy could just keep on hating it all he wanted to. Nobody was going to keep Jack from seeing his best friend. He lifted his bottom off the sill, jumped into the sultry air, and landed with a soft thud on the bare ground below. With a final glance over his shoulder, he grinned and raced into the freedom of the night.

Jack crawled over the back gate and took off between rows of bright leaf tobacco, slapping at the plants as he ran. It wouldn't be long before the easier period of regular chores would end and first harvest began. Jack hated the long days bent double in the broiling sun, twisting those damned sand lugs off the bottom of their stalks. Unlike most of his friends' fathers, Daddy didn't give Jack a plug nickel for all of the backbreaking labor. He'd be glad when their tobacco was hanging in the barn and he could hire himself out to the neighbors. Zeke's grandpa had already offered Jack extra work and he planned to accept, even if he had to sneak off to do it.

At the far end of the tobacco field, Jack entered the woods where a small creek formed the eastern boundary between the Blevins and Taylor farms. When the boys were little, Jack and Zeke played together as soon as they could wade the creek. Jack wasn't sure why his father had changed so much toward Mr. Taylor. Zeke's grandpa was a nice man even if he was colored. He helped anybody who needed it no matter who they were. When Mama's daddy died, it was Mr. Taylor who placed an arm around Jack's shoulders and spoke to him of the natural order of things, of the turning of the seasons, and the hope of heaven. All Arnold Blevins did was to tell him that crying wouldn't change anything so stop acting like a girl, just like he had when their baby brother died.

Another field, this one planted in cotton, brought Jack to the edge of the Taylor's yard. Bright moonlight painted the outhouse a ghostly blue. He passed through its long shadow as he crept up to the house.

Tapping on the windowsill, he whispered, "Zeke, you awake?"

"Ssh! I ain't talking to you."

As Jack peered through the open window, he could see Zeke clearly propped up on one elbow on his bed. His skinny arms and legs protruded from what must be brand new underwear that was too large for his slight frame. His ebony skin looked all the darker for being set against snowy bed sheets that had been boiled in the wash pot to within an inch of their lives. The contrast made it look like Zeke was floating in midair. Jack bit his lip to keep from laughing.

"I guess you ain't the one who got the rods and reels from out of the bushes then?"

"No. Now go away before you get me in more trouble."

"Do you think your grandpa could have found them?"

"Grandpa ain't got 'em." The quiver in Zeke's voice was unmistakable as his head and upper body filled the window opening. "He tanned my hide good and it's all your fault. I ain't going no place with you ever again."

"Aw, Zeke. Don't be like that. I'll make it up to you. I promise."

"And just exactly how you gonna do that? Grandpa saved for a whole year to pay for them rods and reels. Now he says I gotta work off the price."

"I'll give you all the money I make working tobacco this summer. I can't do no more than that unless I find extra work."

Zeke might have continued with another acidic retort, but a hand appeared on his shoulder.

"What are you boys up to now?" Mr. Taylor's face joined Zeke's in the open window.

"Mr. Taylor, I'm awful sorry about your stuff. It's my fault they got stolen and I'll pay for them. Please don't punish Zeke."

Mr. Taylor was silent for a moment and then said, "Jack, you might as well come on around to the front porch. Bending over this windowsill isn't doing my tricky back any good."

Jack slipped around the side of the weathered clapboard house and stepped headlong into a climbing rose that ran up onto the eaves, around to the front, and down the first four by four that supported the porch roof. Its delicate pink buds created a fragrant arbor through which to view the sunset at the end of a long summer day. Zeke said that his grandmother planted it when she and his grandfather were first married. She gave the rose so much loving care that the family joked it was her first child. When she died, Mr. Taylor continued the pampering and hand watering in her memory.

Zeke loved the plant as much as his grandmother had, and so when he was big enough to lug the watering can from the well, he took over its care. Jack couldn't say he had ever felt that kind of attraction for any plant, especially one that bit you if you got too close. He backed away from the rose's trailing runners as he picked thorns from his bare chest.

When they were all settled in porch rockers, Mr. Taylor drew a long breath before speaking. "Jack, I appreciate that you want to pay for the rods and reels. You bear some of the responsibility for them being stolen, but Zeke could have said no when you asked him to take them without permission. You know the difference between right and wrong, don't you son?"

Zeke didn't meet his grandfather's eyes. His chin practically touched his chest as he nodded in reply.

"I'm bone weary and I'm going to bed. Here's the receipt for the missing things. I'm going to let you boys decide how much each of you should put in on the replacements."

Jack's eyes grew wide when he held the piece of paper up to the light of the oil lamp that Mr. Taylor left on the porch. "Man, it'll take both of us forever to earn enough."

He looked over at his friend and felt a stab of remorse. Tears dripped from Zeke's chin and his lower lip trembled. Jack knew how much it cost Zeke for those tears to be seen.

"Hey, don't worry so much. We'll get it done. There ain't nothing we cain't do if we stick together. Right?" Jack plastered a smile on his face and gave Zeke's shoulder a nudge.

With a second nudge, Zeke's lips curved into a feeble smile. He wiped the tears from his cheeks and whispered, "Right."

Jack had no idea where they would get that much money, but he wasn't about to say so out loud. It wasn't just the year age difference between them that stilled his tongue. Zeke had been tender with his feelings ever since his folks were killed. He was a worrier, too. Jack sometimes made fun of his buddy for acting like a baby, but he walloped the daylights out of anybody else who tried it. That was something, considering Jack was a good head smaller than the other boys his age. They would have picked on him too, if he hadn't been so tough.

The boys rocked in companionable silence for a while as Jack mentally calculated how many pounds of tobacco it would take to repay Mr. Taylor. He finally gave up. He couldn't do that much math in his head.

"You want to go swimming tomorrow evening?"

"Naw. Better not."

"How about pitching some horseshoes?"

"Maybe."

"Dominos?"

"Yeah. That should be okay."

Jack mentally sighed. It was going to take more than a little reassurance to bring back the Zeke who joined him in adventures. Whenever he was upset, Zeke became a real homebody. Right now, it seemed like he was afraid to leave the porch.

Jack cocked his head to one side and eyed Zeke. He knew of at least one thing that sometimes brought Zeke out of his funks. "Tell me again why your grandpa makes moonshine? Him being such a churchgoer and all, just makes me wonder."

Zeke's head snapped up and his eyes blazed. "He don't make moonshine to sell to white folk. He only sells to our people. He hardly charges anything, just enough to cover what it costs to make it and to have a little money extra so he can buy stuff, since coloreds have to pay cash at the store. How many times I have to tell you this? You deaf or just plain stupid?"

"Well, sometimes teacher says I'm stupid and Mama says I'm deaf most of the time, but they ain't neither one right. I just like to get a rise outta you." Jack launched himself at Zeke, threw him on the floor, and began tickling.

Between gales of helpless laughter, cries echoed from high porch ceiling. "Stop!"

"Say you'll pitch horseshoes with me tomorrow."

"No."

"Say it."

"Okay."

"That's better."

Jack stood up and held out his hand. He hadn't pressed for swimming. Just getting Zeke off the porch was enough. Zeke looked up, his eyes wary at first, but finally accepted the offer of help and allowed Jack to pull him to his feet.

Chapter 12

For Liz, their Ponte Vedra weekend was over in a heartbeat. As they lingered in the driveway listening to thunderheads rolling in from the Atlantic, it occurred to her that the weather had mirrored her moods all weekend—sunny when she arrived, dark and depressing now that they were about to part. Jonathan wanted and needed a happy, smiling girlfriend, so she bit the inside of her cheek hoping that would keep the tears at bay. When Jonathan pulled her into one last embrace, his kiss was as passionate as if they hadn't just spent two intense days and nights rediscovering the delights of one another's bodies.

"I'm going to miss you, Baby."

"Miss you more." Liz's voice cracked, causing Jonathan to pull away and look into her eyes.

"Hey, I thought big time professors didn't cry." He brushed his fingers across her cheek where a single tear defied her determined effort to keep it contained by tilting her head back. "Come on, professor lady, give me a smile. It's the least you can do for your warrior man."

Liz wasn't particularly fond of Jonathan's pet names for them, but he was so earnest in his awful attempt at humor that a giggle, sounding more like a hiccup, escaped her trembling lips. She absolutely hated crying in front of anyone, even Jonathan, but the stress of his recent deployment had caught up with her.

"I'm sorry to be such a baby. I just missed you, that's all. I worry when I don't hear from you."

A frown creased his brow. "I swear, Liz, we've talked about this at least a hundred times. I call or e-mail when it doesn't violate orders." The edge in his voice was a warning.

"I wasn't criticizing. I was simply stating a fact." Liz felt her temper rising. The last thing she wanted was to end their nearly perfect weekend with a fight. When she spoke again, her tone was conciliatory. "Please forget I said anything. You don't have a choice. I know that. I'm just a silly girl sometimes."

Looking a little chastened, Jonathan lifted her chin and kissed her again, then said, "If you don't leave now, it'll be dark before you get home. I don't want you driving at night on unfamiliar roads. See, you're not the only one who worries."

Her Prius followed his Vette until her turn back to Gainesville appeared. She sounded her horn and he waved from his open window, then he disappeared from view. The drive that had been so beautiful when she was eastbound on Friday, now took on a gloomy, foreboding quality. Rather than seeing verdant wetland glades set aglow by filtered sunshine, the terrain became a primordial swamp, full of insects, alligators, snakes—creatures locked in a violent struggle for survival.

On both sides of the road, Spanish moss draped cypresses took on the appearance of tall, elegant aristocrats fallen on hard times, reduced to wearing heavy, matted rags. Rain finally caught up with her halfway through her trip. She switched on the wipers, wishing that time and the weather had been suspended at about 4:00 p.m. Friday afternoon. The delicious memory of their hours together in the bedroom overlooking the ocean would have to last for longer than she thought she could bear. Jonathan's duty schedule was turning into a real problem.

The week following their reunion was filled with classes and students clamoring for office appointments, leaving little time to think about missing Jonathan. Nights when she was too tired to be productive, however, were another story. Liz tried all of her usual antidotes to loneliness or boredom—chatting on-line with Seattle friends, reading the latest bestseller, flipping channels—with varying degrees of success.

When Friday afternoon arrived, Liz simply couldn't face the loneliness, so she climbed into her car and headed north. She pushed all of her worries behind a mental wall—her half written novel, the incomplete outlines for the new courses, the stack of term papers needing grading—all of it could wait. She needed the distraction and the comfort of the one thing that was hers alone.

After brandishing her inter-university ID at no fewer than three checkpoints, she was finally admitted to the rare documents collection, a rather grand title for the moldering back issues of the Columbia Tribune and a complete set of Civil War Confederate personnel indices. After the accompanying library clerk closed the collection room door, gooseflesh popped up and Liz shivered involuntarily. Her shorts and t-shirt felt as though they had just turned to tissue paper.

The clerk went to a drawer and removed white cotton gloves. "Put on these before handling the newspapers."

"Why hasn't the college put them on microfiche or scanned them? The oldest copies must be on the verge of disintegration."

"No money and not enough personnel. That's why we keep it next to zero in here. There's a lab coat on the back of the door. We keep it on hand for the uninitiated."

"Thanks. If I come again, I'll dress for the occasion."

The young man laughed softly. "That would be wise.

Well, I'll leave you to your work. Let me know if you need anything."

The lab coat was clearly intended to fit all comers. It floated around Liz like a caftan, but at least she was no longer in danger of frostbite. After rolling the sleeves up several turns, she pulled a big hardbound volume from the shelves and lugged it to the room's only table.

The old newsprint rustled dryly as Liz turned to Friday, June 20. This edition of the then weekly newspaper seemed the one most likely to include a report on Capone's visit since he had arrived the previous Friday. She skimmed the entire paper, but found no mention of him. A frown creased her forehead. A world famous gangster had been in town for over a week but the editor of the local paper hadn't deemed it newsworthy. The only thing the editor seemed concerned about was what appeared to be a personal crusade against local vice. His editorial reminded readers that he, Silas Barnes of the Columbia Tribune, was the only voice crying out against the sins and illegal acts that were perpetrated every day and every night by degenerate, immoral persons. The piece railed on for several paragraphs, but never put forth any specific names. Liz smiled and turned to the police reports out of curiosity.

She wondered if the sparsely populated county could possibly have been the hotbed of moral turpitude Editor Barnes described. She read down a very short list of tickets for speeding, public intoxication, and disturbing the peace. Nothing very out of the ordinary, unless a missing person report on one Big Charlie Blankenship, resident of O'Leno, Florida, had special meaning. Liz supposed it might for the common law wife who reported that she had last seen her husband the previous Saturday afternoon in the company of an unknown woman. The item ended by asking any member of the public having knowledge of Mr. Blankenship's whereabouts to please come forward. Liz grinned. Sounded like Big Charlie might have tired of the semiofficial Mrs. Blankenship and hightailed it out of town with a new girlfriend.

Chapter 13

The sight of DeWitt behind the wheel of a Columbia County Sheriff's vehicle parked at the hotel curb startled Meg. She was expecting his old pickup truck with inner tubes tied down in back. She put the picnic hamper on the sidewalk and leaned through the passenger window.

"Hey, you promised me Ichetucknee. Remember?"

"Sorry, honey. We've got something more important to do than float around the springs."

"And what could be more important than clear cold water on a day like this? It must be close to a hundred."

"Zeke Taylor. Warning him can't wait any longer."

"Has something else happened?"

"No, but I have a feeling it's about to. The wrong folks seem awful stirred up. I asked the boss if we should talk to Silas Barnes about all those editorials, but all he said was freedom of the press, son, goddamned freedom of the press." DeWitt's imitation of Sheriff Ike Darnell's twangy drawl was pitch perfect, making Meg laugh despite her disappointment.

"Hop in so we can get on with it."

DeWitt only drove the car on official county business and never let Meg go with him. He must be really worried to risk the sheriff's anger over a civilian riding shotgun.

The air blowing through the car's open window was the only relief from the heat that Meg was likely to get, so she propped her arm on its ledge and leaned out for the full effect. After about 40 miles, the turn off for Ichetucknee Springs blew past in a cloud of powder fine dust.

Coughing and wiping her face with a handkerchief, Meg moved closer to DeWitt. "Mrs. Simmons was sitting on the porch when we went past. I'm sure she saw me hanging out the window. I guess we don't have any choice now but to go by to see my folks. I'll never hear the end of it if we don't."

DeWitt lifted a wary brow. "Your daddy doesn't like surprises, especially when they involve me."

"Don't mind him. That's just his way. It doesn't have anything to do with you personally."

"I'm not so sure. The last time I dropped by unannounced, he met me on the porch with a shotgun."

"He keeps that thing by the front door. Everybody gets the same welcome unless he knows they're coming."

"I suppose he tells everybody that mixed breeds have no business seeing his daughter?"

Meg sighed and ran her fingers along DeWitt's cheek. "I'm sorry, darling. Daddy's just gotten plain mean. I don't know how else to explain why he acts the way he does."

DeWitt put his arm around her shoulders and pulled her closer. "That's another reason we should set the date. We need a home of our own where your daddy can't interfere in our lives."

"We'll have it one day."

Meg felt DeWitt tense. "Not one day. Someday soon. I don't know how much longer I can stand this waiting."

Rather than risk an argument, Meg silently reached up and kissed him on the cheek. DeWitt suddenly swerved onto a single-track lane. Without taking his eyes off the road, he pulled her around against his chest and covered her mouth with his as he steered the car to a stop under the low hanging branches of a huge old oak.

In a moment, her arms were around his neck. Their breathing became ragged as his hand slipped beneath the thin fabric of her summer frock and caressed her breast, teasing the nipple until it was hard and erect. When his hand glided under her skirt and began gently stroking her thighs, she gasped in rhythm to the soft throbbing deep within her. With that small part of her mind not inflamed by desire, she realized that they had to stop before they went too far. One of them had to be sensible.

She broke the kiss and drew back, "DeWitt, we—"

"I know, I know. We shouldn't. We can't." The heaving in his chest began to subside. "Meg, this is driving me crazy. I love you and I want to marry you now. Not next week, next month, or next year. How much longer? Just tell me. I can stand it if I know how long."

"When we can afford a place of our own." Meg's voice was quiet but firm. She hated fighting with him, but in this she was determined to the point of pig headedness.

DeWitt stared straight into the rearview mirror as he jerked the gearshift into reverse. He neither spoke to nor looked at Meg for the rest of the journey.

When they bumped to a halt in the Taylor's front yard, he got out and slammed the door. "You talk to the boy while I see old Mr. Taylor. I'm here to question him about rumors that he runs shine. Understand?"

Tears threatened to roll down her cheeks, but Meg refused to cry. She was right and they both knew it. Angry and frustrated, she flung the car door open and followed DeWitt onto the front porch where he banged on the screen door. The buzzing of an electric fan set at high speed floated through the open windows and front door.

"Don't break it down. I'm a coming. Just slow is all," Mr. Taylor rumbled from somewhere inside the house.

His feet shuffled over the bare floorboards as though each step hurt. When he appeared in the screen's frame, his once tall body looked bent as though the burdens acquired over his many years of life were finally too great to support.

"What can I do for you today, Deputy?"

"We need to talk about that curl of smoke I see coming up out of your woods from time to time."

Mr. Taylor craned his neck and peered at the forest running along one side of the yard. "Can't say as I know what you mean. Them woods woulda burnt up as dry as it's been if there was a fire in them somewhere."

Meg sensed DeWitt's irritation in the squaring of his shoulders and stepped out from behind him. Mr. Taylor's expression changed from one of wariness to gentle puzzlement.

"Well, if it ain't little Meg Blevins. My goodness. Look at you all grown up. How time do fly."

"Hello Mr. Taylor. How've you been?" Meg was saddened to see how much he'd aged. His hair was completely white now and his eyes held sadness as deep as a well.

"Cain't complain except for the rheumatism in my lower back. Acts up now and again." He turned toward DeWitt. "This ain't no social call, but don't mean I cain't be hospitable. Have a seat and I'll fetch us some iced tea."

When Mr. Taylor turned toward the kitchen, Meg noticed a pair of dark eyes peering at them from the hallway. A small boy grinned at her and waved shyly.

Seeing her opportunity, she called, "Hey Zeke. Jack tells me you got a new cat."

"Yeah. It's a mama cat. Wanna see her?"

Zeke came onto the porch, took Meg's hand, and led her around back to the chicken coop where a small calico nursed three young kittens in a hay lined box intended for the hens' use.

"You can pet 'em if you want to. She won't scratch."

Meg extended her hand and let her fingers drift over downy fur. All four felines purred like the engines of well-tuned automobiles. Mama Cat leaned over her brood, pink tongue darting from one drowsy head to the next, giving Meg's fingers a going over in the process.

"You can have one when they's weaned." Zeke's small dark hand reached into the box next to Meg's. He scratched Mama Cat behind her ears. In response, her motor revved even higher.

"She sure likes you, Zeke."

"Yeah. I pulled her outta the river. Me and Grandpa saw a man throw a sack in the water. It was wiggling and squalling to beat the band. She used to follow me everywhere until she had the kittens."

Here was her opening. "Zeke, I need to talk to you about the river, about the night you and Jack saw a man throw something big in it, the thing that went down the sinkhole. Have you told anyone about what you and Jack saw?"

Zeke looked up at Meg, fear clouding his soft black eyes. He shook his head and resumed petting the cats.

"Good. Don't ever tell anyone." Meg stooped down until they were eye level and turned him to face her. "Promise me, Zeke."

"Okay." His voice was hardly above a whisper.

"Really, Zeke. It's terribly important that you and Jack keep the secret. Something awful might happen if you don't."

"I said okay. I'm not stupid ya know."

The high pitch of the boy's voice told Meg her warning had hit a nerve, probably because he'd already seen his share of awful happenings. When he was only four, he watched helplessly as his father and mother died while trying to save his baby sister from their burning home. A question of arson arose briefly because Zeke talked nonstop about a strange white man running away from the house just before it burst into flames, but it led to nothing.

Even though she was a child herself at the time, Meg was puzzled that no arrests were made when Zeke gave such a clear description. She had wondered ever since if the sheriff didn't want to spend the man-hours on the deaths of three colored people, or if four-year-old Zeke had simply been mistaken. She hoped for the latter, but knew the truth was more likely to be laid at the sheriff's door.

Meg slipped her arms around the boy and pulled him to her. A tremor ran through his small frame. "I know, Zeke. Jack's told me how smart you are." Meg felt guilty for frightening this sweet, small boy. She hugged him closer and continued, "I can't have pets in my room at the hotel, but Mama said she was on the lookout for a calico because they're such good mousers. Could she have a kitten?"

Holding him at arm's length, Meg was relieved to see his frown lighten as he nodded. "Grandpa said one female cat is enough. I been worried about finding a home for the little girl. Think your mama would take her?"

"Calicos are always girls, so I don't think it'll be a problem."

Zeke's trusting smile tugged at Meg's heart, stirring something fiercely maternal. She sighed and wondered if she was a fool to continue delaying marriage. She and DeWitt had talked about how many children they wanted. Two boys for him and a little girl for her. When she was a child, Meg believed that having all of the answers would come with adulthood, but life was showing her just how wrong she'd been.

Chapter 14

Liz decided she'd been abandoned in a meat locker. Shivering, she pulled the borrowed lab coat closer and this time read the Columbia Trib June 20 edition cover to cover, but still found no mention whatsoever of Scarface—absolutely nothing. She flipped through the pages a second time and then a third, her intuition whispering that there had to be more here than met the eye. Chin resting on her upturned palm, she gazed thoughtfully at the tall pines just outside the window. It just didn't add up. The editor, who was so concerned about crime, hadn't written a single word about the visit of a world famous gangster. That would have been big news in any news market in the nation. Curious, she scanned back through the issues until she found his first anti-vice editorial dated January 24, 1930.

My Dear Neighbors,

Columbia County residents know of the recent loss of five young men, but how many know the true cause of the highway carnage that stole them from us? Surely not you, dear reader. If the peaceful and law abiding citizens of Columbia County knew, they would surely rise up in arms. If they but knew of the sinister persons in our community lying in wait to ensnare the unwary and beguile the innocent, they would lock their children up and never let them venture from home. If they but knew of the vile and illegal acts that sully fair Columbia's name, the hue and cry would surely be heard all the way to Tallahassee. But therein lies the problem. Our citizens apparently do not know for no voice has uttered so much as a whisper in protest.

It is time for a champion to open the eyes of our good people. But who will don the mantle of justice? Who will arm himself with the sword of righteousness and do battle with the evil that lurks in our secret corners and alleyways? Since no one has thus far been willing to put his name forward, I, your editor, humbly offer my services in this cause. In the coming weeks, months, even years, if needs be, The Columbia Tribune will not stand down until every liquor distillery, every purveyor of illegal alcohol, every gambling parlor, every house of ill repute within the boundaries of this county is broken or burned to the ground. We will not stop until our daughters and wives are safe from the degenerates who roam among us. We will not cease until our sons are no longer tempted into the ways of wickedness that lead them to their doom. That is my solemn promise.

Turgid was the first thought that came to mind at the end of the mercifully brief editorial. Dripping sarcasm was the second. Editor Barnes appeared to be a man whose disdain for his neighbors was equaled only by his elevated opinion of himself. Liz skimmed through the following months of editorials and police activity reports, but nothing interesting or particularly new presented itself until the edition dated Friday, June 27 where an item at the bottom of the front page caught her attention.

Local Women Lynched

Two local women were found beaten and hanged in their places of residence. Jesse Jardine, white, of North Valdosta Highway and Alma Stone, Negress, of NE Washington Street died in the early morning hours of Saturday. Other women living in the residences reported being awakened by loud voices and sounds of violent scuffles. The women were unable to identify the assailants because they locked their bedroom doors and did not come out until the attacks were over. The deceased women were each found with ropes around their necks hanging from front porch beams. A large wooden cross blazed in the front yard of each house for some time after the bodies were taken down.

Liz knew that the occasional Caucasian was on the receiving end of the Klan's perception of justice, but what was so special about these two women? Liz read the paragraph again. Perhaps the answer lay with their living arrangements. There was no mention of husbands, children, or survivors of any kind. Surely the reporter writing the article would have said if any of the women living together had been related. One white woman and one black, both lynched on the same night. There had to be a connection. Liz wondered what Editor Barnes had to say. She turned to the editorial page. Among the paragraphs she had come to expect, a couple lines popped out.

Regardless of the method, our community is surely better off without the likes of Jesse Jardine and Alma Stone. Their houses of ill fame will soon stand empty of the women and girls, who until the small hours of Saturday morning, sold themselves within their walls.

That was all. No mention of Capone having left town earlier in the week. She was no closer to solving the mystery of Capone's stay than she had been before, and now she seemed to have stumbled onto a new puzzle. Liz tapped her pencil against her notepad and considered the implications of what had been written, and perhaps more importantly, what had gone unsaid. There was no mention of white sheets and the men who hid beneath them. Klan members' identities were usually known in the small towns and rural communities of the South during that period in history, but if one did not already understand what the burning crosses meant, it would have been as though the Klan hadn't existed. That seemed unlikely.

As she turned to the next week's edition, Liz's cell phone began vibrating against the table.

"Where are you?" The caller's voice had an aggrieved quality.

"In Lake City, Jonathan. Where are you?"

"Your living room."

"I thought you had duty this weekend."

"It got changed. When're you coming home? I'm hungry."

Liz remained silent as she experienced a moment of exasperation.

"Liz?"

"I'll be there in about forty-five minutes. If you can't wait that long, go get something on your own."

"Hey, if you're going to be a grouch, I can go back to Jacksonville."

"Sorry. I'm just frustrated. My research isn't going very well. See you soon. I'll cook us a nice meal."

She flung the lab coat onto its hook, grabbed her belongings, and raced for the car.

With her common sense doing a tap dance on its warning bell, Liz hit the interstate and accelerated to well over the speed limit. Whizzing past other traffic, her eyes flew to the dashboard clock every few minutes. The digital minutes seemed to advance every twenty seconds or so. A glimpse of state trooper yellow and black lurking behind an exit sign made her heart jump and she eased up on the accelerator, but she shook with frustration. Glancing in the rearview mirror for flashing blue lights, she caught the image of a young woman with rather wild eyes. For a moment she didn't recognize herself. Shocked, she suddenly wondered who she was becoming.

When had jumping at Jonathan's slightest whim become such a habit? She let the car slow to a lawful 70 mph and breathed deeply. If this were a problem related to her research, she would analyze the facts before forming a conclusion. On the pro side, she loved Jonathan. He was good looking. Charm dripped from every pore when he wanted it to. He worked in a macho field and should be on recruiting posters wearing his pilot's uniform. He was thrilled when she moved to Florida. He was a great lover.

On the con, his charm was too often reserved for social situations. He could be selfish and demanding in private. He expected his schedule to determine their time together. Cleaning and picking up after himself was outside his skill set. But most frustrating, he refused to utter the words that would mean everything to Liz.

Oh Lord, this isn't solving anything. She jabbed the radio on button. *Hell girl, just admit it. The only fact that really matters is on the pro list. You love him and want to spend the rest of your life with him.*

Without warning, a nasty thought popped into her head. She turned up the music to drown it out, but it wouldn't be thwarted.

But does he love me as much as I love him?

For the first time, it occurred to her that he might not, that this might be a repeat of her last relationship, the one that ended with her left alone and feeling deeply rejected. Her stomach clinched. A cold, jagged knife thrust deep into her heart. Her knuckles paled as her grip on the steering wheel tightened in response to the turmoil whirling through her mind. But the worst part? She had turned her life upside down for a man who wouldn't say three simple freaking words.

Damn, what a mess.

Chapter 15

"Did he understand?" DeWitt shouted over the truck's rattling as they bumped along the washboard road leading to Meg's parents' farm.

"Yes. I'm afraid I scared him."

"Zeke needs to be scared and so does Jack." The edge in DeWitt's voice told Meg that he was still upset with her.

Looking for a neutral topic, she asked, "What did Mr. Taylor say? He's such a nice man. I'd hate for him to be in trouble."

DeWitt cut his eyes at her. "He and I do this little dance about every six months. I ask him if he's making moonshine. He denies it. The smoke in his woods stops for a while and then one day it starts again."

"I'm glad he hasn't been arrested, but why not?"

"What the boss doesn't know won't hurt him. Mr. Taylor's a small time operator. He needs the money and I like him. Are those reasons good enough? Do they meet your high standards?"

"Please don't be like that. You know I love you. I want to get married as much as you do, but how long do you think we'd be happy without a home?"

"We'd be like most couples just starting out. We'd rent a room somewhere."

"And have nothing of our own."

"You're wrong. We'd have each other."

Meg couldn't argue with that and she didn't want to. She focused instead on the turn up ahead. She dreaded stopping by home, but it was a small community and word that she had been in the neighborhood would reach her parents sooner or later. If they were lucky, only Mama and Jack would be around. But when the car pulled to a stop in the yard, her spirits sank. Daddy sat on the front porch removing his work boots. He looked up at the sound of tires crunching on the gravel driveway. Then he frowned.

"Looks like your pop is thrilled to see me."

"It's probably the car."

When they were on the porch steps, Meg's father snarled, "Everybody in the community's going to think something bad's happened with that blamed police car sitting in the yard. Folks'll be making up tales for sure."

Meg couldn't help smiling. "Daddy, would you rather we hadn't come by? The neighbors would've made a lot out of that too, now wouldn't they?"

"Well ain't you just the sassy little miss. I ought to turn you over my knee for backtalk."

"Daddy, I'm a grown woman who earns her own keep. I'm too old for spankings." The older she got, the more determined she was to stand up to her father's ill tempers and bullying. "Where's Mama?"

"In the kitchen, where else?"

They left her father on the porch grumbling to himself and followed the dark central hall to the back of the house. Meg's mother turned from the stove at the sound of their footsteps. Sweat poured down her beet red face and her hair clung to her head in damp curls. She dropped her long-handled spoon onto its rest and smiled tiredly.

"What a wonderful surprise. I didn't expect to see you for another couple of weeks or so."

"Hey Mama." Meg crossed the kitchen and gave her mother a hug while her gaze wandered over shelves and counter tops. "Looks like you've got enough beans canned to last all winter."

"Garden came in real good this year." Mama ran a wet dishcloth over her face and pushed the hair out of her eyes. "I'm glad for a break. How about teacakes and iced tea?"

They had been seated on the back porch for about five minutes when the screen door slammed and Meg's father joined them. He glared at DeWitt and Meg.

"People are talking about you going around with this mixed breed. I told you no good would come of it."

DeWitt's face glowed red and the ice in his tea sloshed against the glass. Meg saw his free hand clench at his side. She glanced at her mother who dropped her eyes and picked at an invisible spot on her apron. "Daddy, I couldn't care less what those old coots you go hunting with think or say. DeWitt and I are going to get married someday and you might as well accept it."

"I may put up with it, but don't mean I'll like it."

"Mr. Blevins, you may not like me or my people, but I love Meg and I'll be a good husband to her. Meg, we've got to go if you're going to be back at the hotel in time for your shift."

DeWitt didn't even look at her or wait for a response. He strode through the house and out to the car. Meg scrambled to get in as the engine sparked to life. Glancing back through the rear window, she cringed at the clouds of dust the speeding tires kicked up. The sediment would drift through the open windows and onto Mama's freshly polished furniture.

"DeWitt, I'm sorry. Please don't let him get to you like that."

A long exhaled breath eased the tension radiating from DeWitt's every pore. Meg stroked his bare arm and laid her head on his shoulder.

"Meg, promise me you'll forgive me when I straighten him out one day. I won't put up with his crap forever."

"I don't expect you to, but remember that Mama and

Jack have to live with him all the time. See, it could be a whole lot worse." She grinned and poked him in the ribs. When the corners of his mouth turned up, she poked him until he laughed and grabbed her hand.

"Stop it. Do you want to cause a wreck?"

"No, I just want to see you smile. You have the most beautiful smile I've ever seen."

He leaned over and kissed the top of her head. "Flattery won't get you anywhere, but giving me the answer I want will."

"It won't be long. We're almost there."

DeWitt's smile faded as quickly as it had come. Silence reigned for the remainder of the ride to town. When he parked in front of the hotel, DeWitt's arms flew around Meg. He kissed her hard. As much as she loved his kisses, this one felt as though it was tinged with something more than passion. When she pulled back to catch her breath, she saw that his eyes glittered in a way she hadn't seen before.

"You're angry. I'm sorry. I wish it were different."

"It will be. You need to give me an answer soon. I'm not sure I can wait forever."

"Oh, DeWitt, I wish I could just throw caution to the wind, but I don't want to end up like those poor souls I see everywhere. Half a dozen kids and not two nickels to rub together. They can't even afford a doctor when someone gets sick."

"That's what you think of me as a provider? Is it?" DeWitt's face glowed like the stoplight at the end of the block.

"That's not what I meant. It's this terrible depression. DeWitt, please. I love you and I don't want to fight."

"I don't want to fight either, but I need an answer."

"I can't talk any longer. I'm going to be late. See you in the morning?"

"I'm not sure. I have stuff I need to do. There's an important decision I got to make. And I need to make it by myself."

Meg got out of the car feeling as though she had been punched in the chest. She prayed she misunderstood. Surely he wasn't thinking about breaking their engagement. But for the first time doubt clouded her vision of the future. Dewitt told her everything, at least she was pretty sure he did. He said it helped him to talk things over with her. But ending their engagement was the one decision he would make without her.

She stood at the employee time sheet staring into space when a jolly voice made her jump.

"Penny for your thoughts, pretty girl." Albert grinned at her from behind the front desk.

"My thoughts aren't worth a penny."

Albert cocked a paternal eye at her. "That deputy giving you a bad time? If he won't do the right thing, I'll have a word with his boss. Ike should be in here sometime tonight."

To her dismay, tears rolled down her cheeks before she could stop them. "Oh, Albert. Please don't do that. DeWitt's not the problem. He'd get married tomorrow, but we don't have enough money for a house of our own."

Albert harrumphed and placed a soft fleshy hand on her arm. "Darling girl, if you're gonna wait for that kind of cash with times the way they are, you're likely to end up an old maid. Marry that boy and grab what happiness you can. I've seen the way he looks at you. If ever a man was in love it's DeWitt Williams."

Meg leaned across the desk and gave Albert a kiss on the cheek. "Thanks. I needed to hear that right now."

"If I'd known that's all it takes to get a pretty girl to kiss me, I woulda opened a matchmaking service a long time ago."

Meg gave Albert a watery smile. "Take some advice from me. Stick with what you know." She signed in and fled to the changing room.

The restaurant contained mostly local families, many of whom came every Wednesday for a late supper after prayer meeting at one of the downtown churches. As Albert predicted, Sheriff Ike Darnell sat with his wife and daughters in the center of the room greeting everyone who passed. When Ike's plate was empty, he left his family and started making the rounds. DeWitt said that election years brought out the best in Ike: glad-handing, kissing babies, charitable contributions to the poor, rides to the election polls for shut-ins—the list of good works was long.

The free barbecue dinners were especially popular. The number of hogs sacrificed every four years on the altar of re-election had increased to the point that several sties were emptied over the course of an election season. The voters were happy. The farmers were happy. Everyone was happy except, of course, the hogs.

Albert waited to come in for his evening coffee break until the room was nearly empty. When Ike saw him, he called across the room, "My pre-election picnic's coming up. Will we be seeing you and your lovely wife?"

Albert grinned. "Wouldn't miss it, Ike. Your boy cooks the best barbecue in the county."

Meg pursed her lips and raised her eyebrows at Albert, who pretended she wasn't in the room. Albert nodded again to the sheriff and left with a steaming mug and a saucer of pie. Her boss kept his political leanings a dark secret and was, therefore, invited to every event by every candidate. It was quite a feat in a town where a child's head cold might be reported in the Trib on a slow news week.

As she wiped down the empty tables, Albert's words played over and over in her mind. She glanced at Mrs. Darnell and her daughters conversing in the restaurant doorway and wondered if that would ever be her, a mother with children she loved and was proud of. DeWitt seemed on the verge of issuing an ultimatum and she wasn't sure what her answer would be. She loved him with all her heart and wanted to have his children. In fact, their physical relationship was something that she ached for just as much as he did. Was financial security worth losing the man she loved?

Visions of life without DeWitt swirled through her mind. When tears welled up again, she swiped angrily at them, shook her head, and focused on upending chairs onto the tables. She wondered if DeWitt would come in for breakfast tomorrow morning or still be angry enough to skip it.

Oh Lord, life was turning into a real mess.

The colored man who swept floors and did the heavy work started with his push broom, raising little puffs of dust that made Meg sneeze. She wondered in irritation why the floors weren't oiled more often and stepped into the lobby to get out of his way. The reception area was usually empty at this time of night, but the sheriff's wife and girls were huddled in a seating area near the entrance. Meg decided Ike had followed Albert into his office for a round of politicking.

She nodded to the Darnell women and picked up a hamper of clean laundry awaiting transport to the floors above. She would spend the rest of her shift sorting linens and making up unoccupied rooms. Most of the hotel's employees confined themselves to one type of work, but since she got free room and board in addition to her salary, Meg did whatever was needed. It was an unusual arrangement, but it meant that most of her earnings could be put away for the future.

She waited by the elevator's metal gate with the hamper on her hip. Her free hand went to her neck just below the base of the skull and massaged her aching muscles. They felt like rocks and thumping had begun in her temples. Soon her stomach would be upset and her period would start. There wasn't any part of her body that didn't rebel against the monthly visitation. No wonder it was called the curse.

The Blanche's elevator, the first one in Florida, creaked up and down on its thirty-year-old cables as though they were much older. While the car lumbered down from the third floor where the suites were located, Meg drummed her fingers on the laundry basket. Since Capone and his men were the only guests on the third floor, she fully expected one of them to step out of the car when it arrived. Capone had been true to his word and kept his men in line, but she still dreaded contact with them, however brief.

The car clanked to a stop, making Meg jump. Her heart rate increased and she considered hiding in a nearby hallway until the gangsters passed out of sight, but then chided herself for cowardice. When the outer gate opened, she squared her shoulders, but her anxiety disappeared like a balloon pricked by a pin.

"Good evening, Mr. Barnes."

The white haired gentleman's features froze, as though he had been so lost in thought he had forgotten his surroundings. When he finally focused on Meg, he slumped slightly, making Meg think he might be ill. She was on the verge of asking if he needed help when he visibly got a grip on himself and bowed slightly before passing from the elevator into the hallway.

"Good evening, Meg."

Meg watched the Columbia Tribune editor making his way to the front exit. Whatever was troubling him, he had recovered enough to resume his characteristic ramrod straight posture. Puzzled, she held the elevator gates open while she considered what the problem might be. It certainly looked like Mr. Barnes had come from the third floor and she concluded that he must have been there to see Capone. It was possible that he had interviewed Scarface about his visit to the area, the usual sort of thing the Trib ran on the community interest page, but somehow that just didn't make sense. Silas Barnes was known to be a proud man who took his moral code seriously, not the type to consort with gangsters.

Some impatient person on an upper floor lay on the elevator's call bell bringing Meg back to reality. She muttered an oath under her breath, boarded the car, and slammed the gates. Something was off here. She knew it was none of her business, but all the same, she made a mental note to mention Mr. Barnes to DeWitt. If she couldn't make him happy with the answer he wanted, at least she could help him in his job.

DeWitt. Thinking of him only increased Meg's frustration. She jabbed the third floor button. The fewest rooms needing attention were up there, so finishing them tonight seemed sensible. As the car crawled upward, cramps wrapped their vice-like fingers around Meg's uterus and squeezed hard. She felt the first dampness a moment later. She taped her foot impatiently while the elevator car groaned and finally settled itself at the third floor. Flinging the gates open, she nearly toppled into the gangster who had accosted her on his first night in town. Meg jumped out of his way into the hall as he pushed into the elevator.

The gangster had his hand on the down button when he stopped and called after Meg. "Hey. Ain't you the dame from the restaurant?"

Meg turned back and nodded.

"Goddamned phone out of order down there?" His words sounded more like a threat than a question. "Boss wants some sandwiches and glasses for five brought up to the room. Make it snappy and bring plenty of ice."

Meg's heart skipped a beat. "I'm sorry, sir, but the kitchen's closed. You could go down to the café around the corner if you hurry. They stay open a little later than we do."

The man stepped from the elevator and withdrew his wallet. He shoved a five and a ten into Meg's hamper. "Tell you what. How about you hurry your pretty little ass to anywheres you want, just make sure you come back with them sandwiches." He then turned and walked away.

"Sir, I can't do that. I'm on duty. I . . ."

The door to Capone's suite slammed.

She shifted the laundry hamper and hurried to her room. As she fumbled with her key, she heard the faint sound of the elevator descending. What now? Perhaps that awful man was going to the café after all. She listened for a moment then unlocked her door.

Meg's room was no bigger than a large closet. It was originally intended for a lady's maid or valet traveling with his or her employer, but the world had changed considerably since the Blanche opened its doors in 1902. Two steps into the room and she stood at her chest of drawers where she removed clean underwear and a sanitary pad. The pads were an expensive luxury, but a godsend that she couldn't do without.

After she washed and changed her underclothes, she sat on the bed for a moment. Albert wasn't going to like this, but too bad. Either she went to the café or he would have to go himself, as she doubted he would want the Blanche on Scarface's bad list.

As predicted, Albert was none too happy, but he opened the kitchen for her instead of sending her out. He saw no need to pay the competition when they had a perfectly good ham sitting in the cooler. He took the fifteen dollars and put it in his pocket without giving her any change.

"Albert, you can't keep all of that money! A sandwich and Co-Cola only cost $.75."

"Well now, let's see. There's the room service charge, the after hours charge, the crossing the road charge, food and beverages for five. Fifteen's about right. Wait another ten minutes before you go up." He grinned and left the kitchen.

How like him to leave me to clean up the mess, Meg mentally fumed. Her belly ached, her head hurt, and she was bone weary. She glanced at the wall clock above the kitchen door. Its hands were closing in on midnight. No wonder she felt exhausted. The unmade rooms could wait until tomorrow. She was going to bed as soon as this food trolley was delivered. In a huff, Meg slammed through the service door and out into the elevator passage.

By the time she reached Capone's suite, she had gotten a grip on her temper because a puzzle had pushed the anger aside. There were only four men in Capone's party, so who was the fifth sandwich for?

Chapter 16

Liz scanned the cars in her apartment building's parking area looking for Jonathan's yellow Vette. She was twenty minutes late due to a traffic standstill just before the Alachua exit. When she tried to call to let him know she was running late, he hadn't answered. Now she had a terrible premonition that he had given up and at best gone to dinner without her, at worst left for Jacksonville. She tried his cell number again.

"Hey, Babe. Where've you been?" Laughter, loud music, and the sound of ice clinking against glasses played in the background.

"I'm sorry. There was a really bad wreck on 75. Why didn't you answer when I called?"

"Guess I didn't hear it ring. I'm at the Gator Den. Why don't you come on over?"

"Jonathan, I've just raced to get here to cook a nice dinner for you. Wouldn't you rather eat at home?"

"Naw. Already had enough potato skins to kill my appetite."

"Okay then, see you in a minute."

Liz pressed the off button before Jonathan could reply. Good thing she hadn't stopped by the store for the steaks she'd planned on grilling. When she turned out of the parking lot onto West University, her tires squealed in protest as she stamped on the accelerator. Within moments, blue lights flashed behind her.

The young officer made a few notations on his ticket pad and came around to the driver's side. His eyes widened when he saw Liz. "M'am, where're you going in such a hurry?"

"I'm sorry, Officer. I guess I'm just distracted." There was no logical way to explain why she was speeding through rush hour traffic on the busiest street in Gainesville.

"You've got a Florida address on your insurance card, but Washington state plates. How did you manage that?"

"I just moved here. My insurance was due, so I had them send the card to my new address."

The officer wore an expression of polite disbelief as he started writing again. "Well, maybe a ticket will help you pay attention to the speed limit and remind you to get your Florida plates and license before you take this baby out to the races again." He whipped the offender's copy from his clipboard and handed it to Liz.

Great! Just wonderful! A hundred fifty dollar fine.

Exactly how she was going to pay it was yet to be determined. Liz was still paying for the damned car, which needed new tires before she could get it inspected, and her three month apartment lease was up at the beginning of November. Moving would cost money that she really didn't have, but she really wanted to be closer to campus. She steered out into traffic and traveled the next few blocks at a much more sedate speed.

At the end of a long block, the Gator Den hove into view and she put on her turn signal. After circling the parking lot three times, she finally cut off another car and pulled into a vacated spot. The other driver shot her the bird and yelled something that sounded like he was questioning her virtue or her parentage or both. Liz walked through the bar's door without looking back. She tried to raise some righteous indignation, but she knew the young man had a right to be angry. She only hoped he wasn't one of her students.

Liz's gaze swept the room while she pushed her way through the Friday evening crush. When she finally spotted Jonathan, his emerald eyes were looking meaningfully into a beautiful blonde's big peepers. He leaned in across the table and whispered something apparently hilarious in the girl's ear. Her laughter rang above the din of the overflow crowd. She must have been all of eighteen, if that. Even worse, Liz had seen the girl earlier that week.

"Hello, Baby. Here. Let me grab you a chair." When she was seated, he continued. "This is . . . what's your name again?"

"We've met." Liz matched the girl's wide-eyed stare until she muttered something about needing to do homework and fled.

"She's one of my students. That's why I hate coming here. I've told you that several times."

"Yeah, but they have the best burgers in town. Can I order you one? I've eaten."

Liz smelled the odor, onions and beer, when Jonathan leaned over to give her a peck on her cheek.

"Sure. Why not?" There was no reason for her to starve just because she wanted to throttle her date.

When Jonathan rose, Liz saw several female heads turn and follow his progress toward the counter. After he disappeared in the crowd, one of the girls turned back to Liz. Sure enough, another of her students smiled at her from the next table. The girl leaned over to her companions, whispered something, and then all three giggled. Liz could feel the flush crawling from her throat up onto her face.

That was enough. She wasn't about to sit there and eat a burger she didn't really want while being scrutinized by children that she would see at 8:00 a.m. on Monday morning. She rose with as much dignity as she had left and nodded at her student. Halfway to the order counter, she bumped into Jonathan.

"You going to the ladies? It's the other way."

"No, I'm leaving."

"But your food's already been ordered."

"Try to cancel the order or leave it. I really don't care." Liz marched toward the door while shouting over her shoulder, "You coming or would you rather stay here and flirt with teenagers?" She didn't look back to see if he followed.

Long after eating a salad in her apartment, Liz heard the Vette's familiar rumble. She was in bed, but hadn't slept at all. The clock on the bedside table showed 1:00 a.m. She quickly yanked off her gown and threw on an old t-shirt. She had no intention of looking like she was anxiously awaiting him to grace her with his amorous attentions, delightful though they were. He knocked just as she zipped up her jeans.

She waited thirty seconds and opened the door.

"I'm not in any condition to drive back to Jacksonville tonight. Can I sleep here?"

"You've got a key. Why didn't you use it?"

"Couldn't get it in the lock. You sleeping in jeans these days?"

"I've been grading papers. Hadn't gone to bed yet." Why she felt the need to tell lies now was beyond reason.

Jonathan fell through the door and landed halfway onto the sofa where he crawled the rest of the way, curled up like a cat, and promptly began snoring. As angry as she was, Liz knew from the weather report on the 10:30 news that the first cold front of the year was due. She grabbed a blanket and threw it over him.

After a night of fretful, broken sleep, Liz awoke much later than usual. When she glanced at the clock on her nightstand, it read 11:00. One of the things that had enticed her to rent this place was its coffee bar in the master bedroom, a very hip convenience for a girl who was decidedly not a morning person. She made herself a cup and padded back to bed.

The knob on her door turned and Jonathan poked his head in. "Hey. Sorry about last night. Am I forgiven?"

"Why should you be?" Liz was still angry.

"Look, I know I acted like a pig. I admit it. But I came to Gainesville last night without calling first because there's something I need to tell you in person."

A spark of fear mixed with irritation stirred within Liz.

"Can I have some of that?" Jonathan pointed at her coffee.

"Of course. You know where it is."

Jonathan strode over to the coffee bar and poured a cup to which he added four sugars and creamer. Just thinking about that combination hitting a hung over stomach made Liz queasy, but Jonathan showed no signs of running for the toilet. She found herself adding his ability to bounce back so quickly from a night of drinking to his list of offenses. He shouldn't be so damned energetic. A night of disturbed sleep had left her with a pounding head and feeling at least one beat behind the tempo. She wasn't sure she could deal with distressing surprises this morning.

Bringing his cup to the bed, he dropped down beside Liz and kissed her lightly on the lips. She glanced at the spilled sugar and drops of creamer scattered across the coffee bar's gleaming granite and felt her irritation grow. Not once did he ever think that someone had to clean up the mess.

"Hey, I'm an inconsiderate jerk sometimes. I wouldn't have flirted with that girl if I'd known she was your student. Besides, it didn't mean anything."

"Jonathan, the flirting was just the last straw. You know why I hate the Gator Den, yet you went there anyway. You couldn't wait twenty lousy minutes. With you, it's everything right away all the time."

"I went on duty at midnight and left for Gainesville as soon as I got off. Hadn't eaten anything since supper Thursday."

"Well, you could have said something. Then I wouldn't have raced like a maniac to get here so I could cook!" Liz surprised herself by the shrillness in her voice. Even to her own ears, she sounded like a fishwife.

Jonathan turned a distinct shade of puce. "Look, I didn't come here to argue with you. There's something you need to know and I thought it would be better to tell you in person than over the phone." Liz's brows rose in surprise. "Yeah, even I can think of someone else occasionally, hard as that is to imagine."

Liz's anger evaporated. "What's wrong?"

"Baby, this is as hard on me as it is on you. Please believe that."

"Okay. Don't keep me in suspense. Out with it."

"I'm being transferred to Spain after the first of the year."

"Spain? Do we have a base there?" Liz knew it was a stupid question as she was asking it.

"Of course. My whole squadron is being sent there. We share the base with the Spanish Navy."

"Where in Spain?"

"Rota. On the Atlantic Coast."

"But what about us? I gave up my life in Seattle to move here to be with you."

A surprised expression crossed Jonathan's face. "Well, you can come along if you want. Rota is a resort area with a pretty nice beach."

"I can't leave my job in the middle of the academic year after only one semester. No university would ever hire me again."

"I can't help what the Navy decides to do. It's their call, not mine." He turned from her and looked at the trees outside her window.

"Jonathan, do you really care whether I move to Spain?"

He paused for several beats before answering, "Sure."

Damn him, damn him! He still wouldn't say those three words she desperately needed to hear.

"I don't know. I'll have to think about it."

"Got anything to make for breakfast?"

Liz nodded. "Take a shower while I get it ready. Eggs and bacon. Take it or leave it."

Jonathan tilted his head slightly to one side as though he was thinking it over. Or maybe he was simply surprised that she was still angry with him. Either way, Liz was in no mood for hanging around the apartment in bed all day, their usual weekend activity.

Liz stood at the range absentmindedly pushing eggs around the pan. The future looked bleak indeed. Her head told her it would be folly in the extreme to pull up stakes once again to follow a man who couldn't commit, but her heart told her that Jonathan was the love of her life and that she would probably never get over losing him.

His arms slipped around her waist, bringing Liz back to the present.

"That smells good. How about a little something sweet after breakfast?" He brushed her hair aside and let his lips wander over the nape of her neck.

Dropping the spatula against the pan's edge, Liz turned so that she could look at him. "Jonathan, I need some space. I want you to go back to Jacksonville as soon as we eat." It came out sharper than she had intended.

"Whoa! If that's how you feel I'll get out now."

"You drop a bomb on me and expect everything to be sweetness and light? I need time to think. I moved across the country for you and now you ask me to leave my new job and go to the other side of the world. How did you think I'd react?"

"Look, it was your idea to move to Florida. Remember? I admit I liked it, but I didn't ask or expect you to do anything then or now."

Liz felt the volcano that had been building since last night explode. "That's really hitting below the belt! But since you brought it up, it looks like I'm the only one who makes sacrifices in this relationship! You're happy as long as it doesn't cost you anything. Well, here's how life really works. You have to give as well as take."

Without another word, he pushed Liz away and strode from the room. The front door slammed shortly thereafter.

Liz stared at the spot where Jonathan had stood a moment ago. There were other ways she could have handled his little surprise besides being sullen and kicking him out. As much as it hurt, he was right. He hadn't asked her to uproot her life for him. It had been her idea and her decision. Jonathan had been pleased, but in all honesty, he had also been surprised.

Acknowledging that he might not care as deeply as she did made her head swim. She sat down on the floor and rested her forehead on her knees. Sobs shook her body until she slumped over onto the cold tiles. They pressed into her cheek, but she welcomed the discomfort. It gave her something to focus on other than the pain tearing her apart.

Her phone rang and Roberta's name popped up on the caller ID. Liz didn't have the energy or the courage to talk to her editor at the moment so she let it roll to voice mail. She sat up and leaned back against the cabinet. Crying wasn't going to solve any of her problems and sitting around the apartment all weekend feeling sorry for herself would drive her into deep depression, but she just couldn't face anything work related. She felt overwhelmed to the point of inertia when she thought about the stacks of ungraded papers waiting on the coffee table or the barely begun new course proposals. She could try to work on her novel, but her creativity was at its nadir.

She pushed herself to her feet and shuffled to the bathroom. The mirror above the sink reflected a mess of a woman. Swollen eyes, tangled hair. A perfect complement to her tangled, messy life. She sucked on her lower lip and wondered how to keep utter despair at bay. As much as she would love to give in to hysterics, she couldn't afford to become nonfunctional. Her career rode on her success at Florida.

She leaned over the sink and splashed water over her face. Getting lost in the past had always been her antidote to worry or unhappiness. Maybe returning to Lake City would blot out last night and this morning. She would take a room near the Blanche. That might provide an atmospheric distraction as well. She could finish her search through the Columbia Trib, spend the night, and maybe find someone to interview on Sunday. After showering and throwing on her most comfortable jeans, she looked in the mirror again. The woman looking back was shinier, but no happier. Determined to block out her pain, she locked her apartment door.

The traffic north on I-75 was almost as heavy as that in the southbound lanes, filled as they were with snowbirds headed to the Gold Coast for the season. Snowbirds was a term Liz had just learned, but it accurately described the travelers fleeing frigid northern winters. Since it was now well past noon, Liz decided to check into the Blanche first and then look for a place to grab lunch.

Liz struggled into a parallel parking space in front of the old building and stepped onto the narrow sidewalk. As she surveyed the area, it was like being transported back to a simpler time. It was easy to envision Model T's and farm wagons sharing the two-lane street and ladies in hats and gloves going in and out of shops. Liz looked up into the sun and shaded her eyes.

Hotel Blanche etched in concrete was set at the top of the building's third floor brick facade. From all appearances, the Blanche took up most of the city block. Liz wondered how the hotel could make it since the interstate bypassed the downtown by several miles. When she glanced at the entrance, she began to get a clue. Blanche Center in cream lettering stood out on a dark green awning. A peek through the locked glass front doors showed a freestanding marquee filled with the locations of county government offices. She cupped her hands around her eyes and peered through the glass to get a peek inside.

The lobby was much as it must have been during Capone's stay. Black and white tiles covered the floor, which led past what would have been the reception desk to a hallway containing an early vintage elevator. Six foot tall dark wainscoting covered the lower walls with cream-colored plaster above, extending to the twenty-foot ceiling. Embossed brass fixtures completed the turn of the century atmosphere. Back in its day, the Blanche must have been an island of gentility in a sea of agricultural swampland.

Her growling stomach reminded her that she hadn't eaten anything but a salad since noon yesterday. A little café around the corner from the hotel entrance announced dinner served 11:00 to 2:00, supper 5:00-8:00. She had five minutes. She trotted across the side street and through a door with 7 Lakes Café, Serving Fine Southern Cooking Since 1920 painted in gold letters on its glass.

A waitress, who looked to be in her seventies and wearing an old-fashioned shirtwaist uniform, greeted her. "You just made it, Honey. Sit anywhere you want. Be with you in a minute." Ethel, according to her nametag, shoved a menu into Liz's hand and disappeared behind a swinging door.

Liz chose a table next to the window. Sitting at the laminate top surrounded by chairs whose frames were a continuous L curve of chrome was like stepping back into the fifties. The wall decorations and Coke signs contained images that Liz had only seen in her grandmother's ancient magazine collection. The menu apparently hadn't changed one iota since the Eisenhower era either. Offerings were southern fried, country fried, pan-fried, boiled, or prepared with mayo. Only one lonely little dinner salad served with Ranch or French hovered at the end of the list of sides.

Ethel reappeared. "Whatcha gonna have, Hon?"

"Do you think you could put some of the sandwich turkey on the house salad?"

"You wantin' a chef salad ain'tcha? How about I ask the cook to put a little ham, cheese, and boiled egg on it too?"

With such a kind offer, Liz could only answer, "Thank you. That would be wonderful."

"What kinda dressing you want?"

"Nothing please."

"Dry? You ain't from around here are you, Hon?"

"I've just moved from Seattle to Gainesville. I teach at the university."

"Whatcha doin' in Lake City?"

"A little research into the Blanche's history."

"You must be the girl lookin' for old copies of the Trib. Ever find 'em?" Liz must have looked surprised because the waitress continued without waiting for an answer, "The editor's secretary eats lunch here most days. She gets lonely in that office all by herself so much. Talks up a blue streak when she comes in."

Liz decided Ethel might be the goldmine of information she sought. "I did finally find the copies at the junior college. Have you lived in Lake City long?"

"All my life. Family on both sides has been here since the early 1800's. There ain't much I don't know about county history."

"When I've finished at the college, may I interview you? At your convenience, of course."

"Sure. I like talking about the old days. I work everyday except Monday. Come by whenever you want to. About this time of day is good, then we can sit here in the café and have some iced tea while we talk."

Lunch completed, Liz considered her next stop. With the flow of travelers on the interstate, she decided not to wait until evening to find a room. She backtracked to 75 and paid a premium for the last one at a national chain. Not many people wanted mini-suites these days. The pain in her pocketbook, however, couldn't hold a candle to the pain still punching her in the mid-section at the most unexpected moments, like when she realized the hotel clerk's eyes were the exact green of Jonathan's. Unusual color, hard to find, until you didn't want to see it.

She drove out of the hotel parking area and punched the accelerator. The tires squealed and the car fishtailed. Liz tightened her grip on the wheel, got the car under control, and brought it back down to the speed limit. Driving recklessly seemed to be becoming a habit, but her heart's pumping told her she wasn't cut out for the danger. When she pulled into a parking slot at the junior college, she was doing a sedate 15 mph.

She no longer needed the loaner lab coat. She pulled a sweatshirt from her book bag and slipped it on before going to the shelf for the big volume containing the 1930 Columbia Trib issues. Picking up where she left off, Liz turned to the next Friday, which happened to be July 4. Editor Barnes had abandoned his crusade against vice for once in favor of a patriotic tribute to the nation, so she turned to the police report and scanned down the column until her eyes locked onto an item.

Joseph Johnson, Negro, was found hanging from a tree in his front yard in the early hours of Saturday, June 28. Johnson, also known as Keno Joe, was a resident of O'Leno for forty years. Ashes from a large fire were also present in the yard of the home located on the Santa Fe River.

Keno. Now that made things interesting. First, two ladies of the evening and now someone who had a gambling game for a nickname, all of whom were lynched beside burning crosses. And then there was O'Leno. This was the second time it had been mentioned in the police reports. Liz looked back through the issues. There it was, June 14, the last time that anyone had seen Big Charlie Blankenship. Could it be that he hadn't run off with a girl friend after all? That perhaps his disappearance had some connection to the crime wave plaguing the purveyors of vice in 1930 Columbia County, Florida? Whatever the answer, it certainly looked like the KKK was answering Editor Silas Barnes's call to action.

Chapter 17

Meg rolled the trolley from the elevator and headed toward the pretentiously named Presidential Suite. As far as she knew, no presidents had ever stayed at the Blanche, but she supposed the owner could always hope. The only sound in the dimly lit hallway came from the ironstone plates clattering as the trolley moved over the thick carpet runner.

Meg wheeled up to Capone's door and started to knock, but raised voices stayed her hand. The thick walls and door muffled some of the words, but she caught enough of the loudest exchange to make her heart race.

"You can't talk to the boss that way!"

"I can and I will. I'm the law in this county and what I say goes. Capone, you and your men need to leave town no later than tomorrow. It's best for everybody. Is that clear?"

The rest became muffled again until the door opened and Sheriff Ike Darnell filled its frame. His eyes widened when he saw Meg.

"Miss Blevins." He nodded and made his way toward the elevator.

Meg hesitated just outside the door.

"Hey you! Girly. Bring da food in." Vito, the gangster who had given her trouble that first night, beckoned with an elaborate gesture.

As she passed, he swatted her on the bottom. She increased her pace while the hoodlum laughed.

"Ain't she just the prettiest little thing you ever seen?" The man's attempt at a southern drawl was ludicrous and insulting.

Meg kept her eyes glued to the floor until she reached Capone.

"Sir, would you sign the check, please?" She was afraid to address him by name, real or alias.

"Gimme that. Boss don't sign for nothing."

Meg nodded and handed the room service bill to the henchman.

"Where should I set up, sir?" She directed the question to no one in particular and didn't make eye contact with any of the men.

The henchman looked to his boss, who waved his hand in the general direction of the marble fireplace. Meg rolled her trolley across the room, moved a small table from the alcove created by bay windows, and laid out the meal. Set up completed, she made for the door but as she passed Vito, he grabbed her arm and turned her to face him. In one swift motion, he stuffed money into the front of her uniform. He held her for several beats while gazing into her eyes. To her horror, Meg felt tears welling up. The hoodlum leaned in. Meg was sure he would try to kiss her or worse. Terrified, she could only stare at the man like a small animal mesmerized by a cobra.

Without warning, he planted a quick kiss on her cheek and laughed. "I do believe this one's pure as the driven snow."

Capone's second-in-command came to life. "You heard the boss the first time. Leave her be."

Vito looked at the man, smirked, and released Meg's arm. "Well, kid, I don't have to take a woman if she don't want it. I got plenty begging for it. You run along now and be a good little girl, you hear?"

Meg walked toward the door with as much dignity as she could muster, but with her hand on the knob, Vito called, "Hey, pretty girl. Tell that fat boss of yours I had to tip you again since he didn't give you no change. I expect the extra to be taken off our bill and the tip stays in your pocket, see?"

Meg nodded and fled. When she was finally in the elevator with the gates closed, she slumped back against the wall. She felt as though she hadn't drawn breath since the hoodlum first touched her. When she looked down at her hands, she saw they were trembling. Sheriff Darnell's words echoed in her memory and her entire body went limp with relief. Thank goodness Columbia County had a sheriff who wasn't afraid to stand up to big time gangsters.

The kitchen was completely dark when Meg pushed the swinging door open with her hip. She parked the trolley just inside and turned down the service hall to the back stairs. Even though staff was allowed to use the elevator late at night, there was no way she was going to risk passing Capone's door again.

Meg closed her bedroom door and turned the key. It felt so strange. It was what people in cities did. Seldom in her eighteen years had she felt the need to secure a door, but tonight she feared the Yale lock might not be strong enough. Her cubbyhole of a room retained all of the day's heat and sweat covered her in an instant. She went to the sink and ran cold water over her wrists, then splashed her face. The headache and intestinal distress brought on by her period were finally easing, but the cramps marched on. Meg leaned against the sink and stared at her reflection in the mirror.

Her face looked bloated and dark circles under her eyes showed how much she needed rest. It had been an exhausting, distressing, and confusing day. Her argument with DeWitt weighed the heaviest, but the puzzle of what Mr. Barnes had been doing on the third floor also played at the back of her mind. Since Mr. Phillips, a.k.a. Al Capone, and his men were the only guests in residence on that floor, she could only conclude that Mr. Barnes had visited the gangsters. Given the editor's very determined anti-crime campaign that began in January and was still in full swing, it was very odd that he would have any truck whatsoever with those men. DeWitt fumed constantly that Barnes was only interested in circulation numbers and was afraid that he was stirring up trouble. DeWitt even argued with his boss, Sheriff Darnell, about trying to get the editor to back off. But Meg believed Mr. Barnes was sincere. Maybe he pushed too hard, but she thought his heart was in the right place.

As to the situation with DeWitt, hard as she tried, no good option presented itself. She loved him and wanted to spend her life with him, but she also wanted to save enough money to buy a home that they owned outright before they married. Marriage meant children and children needed a home that no bank or depression could take away from them. She shook her head in frustration. Lack of sleep wasn't going to bring the answers.

Eying the fire escape hanging outside her windows, Meg decided to leave them closed. Maybe if she turned the ceiling fan on high and slept in her panties, she could make it until morning. After sponge bathing from face to feet, she rejected the towel in favor of stretching out on the bed with droplets still clinging to her face and body.

Throwing the spread back, she lay down on the top sheet, but even with the fan whirling at top speed, sweat soon popped out and trickled onto the bed. Knowing she would never get to sleep in such stifling heat, she put on her lightest gown and adjusted the windows' sashes so that air could circulate. Dying of suffocation was probably a greater danger than harm from intruders. Common sense said Capone's men wouldn't be interested enough in hotel maids to seek out their quarters.

Meg flopped on the bed again, but sleep proved elusive. The scene with DeWitt replayed continuously, keeping her tossing and turning into the wee hours. Images of half a dozen kids, several of them in dirty diapers, living with her and DeWitt in three rooms above somebody's backyard garage vied with scenes of a future spent searching for what she once had with him and never found again. He was the love of her life. She was sure of it.

Mama said she and DeWitt were lucky to have found each other so young. They would have a lifetime together, maybe not riches, but something far more important. Mama was right about most things, but Meg feared poverty more than death. The stress of living hand-to-mouth could kill love faster than the 1918 Spanish flu had killed soldiers and civilians by the thousands. And when affection died under those conditions, it rarely revived. Meg had seen it too often among friends and neighbors, especially after the stock market crash. She didn't know what she would do if DeWitt issued an ultimatum.

Her headache returned with a vengeance. She had a full day tomorrow and couldn't afford to wallow in self-pity any longer. She rolled out of bed and went to the sink. Grabbing a bottle from the medicine cabinet, she gulped down two aspirin and returned to bed. Maybe things would look better in the morning.

The rising sun brought with it a pain free head, but one feeling fuzzy from too little sleep. Meg struggled through her morning routine and arrived at the restaurant only moments before her shift began. She spied Albert having breakfast at the table by the front window. Anger rose like bile and she descended on him mid-bite.

"I will not go back to *Mr. Phillips's* suite ever again, so don't ask. I don't care what the reason is."

"Well good morning to you too, Miss Blevins. Have a seat and tell me what's on your mind." Albert grinned up at her, increasing her agitation and bringing heat to her face. Sometimes his perpetually sunny outlook was simply infuriating.

"I'll stand, thank you very much." The story of her most recent Capone encounter poured out in a stream of anger, fear, and frustration, ending with, "And you better take that amount off their bill like I told you the first time if you know what's good for you."

Albert looked taken aback. "I'm sorry Meg. I had no idea it would be like that."

To her dismay, she felt tears forming. "After everything that's been reported about him, how can you say that? You just didn't want to be bothered last night, did you?"

He had the good grace to look truly contrite. "I guess you're right. I was tired and wanted to go home. I'm really sorry."

Meg nodded and went to get her order pad. If she continued to talk with Albert, she feared she would say something they both would regret.

Through the restaurant's glass doors, she could see one of Capone's men stepping from the elevator with the bellboy in tow. His luggage cart was mounded over and the boy struggled to get it over the elevator's lip. Relief flooded Meg. It seemed that Capone had taken Sheriff Darnell's warning seriously. She added that to her list of things to tell DeWitt.

For the rest of the morning, Meg's attention remained glued to the front door, but the person she awaited so anxiously never appeared. When breakfast officially ended at 10:30, she knew he wasn't coming.

Chapter 18

Anxious to see if Editor Barnes might inform the connections Liz thought she was seeing among the 1930 murders, she quickly flipped to the July 11 editorial page and read his comments.

My Fellow Citizens:

As you will be aware, a rash of lynchings, for they can be called nothing less, has broken out in our fair community and there are some who would lay their genesis at the Tribune's door. These persons would have you believe that this editor has intentionally stirred up the vigilante element that has been so active of late. They accuse this writer of desiring and promoting the unhappy ends that have come to those persons alleged to be controlling vice in Columbia County.

While comments decrying the low state of morality among those persons degrading our community's reputation have certainly appeared in this column, it was never their purpose to elicit violence. The sole intention from the first has been to inform the public, a public seemingly as apathetic now as it has been in the past toward criminal activity. And lest one dismiss these killings as justice meted out to an inferior and deserving race, consider this: two white persons, one of them a woman, can be counted among those who met with violent ends. This writer can only speculate at what will finally get the attention of the good people of Columbia County.

Liz stared at the article and thought about what Barnes had written. It dawned on her that he mentioned two whites.

She only recalled one. She quickly turned to the police reports and found two simple entries.

James "Jamie" Tuttle, white, 40, found dead in the front room of his home in Five Points. The cause of death is reported as gunshot through the heart. There were ashes of a recent fire in the front yard of the home.

Moses Jackson, 55-year-old Negro, found hanging from a tree in the front yard of his home. A cross blazed beside him when neighbors came to cut him down.

Liz shoved the big volume of bound newspapers away and turned to the spiral where she had been jotting down notes. She felt the need to get a handle on the information she'd collected. She read everything through again, this time making a chart of the pertinent data. After looking over the spreadsheet, she concluded that Editor Barnes knew more than he revealed in his articles. For one thing, he didn't state the names of those he railed against. Was it because gambling, moonshining, and prostitution had been so out in the open he felt it unnecessary to print the names of those involved? Perhaps. Law enforcement in rural backwaters sometimes took a very lenient view of such things. They were often undertrained or too shorthanded to deal with what was viewed as petty crime.

As to the lynchings, Liz made a note to search later Trib editions, but she suspected that the killers were never brought to justice. In the case of Klan lynchings and other acts of racial hatred, law enforcement too often simply looked the other way. Even worse, officers of the law were sometimes directly involved in the evil perpetrated by the KKK. Her study of history had shown that it was a sadly all too common occurrence across the pre-civil rights South.

Alternatively, Barnes might have been afraid, but his crusade led her to believe otherwise. And who were his accusers? What Barnes had left unsaid was as important as what was on the page in black and white. He denied any responsibility for a call to violence, but as far as she could tell, he hadn't written anything to dissuade those carrying out the lynchings until this article. Taking umbrage at being accused of stirring up trouble was the first time he had come close to denouncing it. The KKK seemed the guilty party, but Barnes hadn't even mentioned them in his editorials. He merely made a veiled reference this one time. Barnes seemed to be walking a very fine line.

Then there were the questions that any investigative reporter would have asked long ago. Why this particular time for his crusade? It seemed probable that the community had long viewed vice activities as victimless crimes and had never really cared much about ending them. Liz tapped her pen on the table as she stared at the long shadows outside the library window. Who stood to benefit from these deaths? Could someone have been poised to step into a void being created in the area's underworld? So far there was absolutely no evidence that Scarface had any interest in smalltime criminal activities conducted in northern Florida's palmetto swamps and pine thickets. But then why the extended stay?

Perhaps Capone had a local proxy, but who? Liz allowed her imagination to take flight. Could it have been Barnes himself? An intriguing thought. Other than his apparent responsibility in stirring up the Klan, she had no actual facts to support this theory, but a part of her hoped he was involved. She had taken a distinct dislike to his grandiosity and self-adulation.

Liz pushed her chair back and stretched. Her neck and back were tense from having bent over the newspapers all afternoon and her lunchtime salad had worn off some time ago. She glanced at her watch and decided a return trip to the 7 Lakes was in order. Ethel might have the answers she sought, or if not, might be able to point her to someone who did. If she knew as much county history as she claimed, Ethel might even know why Capone stayed here for twelve days in 1930. The sun hovered on the horizon as Liz retraced her route back to the little main street, returning to the parking spot in front of the Blanche.

The café was almost empty when Liz pushed through the door. Disappointingly, there was no sign of Ethel. Since her main purpose wasn't the food, a place out on the interstate would certainly have more varied offerings.

She had her hand on the door handle when a voice called, "Hey, Hon, we're still open. We just ain't very busy tonight. Come on back in and sit anywhere you want."

Ethel's softly wrinkled face with its tightly permed blue-gray halo poked through the kitchen door. She bustled into the dining room with a loaded tray and served her only other customers. Liz chose a table away from the elderly couple that was tucking into fried chicken and mashed potatoes.

In a moment, a menu dropped onto the table. "Know what you gonna have or do you need a minute?"

Liz decided to give in and eat like a local. "What's good tonight?"

Ethel grinned and raised an eyebrow. "Everything on the menu, but if I was ordering, I'd go with the chicken."

"Spoken like a true diplomat. I'll follow your recommendation." Liz looked around the café. "Since you aren't very busy, can I buy you dinner? I'd love the company unless your boss would object."

"I guess I'm the boss this time of day." Ethel nodded toward the kitchen and laughed. "For sure it ain't the cook. I done had supper, but I'll take a glass of tea. Be back in a minute with your food."

Ethel brought her order fairly quickly then turned toward the beverage counter with "be back directly" called over her shoulder. Liz eyed the mounded over plate before her and took a tentative bite. The chicken was melt-in-your-mouth delicious as were the homemade mashed potatoes, garden peas, and biscuits that had to be made from scratch. There may have been a week's worth of calories on the plate, but it was the pinnacle of comfort food and Liz sorely needed that commodity. All afternoon, images of Jonathan's handsome face in various attitudes had intruded despite her resolve to lock the issue of Spain away until she was alone in her hotel room.

The chair opposite Liz scrapped back and Ethel's ample form plopped down. "Well, I'll be. Never thought a skinny little thing like you could put away that much food. Glad you liked it. How about a slice of lemon icebox pie?"

"Only if you'll join me."

"Don't mind if I do." Ethel nodded and rose from the chair.

While the waitress fussed with the stubborn door on the display cooler, Liz reached into her purse and placed a small digital voice recorder in her lap.

Ethel returned with slices that looked to be a quarter of the pie each. When she saw Liz's expression, she grinned.

"This is all there was. No need in leaving one little slice in the pan that'll have to be thrown out in the morning. The cook makes fresh pies everyday."

Liz took a bite and was immediately transported. "I don't think I've ever tasted anything this fabulous."

"I'm guessing you ain't used to our kind of home cooking."

Liz smiled ruefully. "I'm afraid I'm not accustomed to very much home cooking of any type. If it didn't come from a box, can, or the freezer, my mother didn't serve it. I'm afraid I've followed in her footsteps."

"Well, you just enjoy this then. If you was my granddaughter, I'd feed you up for sure."

Liz was touched by the maternal light in the waitress's eyes and wondered why she was still working at her age. Ethel looked to be in her seventies, maybe more. Although Liz would never say it aloud, if Ethel were her grandmother, she wouldn't be standing on her feet all day or lugging heavy trays. As Liz gazed into the kindly face, she thought how lovely it would be to simply chat for the rest of the evening. It had been a long time since she had spent more than a brief weekend with her own grandmother whom she loved dearly. But glancing at the wall clock above the kitchen door, Liz decided she'd better move on to her main objective.

Between bites, she said, "When I was here for lunch, I mentioned my research and you said you enjoy talking about the old days. May I take you up on your offer now?"

"Sure. If I didn't know them, I probably heard about them from Mama and Daddy. There wasn't anything that happened around here then that people didn't know about by the next day."

Liz lifted the recorder from her lap and placed it on the table. "If you don't mind, I find that using this is better than trying to take notes. Writing while someone's talking is distracting."

Ethel eyed the recorder with the suspicion displayed by many older people born before the technological age. She paused for a moment and then said, "I guess there cain't be no harm in it. That way you won't make a mistake about what I say."

"Exactly. What you have to say could be very important and I want to get it down as accurately as possible."

"Well then, fire away."

"What I've read in the old newspapers leads me to think that 1930 was a difficult year for Columbia County."

Ethel nodded. "All the 30's was hard times everywhere, especially for little places like this. Between the Depression and years of bad crop prices, lots of folks around here was just about ruined. And it wasn't just the farmers who suffered. The town depended on good crop prices to bring money in just as much as the farmers did."

This wasn't the direction Liz had hoped the conversation would take, but she smiled sympathetically. "My grandparents talked a lot about the Depression, especially when I threw away anything that could be reused. My grandmother even saved the rubber bands and plastic sleeves that came around the newspapers delivered to her house. She said you never knew when you might need them."

Ethel's expression became stern. "And she was right. I save string and tinfoil myself."

Liz wanted very badly to steer the interview toward the information she needed, but she didn't want to risk seeming impolite or unusually inquisitive. A stranger abruptly asking too many questions about sensitive issues could put off people, especially in small towns. While Liz cast about for the best way to broach her subject, the two women fell into a companionable silence broken only by the ping of fork tines hitting ironstone plates and ice clinking against tea glasses.

When the silence became too long for comfort, Liz decided to take the plunge. "Ethel, you know I'm researching county history, but I don't think I've mentioned exactly what I'm looking into."

"No, you ain't. Figured you'd get around to it eventually."

"I'm particularly interested in the year 1930."

When Ethel didn't comment, Liz ventured, "Do you remember a Columbia Tribune editor named Silas Barnes?"

It could have been Liz's imagination, but Ethel seemed to draw back slightly at the mention of the editor's name. "Daddy mentioned him once or twice."

Liz removed the chart from her purse and placed it so that Ethel could see it. "I've read all of his columns from January through the end of July of that year and I'm a little confused about what was happening then."

"Well, I wasn't born 'til '33, so I may not be much help."

"Perhaps, but I thought you might have heard your parents or grandparents talk about it. It seemed to be a pretty turbulent time."

"Like I said, times was hard. It was the Depression."

Liz didn't know if the waitress was being purposely evasive or simply didn't know anything about events that occurred before she was born. Either way, Liz decided to be more direct. Pointing to the chart, she continued, "This is what I find confusing. Mr. Barnes wrote as though the county was engulfed in a crime wave, but he barely mentioned the unusual number of murders taking place over a short period of time. And when he finally wrote about them, he implied that the victims were criminals who deserved what happened."

Ethel looked at the chart and shrugged. "If you say so. I ain't ever had any reason to read anything that far back."

Fearing she might be pushing too hard, Liz continued with what she hoped was sufficient sympathy. "I can certainly understand that. I haven't gone through the old newspapers in my grandmother's attic either, but she's talked a lot about what happened when she was young. I'm hoping that maybe your parents or grandparents did the same."

Ethel's eyes narrowed. "What do you really want to know?"

Hearing the edge in the waitress's voice, Liz decided she'd better explain herself. "My area of specialization is history of American crime and I'm doing research for an article that I hope will be published in the *Florida Historical Quarterly*."

"And what does that have to do with Columbia County?"

Liz pointed to the chart again. "Well, a lot happened here in 1930. These events may have been connected or merely coincidence. The answer may depend on whether the murder victims were involved in criminal activities."

Ethel stared at the back wall for several beats, then her brows drew together in a frown and she shrugged. "Guess it depends on what you mean by criminal."

Beginning to feel frustrated, Liz made an effort to keep her voice even. "From reading Mr. Barnes's columns, it looks like moonshining and gambling were high on the list. Prostitution for sure. The way he described the two female victims, he might as well have called them madams outright."

Ethel harrumphed and her lips became a thin line. "There was a time in this county when people could do what they wanted to so long as they didn't hurt nobody but themselves."

"That's exactly the problem. It seems like one day vice activities were ignored by everyone and suddenly the next it was very important to have them all brought to an end. Would you take a look at the names and see if you can remember anything you may have heard?"

Liz sensed the older woman's reluctance, and after several second's silence, feared Ethel was on the verge of refusing when she finally nodded. Liz pushed the chart across the table and Ethel studied it for some time. When she spoke, her eyes held a wistful expression. "Daddy used to say that some people and places get to be like a wound that's still infected after the skin's healed over. On the outside, they look normal and healthy, but on the inside, deep down, the corruption's still there. After a while, it just eats up everything from the inside out. He was a deacon at First Baptist. Wrongdoing troubled him a lot."

"Did he ever talk about the nature of the wrongdoing?"

Ethel glanced up with an expression that Liz couldn't quite interpret. It seemed as though the discussion had become painful for the older woman. "They was all sinners. Gambling, moonshining, women—you name it."

"Did your father ever talk about why these particular people were targeted?"

"He said they was the ones that controlled sin in the county 'til the Klan got aholt of 'em."

Liz hesitated, then decided to go for the prize. "Did he know why the KKK chose this particular time to act? Did Silas Barnes have that much influence or was there another reason?"

The shades suddenly dropped in Ethel's eyes and she shoved the chart back to Liz. "It's getting late and I got to close up. Owner don't like it if customers are here after closing time."

As Liz followed the waitress to the cash register, she wanted to kick herself. In her eagerness, she had somehow hurt this kind old lady, but she wasn't sure how nor did she understand precisely which question had caused Ethel to shut down. She gave the impression that she knew more than she wanted to say, which was odd since she initially seemed so eager to talk about the town's history.

The cash drawer clanged open and Ethel held out her hand, her whole demeanor communicating impatience.

Liz donned what she hoped was her most winning smile. "Thank you for talking with me. I'm sorry that I kept you from getting your work done." When the older woman didn't respond, Liz found herself babbling on. "Thank you for recommending the chicken. It was delicious. Do you think we could meet again to talk? Any place and time you like." As a final peace offering, Liz placed a twenty, twice the cost of her meal, on the counter as a tip.

Ethel slipped the cash into her pocket and said, "Come back anytime you want to eat." The emphasis on the final three words was unmistakable.

Liz crossed the street and paused by her car for a moment to take in the little main street after dark. The single car that passed slowed, its inhabitants giving Liz the once over, before the driver accelerated to his previous snail's pace. Heat, lingering from the sunny day, drifted from the sidewalk and the Blanche's rosy brick façade.

It didn't feel like November at all. Liz thought wistfully of the fall color and cool temperatures that were now settled over Seattle. Today's weather report promised a second cold front for later next week, just in time for the weekend that she and Jonathan had originally planned to spend in Jacksonville. Visions of snuggling in front of his fireplace with a good Cabernet vied with an acrimonious scene where they argued about Spain.

Her cell phone started vibrating and she took it from her jeans pocket to see who was calling. When Jonathan's name popped up on the screen, she let it roll to voice mail. She wasn't ready to talk to him until she had had time to think, but her determination didn't extend to ignoring his message. His voice was clear and full of regret for the way he had acted. He said that he hoped she would still come to Jax. He would take her to the best restaurant on the Riverwalk. He really wanted to see her. Being in love with Jonathan was certainly a roller coaster ride. Liz sighed tiredly and got into the Prius.

As a distraction, she mulled over the encounter at the 7 Lakes while she drove toward the interstate. It wasn't unknown for people of that era to talk about loving their neighbors on Sunday and to lynch some of those neighbors during the following week. Ethel's father would have been of the generation when KKK members were sometimes the business and social leaders in Southern communities. He might even have been a member himself, something Ethel might be ashamed of at this point. People hid all kinds of secrets behind the facades they showed to others. Liz groaned aloud as Jonathan's handsome face appeared unbidden.

The Holiday Inn was a working anthill when Liz strode through the sliding glass doors into the lobby. Scowling travelers turned away from the reception desk in disappointment. Rhythmic pounding from the bar announced the presence of a live band of the hard rock variety. Liz wondered why anyone would think that type of music would appeal to the hotel's clientele, but maybe the hotel bar was the happening place for the locals. A group of twenty-somethings crashed through the swinging doors confirming the latter. The day clerk's green eyes startled Liz when they glanced her way. The young man waved in recognition. Liz nodded and hurried to the elevators, glad that her room was on the top floor. Her research conundrum paled in comparison with the life altering decision she faced regarding her relationship with Jonathan.

After a long, hot soak in the Jacuzzi tub, Liz set the thermostat on 65 and put on her oldest pajamas. Their falling-to-pieces softness wrapped around her like a cotton cloud. Comfort food followed by comfort nightwear. The only thing missing was a good glass of wine. Surprisingly, the mini-bar had a nice selection of two glass wines and hard liquor shots. She chose a pinot grigio and plumped several of the half dozen pillows lining the king-size headboard. After crawling between the sheets, she pulled the comforter over her legs. With her nest complete, she had no excuse to put off thinking about Jonathan and Spain.

Despite his self-centeredness and refusal to commit, she loved him passionately, desperately, of that she was sure. Sadly, it was becoming clear to her that he didn't love her with the same depth. For some women, even a well-educated, intelligent mind was no match for a determinedly wayward heart. It made her crazy to admit that her parents and friends in Seattle were right, but she finally had to force herself to see it. At best, he appeared to feel affection for a good lay who always put his desires ahead of her own. His offer for her to follow him to Spain had been tepid, casual even in the offhand way people used when presented with an idea that they should have thought of first but hadn't.

God, she had so screwed up her personal life.

And the hits just kept on coming. The damages were not limited to the personal realm. It was no longer that simple. Her chances to ever work with Roberta again were dwindling by the day. In fact, the predicted fiction money train would probably never leave the station. And if she didn't get something together for the new course proposals, her promising academic career at Florida would be next on the chopping block.

As much as it hurt, she knew what her decision about Jonathan had to be. She just hoped she would have the courage to stick with it when they were together again.

Chapter 19

A week went by without a single word from DeWitt and Meg began to fear he had reached a turning point, one she couldn't bring herself to face. During any period of unoccupied time, however brief, she sought to distract herself with anything at hand—wiping down the restaurant tables for a second or third time, wandering the little shops along Main Street, reading far into the night when sleep was elusive. At the end of two weeks of silence, despair dogged her every step.

Friday morning was the kind Meg liked. It left her no time to dwell on her problems. She and the two other waitresses kept the order rack spinning from the time they opened until just before breakfast ended. As she finished jotting down her final customers' orders, Meg felt eyes boring into her back and glanced toward the restaurant's lobby entrance. Her heart jumped with joy, but her elation was quickly tempered by a spasm of fear. DeWitt stood framed in the space left by the open double doors and she could feel the tension radiating from him. His natural self-confidence had disappeared, replaced by an awkward hesitancy. He stared at her, silent and unsmiling.

Meg turned in her order and went to the entrance. "Hey. You want breakfast?"

DeWitt's stance relaxed a little. "Yeah, the usual. Sit with me?"

"Pick a table while I get your order."

Meg had prayed for this moment, but now that DeWitt had finally shown up, she wished . . . Oh Lord, she didn't really know what she wished. Being kept hanging had been torture, but facing the possibility of a breakup made her heart bang against her breastbone until she felt lightheaded. While she waited for the food, Meg leaned against a kitchen counter fighting back tears. They had seen each other every day for the past year, and now that life without him stared her in the face, Meg knew the answer he had begged her to give him for so long. She would agree to set a wedding date, caution be damned.

But as she watched the cook tossing three eggs over easy, another emotion began to flex its muscles. If staying away had been his way of pushing the issue, it had worked, but Meg felt anger mixing with her fear. Like a bolt of lightning during a ferocious thunderstorm, a new thought struck, one Meg could hardly bear to acknowledge. Getting away from the farm had given her a taste of independence most of her girlfriends only dreamed of and now DeWitt wanted her to give it up. Perhaps she had been unwittingly dishonest with both of them. Maybe it was marriage she dreaded, not poverty.

Damn, damn, damn! Why couldn't things just stay the way they were?

A finger poked her shoulder, making her jump. "Good grief, girl, what planet are you on? I asked if you'd like for me to cover your area while DeWitt's here and you didn't hear a word I said."

Meg blinked and forced herself to concentrate on the waitress standing beside her. "Thanks! That's so sweet of you."

"Honey, if I had that man waiting for me, I'd get over there before somebody moved in on him. Go on. I'll bring his order when it's ready."

Despite the inner turmoil, Meg managed a smile before she fled.

She stopped just the other side of the kitchen door and watched the corner where DeWitt waited. The table for two was tucked behind potted palms in a secluded location by design. Albert had set up the spot personally, proclaiming that he was really a romantic at heart. Behind the palms, DeWitt moved as though he was shifting in his seat and then the fronds parted just a little. He had to have seen her, so Meg walked across the room to the table. She hoped that he didn't see her hands trembling as she reached for a chair and sat down. His eyes met hers across the table.

After a silence that seemed to stretch for hours, he said, "How you been?"

"Not great. You?"

"The same."

The waitress with DeWitt's order cleared her throat loudly and stepped around the palms. When she was gone, he began pushing eggs, sausage, and grits around his plate, but took only occasional bites.

Meg couldn't stand the silence any longer. "DeWitt, I've done a lot of thinking and . . ."

"Me too." He jumped in without even letting her finish. Meg felt as though a blade hovering above her head was about to drop. "Baby, I found out something. I may be frustrated that we're not married, but that don't hold a candle to how much it hurts not seeing you. I can wait. Guess I don't have a choice. Seems like I can't be happy without you."

All the air left Meg's lungs and she found herself gasping as tears rushed down her cheeks.

"Lord, darlin', I thought you'd be happy. I'm willing to do things your way. What on earth's the matter?"

When she caught her breath, she managed to chirp, "I was so afraid we were finished."

DeWitt got up and put his arms around her. "I'll love you as long as I live and I'll wait as long as I have to." He brushed a strand of hair from her eyes and covered her mouth with his. She melted into his embrace, forgetting everything except that she loved him.

He pulled back and looked into her eyes. "Do you think you could get the afternoon off? We need some time together."

"I'll see what I can do."

Watching DeWitt walk away with a bounce in his step, Meg felt like she could float across the room. He looked back from the door and grinned, then passed into the lobby. Her answering smile remained even when he was no longer in sight and the release of tension made her giddy with relief until her conscience stung her back to earth. Now that the fear of a breakup had been banished, she found her old reluctance to set a wedding date returning.

It sobered her to admit that she dreaded losing her independence as much as she feared being poor. The memory of everything that she had been taught growing up, every echoing voice of family, teachers, and friends accused her of being a selfish, unnatural woman. As stubbornly determined as she was to make a better life than her mother had, a part of Meg feared the remembered voices might be right. The hardest thing to deal with was how unfair she knew she was being to DeWitt. There was no doubt in her mind that she loved him and that he would be the only man she would ever love. But for the first time, she wondered if she really deserved him.

Deserving or not, Meg was going to grab every possible minute with DeWitt, so she went in search of Albert. As manager, he liked to be present during the hotel's busiest times, meaning he usually arrived around eleven in the morning and left around nine at night. She found him in his office behind the reception area, sugar shell poised over a steaming mug.

Albert nodded toward the coffee pot sitting on his office hot plate. "Hey, pretty girl, want some?" Meg shook her head. "Okay, but stop hovering in the doorway. You look like you've got something on your mind."

Meg did as she was bid and walked to one of the visitors' chairs. After dumping four spoons of sugar into his coffee, Albert sat behind his desk. "Now, what do I owe this pleasure to?"

"Albert, I need a favor."

He grinned and a twinkle brightened his eyes. "I don't know. I just might be out of favors right now."

When Meg didn't smile in return, his expression became serious. "You know I'm just teasing. What can I do for you?"

"I need the afternoon off. There's something that I've got to take care of." Meg couldn't bring herself to tell him why she wanted the half-day. Teasing her about DeWitt seemed like harmless fun to Albert, but for her it felt like he kept punching a deep bruise.

"And just what might that errand be?"

"I need the afternoon and that's all I'm going to tell you. After last week, I think you owe me. Don't you?"

Albert's face fell and he looked hurt. "I told you I was sorry about that room service thing. In hindsight, I should have stayed late and gone up with you, but I took the money off Capone's bill like you wanted. You know I'm not getting any younger and staying past quitting time gets harder every day."

The hint of a whine in Albert's voice grated on Meg's nerves. "Albert! Do I have the time off or not?"

"Of course. You're a hard worker. I know you've got a good reason even if you won't tell me what it is."

"I'll make it up by working an extra shift over the weekend."

"You don't have to do that. This one's on me to make amends for letting you down."

Meg smiled despite her irritation. Just when she was ready to kill him, Albert usually turned around and did something kind. "Thanks. I'll work through the lunch rush so the other girls won't be run to death."

DeWitt showed up a little after two still in uniform. Meg's spirits sank. Problems at work sometimes interrupted their plans. Hiding her disappointment, she put on her brightest smile, went to the restaurant entrance, and kissed him on the cheek in full view of Albert and anyone else who cared to see.

"That's the kind of welcome I like." DeWitt slipped an arm around her waist and jerked his head toward the reception desk where Albert stood pretending to check the register, but was actually watching them from under his bushy eyebrows. "Boss going to let you off?"

Meg nodded. "But you're still in uniform. Are you free?"

DeWitt looked surprised and then he must have understood because a tender expression filled his eyes as he said, "I came straight from work, Baby. Didn't want to waste the time to go home and change. And I've got a surprise. Get your bathing suit."

Meg left DeWitt sipping iced tea in the restaurant kitchen while she flew to her room. When she returned, she asked, "Do you want a sandwich before we leave? The cook won't mind if I make you something."

"Nope. Got that covered. Let's get out of here."

He grabbed her hand and pulled her through the swinging door into the restaurant. The other waitresses grinned knowingly and waved goodbye as the couple passed into the lobby. DeWitt and Meg looked at each other and laughed with the shear relief of having their quarrel behind them.

The day outside the hotel beckoned sunny and cloudless. She was almost giddy with self-satisfied joy when they walked by the reception desk where Albert stood still peering at the registration book. She wanted to tell him how much she appreciated the free half-day, but when he looked up, a troubled expression came over his face. Meg felt confident Albert wasn't angry with her and he didn't really know DeWitt well enough to be upset with him. There were times when Meg thought she really didn't understand the man at all. She smiled and called a cheerful goodbye anyway. Albert responded with a halfhearted salute. Meg decided he could just be an old grump if he wanted. At the moment, she really didn't care what kind of burr he had under his saddle. Nothing was going to ruin her day with DeWitt or any of their days in the future.

DeWitt's old pickup sat in a dusty heap just beyond the front doors. Elderly patched inner tubes poked up from the bed behind the cab, giving the truck an even more ramshackle appearance. Meg grinned and looked back at her boss. She suspected it was the sight of a falling-to-pieces rattletrap disgracing the hotel's entrance that had Albert in such a foul mood. Too bad. It was a hot, humid summer afternoon and a cool river awaited them.

"We're going to Ichetucknee, aren't we?"

"I said I'd take you. I'm a man of my word. Got my sister to pack a picnic for us too."

"Your sister spoils you."

"Naw, it's you she wants to impress. Want to go by to see your folks while we're so close?"

The thought of their last trip to the south end of the county renewed Meg's anger with her father, so she pushed the memory away. "Yeah, I just can't go this close to home and not stop to see Mama. You're sweet to ask. If Daddy acts like a jerk again, we can leave. Mama understands."

The hot, dusty ride over the washboard roads jarred Meg until her teeth rattled, but when the tree-lined springhead came into view, she could feel her tension melting away.

DeWitt parked under a giant live oak and they changed clothes behind some obliging bushes. As sweaty and uncomfortable as she was, though, Meg hesitated at the edge of the water.

DeWitt lifted her from behind. "Standing here looking at it ain't gonna make it any easier."

He waded in even as Meg squirmed to regain her footing. The first plunge took her breath away. The water came up out of the sandy-bottomed spring head at a constant 72 degrees, making it feel frigid when the air was in the high nineties. After swimming around for a few minutes, DeWitt got the inner tubes and they stretched across them, the sun baking their backs, but their fronts blessedly cold. DeWitt splashed water on her shoulders and Meg shivered happily.

"Your lips are blue. Are mine?"

DeWitt nodded. "How about something to eat?"

Meg got an old quilt from the truck and spread it beneath the trees. The picnic hamper contained fried chicken, potato salad, biscuits, and a quart jug of tea. Heaven in a basket after the icy water.

Meg licked the chicken grease from her fingers and glanced at the newspaper lining the picnic basket as she returned its empty containers. "Silas Barnes sure has his dander up."

"Yeah, way too much. And he's getting other people's dander up too."

"He's such a nice man. And he only wants this to be a better place for families. What's wrong with that?"

"The murder rate's suddenly gone up five hundred percent. And I think Barnes's editorials are to blame, but Ike won't even talk to him about backing off."

"You really think there's a connection to what Mr. Barnes is writing?"

"Those folks dancing on the end of ropes were all involved in vice one way or another. They were the local kingpins. So yeah, I think Barnes's editorials are to blame. And I think he's the reason the Klan's moved into Columbia County. We haven't had a lynching here since the early twenties and we didn't have really organized Klan around here before he started writing those damned articles. The closest klavern was Gainesville. In fact, I'm not totally sure all the men responsible for the lynchings are locals. Nobody seems to have a clue who's hiding under the robes that were seen by the few witnesses we have."

"Witnesses? I always heard the Klan never leaves witnesses."

"Well, they did this time. They didn't even bother to threaten the girls living with Alma Stone and Jesse Jardine. Makes me wonder if they didn't want to scare the income producers away."

Meg looked confused for a moment, then understanding darkened her eyes. "Oh, DeWitt. Those poor girls. To have to live like that."

"Yeah, it's a rough life." DeWitt paused and looked thoughtful before continuing, "Even if those people were vice lords, they didn't deserve to die like they did. We should be going after the Klan, no matter where they come from. We should be putting a stop to the vigilantism, but Ike won't even talk about looking for the men responsible. He makes me sick."

"DeWitt, everybody knows about your boss. Daddy says he's afraid to cross the Klan. That's why he wouldn't even talk to Mr. Taylor when Zeke's parents were burned out."

"Meg, that's a load of garbage. Ike's not afraid of the Klan. He agrees with them and a lot of the people who keep electing him think the same way. His brand of law enforcement is just plain evil. The only reason I stick with the job is that I plan to run against him someday and I plan to win."

Meg's heart swelled with pride. Despite her upbringing, she knew with every fiber of her being that the way whites like her father treated coloreds was wrong no matter how much people tried to make believe that it wasn't. She liked the colored people she knew. They were good, God-fearing people who worked hard for what little they had. Meg shook her head and muttered, "Poor Flossie."

"What's the hotel cook got to do with anything?"

"Her nephew died last week. She didn't say of what and she hasn't been back to work. Albert's had to bring their family cook in to cook for the hotel. I hope Joe wasn't one of the lynching victims. It would make his death even harder for Flossie and her family."

"Was his name Joseph Johnson?"

Meg nodded.

"He was also known as Keno Joe. Controlled the keno games for all of the coloreds in the county."

"I would never have guessed. He seemed so nice the couple of times he came by to see Flossie."

"Just because you're nice to people your aunt works with doesn't mean you can't run numbers games. Gambling was how he made a living. These days, people do what they have to do to get by." DeWitt picked up a small rock and took aim. He focused on the piece of flint as it skipped across the water. "Don't guess any of that's true for the big time hoods. Capone didn't seem to be hurting for cash when he was in town. Did you stay out of his way?"

Meg hadn't lied to DeWitt, but she simply hadn't told him anything about her contact with Capone and his cronies, not that he'd been around to tell anyway. DeWitt tended to take some things a little too seriously. "I had to serve them a couple of times."

Something in her voice must have given away more than she intended because DeWitt's head snapped around and he peered intently at her. "Did they try to bother you?"

Meg's gaze followed a blue heron as it flapped into the air. She wasn't sure even now how much she should tell him. "Nothing that I couldn't handle."

"Tell me exactly what happened." The expression on DeWitt's face left Meg no choice.

She began with the restaurant scene and finished with the uncomfortable moments in Capone's suite when she took up the room service trolley. With each sentence, the line of DeWitt's mouth became harder.

"You should have called me as soon as you left his suite. I'd have taken care of that hood. Why didn't you call?"

"That's why I didn't call. I was afraid of what you would do. I didn't want you to get involved with men like that."

"My job is to protect you, not the other way around. Is that everything?"

His anger flamed so brightly that Meg was glad she hadn't called. She debated about revealing the final tidbits she had omitted, but decided that she had gone this far, so the final details couldn't make things worse. "That's all there is about me, but Capone had a couple of visitors his last night in town. I wouldn't have thought much about it, except one of them was just plain odd."

"How so?"

"Mr. Barnes was the first."

"Did you see him coming out of Capone's room?" DeWitt's words came as though fired from a Thompson submachine gun.

"No. But I was waiting to go up and the elevator indicator needle showed the car coming down from the third floor. There weren't any other guests on that floor, so what else could he be doing up there?"

"Did he say anything to you?"

"Nothing other than hello. But he looked odd, like he was sick or had something serious on his mind."

DeWitt was quiet for a moment. His eyes narrowed and then he asked, "And the second visitor?"

Meg recounted the bits of conversation she had overheard while standing outside Capone's door, ending with what the sheriff had said. "He told Capone to leave town. That it would be the best for everyone."

"Are you sure that's what they said? That's all of it?"

Meg nodded. As she watched emotions crossing DeWitt's face, she wondered exactly what she had said to upset him so.

"Get your clothes on. I've got to get back to work."

"But I thought you had the afternoon off. And what about seeing Mama?"

"There's something important I've got to do. Both you and your mother will just have to understand."

Without another word, DeWitt grabbed Meg's hand and yanked her to her feet. His behavior was so uncharacteristic that Meg followed orders without further comment, but with every mile they traveled north toward Lake City, her fear grew. Something she'd said had hit DeWitt like a sledgehammer.

Chapter 20

Liz rested her chin on her fist and stared through her office window. The view onto the lawn below revealed an unremarkable weekday afternoon. Undergraduates scurried to and fro while geese paddling in a nearby pond honked angrily. The fat gander had become Liz's favorite campus fixture. Anyone violating the invisible boundaries of his kingdom got quite a surprise when a furious attack ensued amid much flapping, pecking, and hissing. Today however, Liz watched without really seeing any of it. Her mind lingered seventy miles to the east.

She sighed and leaned back, massaging her stiff neck with both hands and forcing herself to focus on present surroundings. The Capone work couldn't go forward without another trip to Lake City and that wasn't possible until the weekend. She had devoted all of the time today that she intended to exchanging e-mails with infantile freshmen who expected their hands to be held. Thinking about tackling the new course designs made her plain tired. Calling it a day seemed her best option, but going home to the empty apartment was so unappealing.

Jonathan always lurked in the back of her mind, but Spain now loomed like an unwelcome guest at a funeral. Jonathan had to be told and if she didn't do it soon, she knew she would lose the will. She glanced up at the wall clock. If she left now, she could be at his apartment by the time he got home from work. In one swift motion, her purse was on her shoulder.

The route from Gainesville to Jacksonville was familiar enough by now to be driven without complete attention, which was good because as she traveled, Liz would suddenly become aware that long stretches of the two lane road had passed without registering, her sense of time suspended by her all consuming ruminations.

She visualized the moment when she would tell Jonathan she couldn't follow him to Spain. Even though all logic said she must let him go on alone, she desperately wanted some reassurance she hadn't uprooted her life and career for nothing. Her greatest fear was that he would express mild regret, a tepid longing for what might have been.

She now suspected this may have been his view from the moment he knew he was leaving. Liz could hear him saying the right things, but his words would be hollow, without passion. He wouldn't try to persuade her the relationship was worth giving up her career. Leaving Florida after one semester would be the death knell of any future in academia. She would be branded unreliable, a judgment she would deserve. Liz knew she had made the right decision to stay put.

And when she had herself convinced she knew exactly how the scene with Jonathan would play out, another possibility shouted in opposition. Her wayward heart seemed compelled to betray her. It screamed that she and Jonathan had to be together, no matter the cost. She loved Jonathan and needed to spend the rest of her life with him. Without him, years of lonely spinsterhood stretched out before her until all she could see was herself as a stereotype, the butt of jokes—horn-rimmed glasses, hair drawn back in a severe bun, tweed suit, the perfect academic female devoted only to dead people and the dusty tomes of history.

After an hour or so of the tug-of-war between mind and heart, a new concept crept into her thoughts. At first, it was so nebulous Liz was only slightly aware of a disturbing presence lurking in the shadows, but then it appeared full-blown, creating a chill like ice water applied to a feverish brow. Perhaps her obsession—another new idea—with Jonathan wasn't the all consuming, love-of-a-lifetime passion she believed it to be. Maybe she was simply afraid of being alone.

It would explain a lot, like why she continued an engagement with her former fiancé when he had made it clear that her career goals had to be secondary if she wanted to keep him. And like why she followed a man across a continent when he refused to say the three simple words she so craved to hear. God, was she really that big a fool?

Rush hour traffic was bumper-to-bumper on Jacksonville's south side. After she passed under I-295, the Prius crawled along Roosevelt Blvd. until she came to Timuquana where she made a right toward the river. Liz often thought the residents of the medium to high income neighborhood must not be terribly pleased to have apartments catering to Navy personnel in their midst, but she supposed it was the price they paid for having a glimpse of the St. Johns River and a slight opportunity at membership in the country club on its western bank.

Jonathan had been lucky in finding his apartment. If you stood on his fourth floor balcony and looked east, you could see sun diamonds dancing on the water beyond the club's expansive lawns.

The complex's entry gate slid back easily at the tap of the security code. She pulled into a parking spot next to his building and slipped the apartment key he had given her from her key ring. Once inside the apartment, she placed the key on the breakfast bar. Jonathan was expecting his travel orders at any moment, so this might be her only chance to return his key and to retrieve the one to her apartment.

Liz loved the view from Jonathan's balcony. The river flowing gently passed the lovely old country club with its manicured lawns and tree-lined fairways created a feeling of peace and tranquility. She unlocked the sliding glass door and stepped outside.

Leaning on the railing, she admired the view. The setting sun painted the landscape and water the burnished copper that only appears when the weather is just right, like during the soft days of late Indian summer. Jacksonville was really a very pretty city, one she would miss when she no longer had a reason to visit.

The breeze picked up, bringing with it the first hint of real autumn, which came so much later here than it did in Seattle. She had been warned not to expect much foliage color. Several people she knew were planning long weekends in the North Carolina Mountains before the park service closed the Blue Ridge Parkway for the winter.

Maybe next year she and Jonathan could make the same trip. Jonathan would love driving over the Great Smokies with the Vette open to the wind. Liz stopped herself before the daydream got any bigger. Jonathan would be in Spain for at least two years.

A Corvette engine rumbling into the parking lot below drew her attention. Her heart skipped a beat in anticipation of the scene that was about to unfold. She hated arguments, but she hated saying goodbye even more. Her heart beat faster at the thought of the courage she needed to do the sensible thing.

Shit. Why was doing the right thing so hard? Her grip on the railing tightened until her knuckles turned white.

The car pulled to a stop and the engine died. Liz leaned farther over the railing and instinctively raised a hand. She could feel her willpower ebbing away just at the thought of being near him. She mentally chided herself for weakness, but the effort was half-hearted at best.

The driver door opened and Jonathan got out. He hadn't seen her yet. No matter how much her mind told her she shouldn't watch, she couldn't tear herself away from the sight of him stretching his beautiful body. Even at that distance, he looked like he was born to wear the uniform and she really did love him so. Liz sighed and shook her head.

She had always heard Spain was glorious in winter. Maybe New Year's Eve in Rota was possible. Flying home and then to Europe and back would be expensive, but with careful planning she could probably swing it. Her parents would be disappointed, but there was no reason for her to spend the entire winter break in Seattle. She could spend the second half with Jonathan and check out what Spain had to offer an American history professor. Maybe in a year or so, she could arrange some kind of visiting professor agreement with a Spanish university. Elation made her almost giddy. She couldn't wait for Jonathan to get upstairs so they could discuss her plan.

Wanting to laugh aloud with relief, she was on the verge of returning to the living room when Jonathan strolled casually around the Vette. Instead of coming directly to the building, he stopped on the car's passenger side and put his hand on the door handle. Liz froze at half turn and stared. The door swung open and a pair of stilettos attached to long slender legs appeared. When the passenger unfolded the rest of herself from the car, an expensively dressed young woman with shoulder length blonde hair stood next to Jonathan in a way that communicated possession to any other female who might be near. The way she leaned into his shoulder as he put his arm around her told Liz this wasn't their first date. The girl smiled up at Jonathan, who bent down and kissed her in reply. Anyone with even the slightest understanding of human nature could see they were a couple.

Her first instinct was to flee, to run back to Gainesville with her tail between her legs, to ignore what she had just seen until she could pretend that it had been her imagination playing tricks on her. Another glance over the railing, however, showed her that no amount of wishful thinking or outright denial could redefine the relationship of the couple standing in the parking lot gazing into one another's eyes.

Liz's heart split wide open as she watched Jonathan draw his fingers along the girl's jaw, ending at her chin, which he tilted upward to the side so that he could nuzzle the delicate place just below her ear. The gesture was so tender. His arms around that girl were so protective. Liz felt her stomach turn over. She dragged her eyes away from the parking lot and returned to the living room. She stopped short, staring at the breakfast bar where the apartment key lay taunting her. At least she now had the answer to her question from earlier that day. And it was yes, she really was that big a fool.

So, what next? Confront him or leave without a word?

As much as Liz wanted to simply creep away and try to forget Jonathan, it came to her that she must confront him for the sake of her own self worth. Not being able to utter the words *I love you* was one thing, but the outright deception that had clearly gone on could in no way be excused or brushed aside. It wasn't her imagination that he had whooped for joy when she told him about her job at the University of Florida. He had been genuinely happy, even contacting an apartment locator for her while she was finishing the summer term in Seattle. He had looked at all of the choices and had finally narrowed it down to the place she currently rented. After two years of practically living together in Seattle, she hadn't invented the things he had said about growing old together. He had led her to believe he loved her and he had never shown anything but pleasure when she said those damned three words he refused to repeat. Jonathan, the man she thought she couldn't live without, had changed in his feelings toward her and she deserved to know why.

Liz sat down on the overstuffed leather sofa and waited. As she ran her hand over the dark burgundy seat cushions, the strangest idea came into her head. At least now, she wouldn't need to live with Jonathan's taste for the rest of her life. She leaned her head against the sofa back and squeezed the bridge of her nose to stop tears from rolling. Maybe she was losing her mind. It was a possible explanation for all of the impulsive, ridiculous choices she had made this year.

A key turned in the front door's lock. Liz stood up, smoothing her clothing and adjusting her stance so that she faced the door in a position of casual, sophisticated composure. At the rate her heart pounded, she had no confidence she would be able to carry off the impression she was trying so desperately to create, but she was determined to try.

Jonathan and the girl's faces were a study in consternation when they realized they were not alone. Their expressions of guilty surprise were exactly the same, like a pair of illicit lovers in a Hollywood romantic comedy. If it hadn't been so painful, Liz would have laughed aloud.

The girl became wide-eyed and then her face turned bright pink. "You said you'd told her. You promised."

Jonathan had the good grace to appear ashamed. He looked from the girl to Liz and back. His mouth opened, but he failed to speak.

Liz surveyed the child standing next to the love of her life. She couldn't be out of her teens. "Clearly he has broken his promises to both of us, my dear."

That brought Jonathan to life. "Tell me, Liz, exactly what did I promise you? You seem to have forgotten. Coming to Florida was your idea."

"I suppose all the talk about growing old together was just foreplay?" Liz turned to the girl. "Let me see. If I remember correctly, it goes something like this. 'Oh, Baby, it'll still be this good when we're old and gray. When you've got what we have, you never want to let it go.'"

The girl looked like someone had slapped her very hard across the face. She stared up at Jonathan in confusion. "You said those things to her? Exactly like that?"

Liz pressed her advantage. "Sorry, I don't know your name. I'm curious. Has he ever actually said the words *I love you*?"

Another slap. The girl drew a long breath and muttered, "Not yet, but I know that he does. We're going to get a place together in Rota. We've contacted a real estate agent and everything."

Liz grabbed the knife hilt and drove the blade home. "Jonathan, this should be interesting. Say the words *I love you* to her. She needs to hear them right now. Go ahead. Maybe it's only with me that you get tongue tied."

He hugged the girl close, bringing her face into his shoulder as he glared over the top of her head at Liz. "Baby, don't listen to her. She's just bitter. I've been dishonest with her, so I guess she's got a right to be angry. I didn't have the courage to hurt her. In some things, I'm a coward."

The sound of clapping filled the room. "Great performance, Jonathan. Academy award worthy. Honey, he's all yours and welcome to him."

Liz strode across the room without looking back. She held her head high and closed the door without slamming it, a feat that took all of her emotional energy. To hell with her apartment key. She would say she lost it and pay to have the locks changed.

Only when she was a mile away from the apartment complex did she allow herself to think. When she realized she had no memory of getting into her car and saw Jacksonville's downtown skyline growing bigger, not smaller, she pulled into a strip mall parking lot and turned off the engine. Leaning her head against the steering wheel, Liz allowed the tears to roll while her body shook uncontrollably.

The woman who had confronted Jonathan, who had spoken with such sarcasm, was someone Liz didn't know. Her troubled relationships with men were driving her just a little crazy. Well, maybe not crazy, but something within her had changed, broken. Liz glanced at her reflection in the rearview mirror and felt like she was looking into the eyes of a stranger.

The late drive back to Gainesville and the night of tossing and turning left Liz feeling sleep deprived and numb. She prepared coffee, drove to campus, and unlocked her office door as though she was a clinician observing a test subject from a distance.

She sat in her desk chair and turned toward the window. She wasn't sure how long she had been staring blindly at the yellowing mimosa canopy floating just outside when loud throat clearing and someone calling her name brought her back from a place deep within herself. She swung around a little too sharply for politeness.

Hugh's voice sounded shy. "Sorry to disturb you. I did knock."

"You're not disturbing me. I was just lost in thought."

A peculiar expression passed over Hugh's face. It was only when she recognized the deep concern in his eyes that she realized her cheeks were wet and that tears were dripping from her chin. She grabbed a tissue from the box on her desk and wiped hurriedly, feeling red heat crawling up from her throat onto her cheeks.

"Sorry. I've had a really bad day."

"Anything I can help with?"

"No, it's not job related."

"I see. Well, when I'm not prattling on about myself, I can be a pretty good listener."

Something in his solicitous manner infuriated Liz. She didn't want to be an object of pity. She had always hated it. Even when her beloved grandfather died, she refused to allow anyone to say how sorry they were or to help with her grief. Now, her boss was trying to offer consolation in her hour of pain and humiliation. It was beyond endurance.

"It's nothing you can help with or understand. So if you will excuse me, I'd like my door closed please."

Hugh cocked his head to one side and nodded curtly before doing as she asked.

Liz immediately hated herself for the perplexed hurt she had seen in his eyes. He was only trying to help. Of course, that had been something of an unspoken problem between them from the start. He wanted something she wasn't going to give. He was a kind, intelligent guy with whom she had many common interests. And he was good looking in a professorial, Ivy League sort of way. He was the sort of man her parents had always hoped she would marry, but he wasn't her type.

In the next instant, she felt like someone had dumped a bucket of ice water over her head. Until this moment, it had never once occurred to her to ask why she wasn't attracted to Hugh and the men like him who had asked her out over the years. Her boyfriends had always had a glam factor, the guys lots of girls wanted. There had been the quarterback in high school and the rock musician during her early college years. Her most serious relationship, the lost fiancé, had been with a guy who saw himself as the next Brad Pitt, a role his looks and acting gifts were made for. He abandoned Liz for a girl who was devoted to his career, not one of her own.

And now that she was on an introspective path, she could see another uncomfortable truth. She had been the one who had worked at all of her relationships. She had wanted to be with those guys and had done what was needed to maintain their attention until she had fallen desperately in love with historical research in her senior year. Graduate school had been a relationship desert until the actor appeared in the second year of her doctoral chase.

At that point, she had been without a boyfriend for so long she had fallen instantly, madly in love when she saw him playing Stanley Kowalski in a local production of *A Streetcar Named Desire*. He had looked amazing without his shirt. Every oiled muscle shone in chiseled definition under the hot stage lights. It had seemed like they were meant to be a couple when they met later at a mutual friend's party. Not long after, the actor's interests and pursuits started consuming Liz's free time leading to the first in a long string of apologies to Roberta, her fiction editor. It rankled to realize how she had reinvented herself for a man.

Stunned by the sudden epiphany, she began to wonder if she had ever had an equitable relationship with any man. The unhappy answer seemed to be no. She had been thrilled by the risky boys and wowed by the glamorous ones. The men in her life had all been happy to bask in the glow of her adoration and she had been satisfied to give it to them without expecting very much in return.

Long ago, her friends had teased her about only liking bad boys. She had laughed and said she liked them all the more for their wicked ways. She had actually said that she liked bad boys. Hard to believe she could have been so stupid and shallow. Funny how things like that could slip one's mind until a precipitating event brought them rushing back with crystal clarity.

Liz wondered if she would ever have a healthy relationship with a man. What a depressing thing to ask oneself. On the verge of tears again, she angrily shook her head. Perhaps the answer was no, but sitting around on a Friday afternoon brooding was a sure crazy maker. Liz felt like she would explode if she didn't get out of the office. There was actually one bad boy who might help her forget her troubles.

She packed up her laptop, grabbed her purse, and headed for her car. Ole Scarface couldn't leave her or break her heart even though he was proving elusive at the moment. She would finish with the Columbia Tribune articles this afternoon and then visit Ethel at the 7 Lakes Café after the dinner hour rush was over. Maybe Ethel could be persuaded to change her mind about discussing Silas Barnes and his anti-vice campaign. Liz was sure the old girl knew something important. She could feel it in her bones.

Chapter 21

DeWitt dropped Meg off at the hotel entrance with a quick kiss and a warning not to tell anyone what she had seen and heard on Capone's last night in town. The recent events in the county stank like last week's garbage and he was determined to find out who or what was behind it, Sheriff Ike Darnell's lax attitude toward the lynchings be damned.

He shoved the gearshift into first and pulled away from the curb. Vigilantism and murder made his blood boil, but the fact that his boss looked the other way because it was an election year made him sick to his stomach. Every day when he walked into the sheriff's office, he felt dirty, like there could never be enough lye soap or hot water to wash away the contamination.

Worst of all, Meg's revelations troubled him deeply. As much as he hated violence, he would gladly choke the life out of anyone who tried to harm her and he was very afraid that she and her brother were caught up in a situation that would get them hurt or worse.

Passing the town square, he whipped into a parking slot and slammed on the brakes. Lettering painted in gold leaf on the Trib's front window bade all to enter and DeWitt decided to take the paper up on its invitation. Silas Barnes had much to answer for whether he had intended to call the Klan to action or not.

DeWitt strode through the open door and came to rest in front of the reception desk where a girl pounded away on a typewriter. Between the keys' clacking and the squealing of overhead fans in need of a good oiling, the girl appeared unaware of his presence. Under normal circumstances, he would have politely cleared his throat or spoken softly. As it was, he barely held onto his temper while he rapped on the desk.

The girl jumped and glanced up. "How may I help you, Deputy?"

"I need to see your boss."

"Do you have an appointment?"

"No and I don't intend to make one."

"I'm sorry, but he can't be disturbed. He's working on Friday's editorial."

"Perfect. That's exactly what I came to see him about."

DeWitt didn't wait for a reply. He brushed by the desk and marched toward the back of the building while the girl called out for him to wait. When he didn't stop, he could hear her speaking frantically into her desk telephone. The door to Barnes's office flew open and the man himself filled the frame.

"Now see here, Deputy Williams, I'm a busy man. You can't come barging into my office whenever you like."

"Step inside and close the door."

"I beg your pardon?"

"You heard me."

Silas Barnes remained planted in the doorway, his face turning from pink to puce. "How dare you. Does Sheriff Darnell know you're here?"

"Why do you think I've come?" The words flowed so easily that DeWitt was hardly aware of their harshness or the lie they contained. All he cared about was protecting Meg and stopping the violence, whatever it took. He stared down at the editor. "I'd advise you to step into your office. I don't think you want other people to hear what I've got to say."

Barnes's eyes widened and he looked like he might argue further, but something about DeWitt must have changed his mind because he moved aside. When they were both inside, Barnes slammed his door.

"Now you listen to me, young man. I can make or break you and your boss, so this had better be important. Out with it or . . ."

"Or what? You'll sic your Klan cronies on me?"

"What do you mean? I . . . I have no connection with the Klan."

"Really? Every Friday since January you've written about how vice in the county needs to be cleaned up. Well, you've gotten your wish. Our small time vice lords have all dangled at the end of Klan ropes."

"Surely as an officer of the law, you agree that our community had to stop condoning such open, wanton wickedness."

"Maybe so, but explain to me why you never once called for the lynchings to stop. Which is worse? A little gambling and moonshining or murder? Or do you still think the victims deserved what they got?"

"Still think? I never said they deserved anything other than to be shut down."

"Seems to me you need to go back and read your own columns."

"I have never condoned murder. I resent your implication. My column is merely the conscience of this community."

"Then denounce the Klan and the lynchings in your next editorial. Surely the fine people of Columbia County don't condone murder either."

The color drained from Barnes's face. "You don't understand. I have a family. I can't write against the Klan. They'll come after me."

"That's what I thought. You're a coward who folds if it looks like you might get hurt. Never mind that what you wrote got other people lynched."

Barnes's whole body visibly sagged and he stumbled to his desk chair where he dropped down with his head in his hands. "Please. I never meant for people to get killed. I was just so angry when those five boys died in January after a night of gambling and drinking."

"Other people have died in wrecks where moonshine was involved. What was so special about this accident?"

"One of the boys was my nephew, my sister's youngest. She had a heart attack shortly after she learned about the accident. It was the stress. Before she died, she asked me to see that justice was done. I used what power and means I had. You would have done the same for your family."

"Maybe, but that wouldn't have included stirring up the Klan or bringing them into the county to do my dirty work."

"And just how am I culpable in the Klan's arrival? I know no one with that affiliation."

"Yeah? Well, they sure did answer your call, didn't they?"

"I am not to blame for what others do when they read the truth put forth in my editorials. However, I can't say I'm sorry that the criminals have been dealt with. Can you?"

"I would have worked within the law."

"Oh, is that so? Then why has your office never once acted to close down the gambling, the moonshining, the houses of ill repute?"

DeWitt felt a stab of guilt, but it was tinged with anger. The implication in the old man's question hit home. But he wasn't sure who he was angrier with, Barnes, Sheriff Ike Darnell, or himself for continuing working for a man he couldn't respect. "Look, I'm sorry about your nephew and your sister. That was a terrible loss, but it doesn't justify promoting murder. And it also brings us to the question of what you were doing in Al Capone's suite the night before he left town. With all of the local vice lords lynched, that leaves room for a new leader, one who'll consolidate all activities. You maybe?"

"How many times do I have to tell you that I didn't mean for those people to be killed? And for the record, I didn't invite or intend the Klan to get involved in Columbia County's problems. Furthermore, I certainly have no interest in becoming a criminal."

"Then explain your visit to Capone."

Barnes looked confused as though he hadn't understood the question, then answered quietly. "I wanted an interview."

"An interview? Why?"

"This was the biggest news we've had in a long time."

"So what did you want to ask him? He was here and then he left. Not much of a story there unless you know more than you're telling."

Barnes looked like someone had punched him in the gut. "Can you imagine what it's like to be the brightest star in your college journalism class and then to have to come home and run your family's small town paper? I was a cub reporter for the New York Times when my father died. My life was over before it ever really began."

"That still doesn't explain what you and Capone talked about."

An ironic smile curled the corners of Barnes's mouth as the color drained from his face. "Nothing. His men wouldn't let me through the door. And they threatened that if I wrote about him, I might find myself fitted for a pair of cement overshoes. Can you believe that they actually used that hackneyed cliché of the gangster cinema? Cement overshoes." His twisted smile broadened but failed to reach his eyes. "I wondered if James Cagney might suddenly step out from behind the door."

Barnes's face was now so white DeWitt feared the old man was unwell. "Mr. Barnes, do you need a glass of water. I'll get you one."

Troubled eyes met DeWitt's gaze. "No, I'll be all right in a minute. Thank you." Looking ten years older, the editor rose to his feet. "I've told you everything there is. Now, if you'll excuse me, I still have a column to finish."

DeWitt didn't believe for a minute that he had heard everything. He wanted to ask more questions, but he also didn't want Barnes's collapse or worse on his conscience. "Think about what I said, Mr. Barnes. If you aren't involved with the Klan, then prove it by denouncing them. It's time for the lynchings to stop."

Turning on his heel, DeWitt strode from the office and returned to his vehicle. One confrontation down, one to go.

The sheriff's office was quiet when DeWitt entered. He went to the secretary's desk and jerked his head toward a closed door. "He in?"

"Yeah, but in a really foul mood. I'd stay out of there if I were you."

"Thanks, but I'll take my chances."

A gruff shout answered DeWitt's knock. "Geraldine, I told you I didn't want to be disturbed."

Seemed like nobody wanted to have a conversation today. "It's me, Boss."

"Come in." Ike looked up over his spectacles. "Don't stand there like a dummy. I haven't got all day."

"It's about the lynchings, Ike. I've talked to Barnes about stopping his articles."

"So?"

"If he stops stirring things up, maybe the killings will stop."

"Why should we care? The Klan's saving us a whole lot of work."

"But that's exactly the point. It should be that they've increased our workload out of sight. Murder is immoral and against the law. We should've stopped the Klan moving into the county in the first place. But now that they're here, we should be out arresting the Klansmen responsible for the murders."

Ike huffed and put his elbows on the desk. "Who says that the Klansmen are locals? Nobody knows who's under those robes."

"But it wouldn't take too much digging to find out, would it Sheriff?"

Ike's jaw clenched. "Look, Deputy Williams, sometimes murder is murder and sometimes a killing's a community service. You should know the difference."

"But this isn't one killing. It's five, six if you count Big Charlie Blankenship. He hasn't been seen in over a month."

"Big Charlie ran off with a new woman and the other five weren't worth the space they took up alive, much less the holes they're buried in."

"How we feel about the victims or their line of work shouldn't matter. We have a sworn duty to stop crime when we can and to put criminals in jail when we don't."

Ike's expression changed from exasperated to cajoling. "Look, Son, I remember what it's like to be young and idealistic. When you're just starting out, you take the law to heart and want to solve all of society's ills. But then you get older and you realize that society doesn't necessarily want all of its ills cured. Nobody gives a damn that the Klan, local or otherwise, killed off gamblers, moonshiners, and whores. Accept it and forget it. Now I've got work to do and so do you."

Ike lowered his eyes and began shuffling the stack of papers in front of him. DeWitt knew when to push his boss and when to leave him alone. It was definitely time to go.

He should have been patrolling the major roads north of town, but his car turned south like it had a will of its own. It didn't stop until it came to rest in Isaiah Taylor's front yard.

DeWitt got out and went to the front door. He looked through the screen as he knocked. Zeke ambled down the center hall.

"I've come to see your grandfather. Is he at home?"

"Yes, sir. I'll fetch him for you."

In a moment, Mr. Taylor appeared.

"How can I help you, Deputy Williams?"

"Is there somewhere we can talk so that Zeke won't hear?"

"Guess we could walk down to the barn. Wait while I get my hat."

DeWitt could hear Isaiah telling Zeke to stay in the house, that he had private business with the deputy. The walk to the barn was a short one. Once there, the two men went into the dark interior.

"Now what is it that's so important to make me come out here?"

"I know you've heard about the lynchings." The grizzled head nodded. "I'm sure you've made the connection?" Again a nod. "Isaiah, I think you and Zeke are in real danger."

"I'm just a smalltime operator. Why would they come after me? And what can they want with an eleven year old boy?"

"I know about your rods and reels that Zeke and Jack left by the river. I think the body they saw dumped in the river was Charlie Blankenship. Where did you buy the fishing tackle?"

"At the sporting goods store in town."

"That's what I was afraid of. The store marks all the things they sell with their trademark. Whoever found them will have no trouble tracing the rods and reels back to you if they want to."

"I suppose that's true."

"Do you have anywhere you can go for awhile until all this dies down?"

"I got a sister up to Atlanta, but I don't have enough for two fares and I'm not leaving Zeke behind. Besides, I got a garden full of vegetables to can for the winter."

DeWitt reached into his pocket and pulled out his money clip. He removed the only bills folded between the clip's brass bars. "Here. This should be enough to buy two one-way tickets. Get out while you can."

Surprise widened Isaiah's eyes. "I can't take your money. Thank you all the same."

"You can take the money. You've got to."

"I don't mean to seem ungrateful, but I don't take handouts from nobody."

DeWitt sighed in exasperation. "Look, Isaiah, this is no time for foolish pride. I'm serious about the danger."

"I know you are, but I'm not taking your money."

"Then at least stop selling shine. The Klan's already gone after the big producers. It's probably only a matter of time before they start on you little guys. I don't want to see anything happen to you or Zeke."

"You're a good man, Deputy Williams. I thank you for your concern, but we'll be all right. I figure the big boys is all the Klan's after. Seems to me somebody wants to take over as boss. I expect us small producers'll be hearing from him directly and then things'll get back to normal."

The two men argued for another few minutes.

"At least say that you'll think about leaving. If you don't care what happens to you, think about Zeke."

"I done thought about all of it and I've spoke my piece. I ain't changing my mind."

Seeing that Isaiah was immoveable, DeWitt returned to his truck and hit the road again. But all the way back to town DeWitt cursed himself for not dragging the old man and his grandson to the train depot and shoving them onto a train himself. He couldn't shake the feeling that everything was coming to a head.

Chapter 22

"Boy, I ain't giving you a plug nickel for the work you do as part of this family, so stop pestering me. What would you do with money anyway? You got no need for it."

Jack drew a long, slow breath in an effort to control his temper. He knew from experience that his father had to be approached carefully on any issue because Daddy believed a man should rule his family with an iron fist. Said it was God's law. Jack cast about for the best way to make his case. He had promised he would replace the lost fishing equipment and Jack was determined to keep his word.

"Daddy, Mr. Taylor gives Zeke a little share of the crop sale price because he says that honest work should be rewarded. I work honest for you."

"I don't give a damn what Isaiah Taylor does or says. You ain't getting nothing from me. I need every dime we make to pay off the bank loan. I didn't inherit this farm like Taylor did his. Nobody ever give my daddy no forty acres and a mule."

Jack moved farther down the row of waist high plants and bent at the waist so he could grasp a handful of leaves and twist them from the stalk. Cropping tobacco was a hot, dirty job and the leaves tucked under his left arm were gummy with the sweat soaking through his shirt. As he stooped from plant to plant, he considered the best way to broach his other option for earning money. At the end of the row, he straightened up and stretched his aching back muscles. After tossing his armload of tobacco leaves onto the old mule drawn sand sled, he decided to wait for his father, who cast a speculative gaze over his son when he came to the end of the next row.

Jack met his father's eyes as boldly as he dared. "Daddy, I understand about you needing all of our money, but could I work for the neighbors when you don't need me here?"

"Doing what?"

"Cropping tobacco and picking cotton."

His father eyed him with suspicion. "You ain't going to have time to hire yourself out for tobacco. I need you everyday until the last of the crop's hanging in the barn. Just who would you be picking cotton for?"

"Zeke's granddaddy. He said he'd pay me same as he pays Zeke if I'd help him get his cotton picked."

"No son of mine's going to work for a nigger. Not now, not ever. Do you hear me?"

"But Mr. Taylor's a good colored man. You used to say so yourself."

His father's face developed a ruddy tint under its summer tan. "People can change their minds. I've done spoke and I ain't gonna talk about it no more. Now get back to work before I take my belt to you."

Jack mumbled "yes sir" before moving on to another row in the small field.

His daddy had been stern as far back as Jack could remember. Granddaddy Blevins had raised his children like that too, so like father, like son. It could also have something to do with crop prices being bad for such a long time. Daddy had been worried about money forever, but then Wall Street crashed last year, the banks started failing, and Daddy hadn't smiled or uttered a kind word since. Hard times had turned his father mean.

It was something that he and Meg had talked about late at night during her visits home. Jack had made up his mind to leave home when he was old enough just like Meg had done. Unlike his sister, however, he feared he would never be allowed to return, not even to see his mother, at least not as long as his father lived. Daddy expected his only son to stay on the farm and work the fields 'til kingdom come or until the bank took the farm, whichever came first.

But Jack had dreams. One day he was going to hitch a ride to Lake City and hop a westbound train. He would ride the rails as far away from the farm as he could get. He wanted to go to California, see the Pacific Ocean, and become a merchant seaman or join the Navy. He wanted to sail all over the world. He would send Mama presents from China, Africa, France—any place where they sold pretty things. And when he was the captain of his own ship, he would come back to get Mama and Meg—well, maybe not Meg. She would probably be married to that ole DeWitt Williams by then. But he would show Mama all the places she had ever dreamed of going.

"Why're you just standing there staring off into space? Get back to work. I want this field finished before supper," Daddy barked, bringing Jack back to reality.

Jack worked his remaining rows in quiet sullenness. The angrier he became, the faster he worked. When his final armload of tobacco leaves was gathered, he dumped them on top of the pile covering the sand sled and turned toward the woods separating the Blevins and Taylor farms without a word to his father or looking back for his approval.

The creek ran at full tilt due to the summer rain that poured down at 4:00 every day with so much consistency you could set your clock by it. The water rippled around his bare feet and legs, washing away the tobacco field's dust and soothing Jack's riled up emotions. He stopped midstream and splashed his face and hair while he considered what to say to Zeke's grandfather about the work. If he told Mr. Taylor that his father had forbidden him to do it, then he might have to tell why and he was not about to repeat what his father had said. There didn't seem to be any choice but to lie.

A fat orange sun hovered on top of the forest behind the Taylor house when Jack entered the cotton field that led to the backyard. He hadn't really seen Zeke since the night he tried to make it right between them about the lost rods and reels. Even though he had promised to return the next day, it hadn't been possible. Daddy had seen him heading for the woods and had prevented him from leaving the farm. Jack had been kept busy with farm work ever since. He worried about what Zeke must be thinking, but then Zeke knew how Daddy could be so maybe everything would be all right.

As Jack passed between the rows of thigh high dark green plants, he ran his hands over partially open bolls. In about a month, snowy cotton would ride high and puffy on dry brown husks. The field was more than Zeke and his grandfather could handle alone. Mr. Taylor would need to know now whether Jack would be helping with the picking.

Zeke and his grandfather sat in the shadows under a steeply pitched back porch roof, a pile of field corn at their feet. Corn shucks and silks lay scattered about aging handmade chairs. Neither of them noticed him and Jack hesitated at the edge of the yard while he thought of what to say. Zeke was his best friend no matter what anybody thought. Maybe Jack should just act like nothing was wrong since Zeke had always followed his lead. He puckered up and blew a soft whistle, their secret signal. Zeke's head snapped up and his eyes met Jack's. A shy grin filled the younger boy's face and he lifted his hand.

"Come on up the porch, Jack," Mr. Taylor called. "It's too hot to stand around in the sun."

Jack dragged a chair over to the corn pile and started shucking. The trio worked in silence for a few minutes before Zeke's grandfather spoke again.

"We've missed you. Glad you came today. Does your mother know where you are?"

"She said it was okay. We been cropping tobacco since I was here last." The lie mixed with a partial truth made Jack uncomfortable, but he was determined to stay as long as they would have him.

"We're gonna have roasting ears, field peas, and cornbread directly. Want to stay for supper?"

Jack glanced at Zeke who nodded. "Yes, sir. That would be mighty fine. You cook as good as my mama."

Mr. Taylor laughed. "I ain't so sure about that, but we get by. You boys finish up this corn while I get the bread in the oven."

When the screen door slammed, Zeke looked over at Jack. "Deputy Williams come by the house yesterday."

"What did he want?"

"Said me and granddaddy need to leave town cause of the lynchings."

"You gonna do it?"

"Naw. Granddaddy says we'll be okay."

"Maybe y'all need to do what DeWitt says."

"Granddaddy ain't stupid. He knows what to do even if he is colored."

"Hey, I didn't say he was stupid. Why're you so touchy?"

Zeke shrugged his shoulders, but Jack could sense there was something troubling his friend. The boys shucked corn in silence until Jack felt Zeke looking at him. He turned his head, seeing a challenge in his friend's eyes.

"You never come back for the horseshoe pitching like you said."

"Daddy made me stay away. You know how he is."

"Yeah." A cloud descended over the younger boy's features. "Why you suppose your daddy don't like us no more?"

"Aw, Daddy don't like nobody now days. If it ain't one thing, it's another that sets him off."

Zeke appeared to think this over and then said, "It's cause we colored, ain't it?"

Jack stared at the porch ceiling as if a spider weaving her web between the rafters was the most fascinating thing he'd ever seen. He didn't know whether to tell the truth on not. Zeke was really tender about anything having to do with color ever since his parents had died in a fire set for no reason that anybody could see other than they were Negroes.

Jack's gaze dropped to the floorboards, then he glanced up at Zeke from under his lashes and muttered, "I don't know why he acts the way he does. He's just got mean."

The younger boy cocked his head to one side. Jack wasn't sure whether his half-truth had been believed, so he switched to a safer subject. "You think the Yankees'll take the Series this year? Babe's hitting homers left and right."

The boys talked stats while they worked on the corn until Zeke's grandfather appeared at the door.

"You boys talking baseball?"

Two pairs of eyes, one intense blue, the other velvety midnight, turned toward the screen door where Mr. Taylor smiled down on them. Two heads, one covered in a shaggy mop of yellow straw, the other with a crop on ebony curls, nodded in unison.

"Well, come on in to supper then. I like baseball too."

After the blessing, Mr. Taylor looked at Zeke. "Offer the peas to your company, son. I'm hungry. Ain't you?"

Zeke grinned up at his grandfather and nodded. As the bowls of vegetables passed from hand to hand, Mr. Taylor continued the conversation, speaking of teams and players of whom Jack was only vaguely aware.

"The Black Crackers, they're my team. You ever heard of them Jack?" The boy nodded to be polite. "One of these days, Zeke and me are gonna go up to Atlanta, Georgia. Got a sister who stays at Reynoldstown. We'll put in with her and go to a game in Ponce de Leon Park. Yes sir, one of these days real soon, maybe next year, we gonna catch us a train."

Jack remained quiet while grandfather and grandson talked about their proposed trip. It seemed that they must have been planning it for a while. Zeke's eyes lit up as he described a ballpark that Jack was sure his friend had never seen and probably never would. Jack doubted that Mr. Taylor had seen it either, but people had their dreams, and even as a boy of twelve, Jack knew it was a bad thing to shatter a fellow being's hopes for the future.

In a way, he envied Zeke. Although his life with his grandfather had come about through tragedy, it had evolved into one of peace and security founded on a love that the old man showed the boy every day in hundreds of small ways, like sharing the income from crop sales, like never mentioning the lost rods and reels again after that one spanking he gave Zeke, not for losing the gear, but for sneaking and lying. Jack sighed and smiled wistfully as he watched the pair trading opinions as to which team would win the Negro Southern League championship that year.

The trio was pouring sorghum syrup over warm buttered cornbread when someone appeared at the screen door. The figure's face was partially hidden beneath the brim of a big Panama, but Jack knew he was a white man by his hands. Mr. Taylor glanced at the door and pushed his chair back from the table.

"You boys finish your supper while I see to our visitor." He went out onto the porch, then both men went down the steps and disappeared around the corner of the house.

"Who's that? I ain't ever seen him before." Jack jerked his head toward the place where the two men had stood a moment before.

"You saying you seen all the folks they are in Columbia County?"

"I guess not. So who is he?"

Zeke's eyes grew big before he grinned just a little. "He Granddaddy's biggest customer now Moses Jackson and Jamie Tuttle done got theyselves lynched."

"Why's that?"

"Ain't you heard about all the lynchings?"

"Yeah. So?"

An exasperated expression crossed Zeke's face. "Sometimes I wonder if you know anything important. All those folks been hung? Well they all, every one of them, was big shots running stuff that's against the law."

"Such as?"

"Well, Moses Jackson and Jamie Tuttle, he's a white guy, they owned the moonshine routes in and out of this county. And that Big Charlie Blankenship over tuh O'Leno? Folks think he ran off with a new woman, but Granddaddy thinks he was the body you and me saw go down the sinkhole. He was big over the gambling for white folks. Not long after that, them hussy women was lynched. And then Keno Joe." A puzzled expression came over Zeke's face. "You know, it's always been us colored folks before, but this time half of the folks are white. It's getting to be a strange world when the Klan takes out after their own kind."

"You wasn't supposed to tell what we saw at the sink hole. I know DeWitt talked to you. Meg said he did."

"I ain't gonna keep something like that from Granddaddy."

Jack mentally added another item to the growing list of differences between Zeke's family life and his own. He didn't want to tell his father anything, couldn't really. Daddy never listened to anybody—not Mama, Meg, or him.

The boys fell silent. Speaking of the lynchings had ruined the feeling of easy companionship that they were trying to reestablish ever since the night by the sinkhole. Sometimes being Zeke's friend was a hard road that had to be walked carefully so accidents could be avoided. The loss of the fishing equipment and the sinkhole incident had been decidedly unfortunate bumps on that road.

When Mr. Taylor returned, Jack helped with the washing up. With the last dish back on its shelf, he placed the damp dishtowel on the drying rack. “Well, I guess I better be off home. Thank you for a mighty fine supper, Mr. Taylor.”

“You’re welcome, Jack. Don’t be such a stranger from now on.”

Jack shuffled his feet, dreading leaving the comfortable easiness he found with Zeke’s grandfather. “I’m real sorry about the fishing tackle.”

“I know you are, son.”

“I’ll work off those rods and reels as fast as I can. I promise.”

“I know that too. You’re an honest boy.”

“We’ll be finished with our tobacco by the end of August. When do you think your cotton will be ready?”

“First or second week of September.”

“I’ll be back then for sure.”

“That’ll be good.”

“But it’ll have to be after school and on Saturdays.”

“I already planned for that, Jack.”

With all of his excuses exhausted, Jack play punched Zeke’s shoulder. “See ya.”

Zeke’s face split with a grin as he returned the affectionate tap. “Yeah, see ya.”

A full moon’s glow painted the world pale blue by the time Jack made his return trip through the cotton field, the creek, and the woods. At the edge of the tobacco field, he was drawn up short by headlights turning in at the cow barn. Jack wondered where his father had been this time of night, but then Daddy had been leaving the house at night with unusual frequency of late, and nearly every Saturday night for a while now. He refused to say where he went. Just got up from the table, went to the barn, and drove away. Jack decided to spy on his old man.

Jack crept to the barn's sidewall and looked through the opening between two planks. A shadow moved across the pile of corncobs just on the other side of the wall. Jack could almost reach out and touch his father as he moved around, kicking cobs out of his path. The boy held his breath as the rusty hinges of the bin where they kept the seed corn creaked. Kernels in their toe sacks rattled a little as they were shoved aside, then something that sounded like fabric rustled and the lid thumped closed.

Jack tiptoed to the front end of the outer wall. When his father headed for the house, Jack turned the corner and started inching toward the barn door, but half way across the yard, Daddy stopped and peered over his shoulder. Jack froze, willing himself to be invisible in the depths of the barn's long shadow. His old man's head swung from side to side like a wolf sniffing the air for prey and he started back toward the barn.

Jack silently edged backwards until the side wall's weather smoothed boards pressed against his shoulder blades through the thin cotton of his shirt. His father entered the barn and the seed bin's lid squealed again, followed by the sounds of toe sacks being shifted and dropped. Another protest from the lid's hinges and all was quiet. Nothing but the crunch of Daddy's boots on the driveway's dry sand broke the silence.

Jack waited until he heard the screen door on the back porch slam, then he hurried into the barn and headed straight for the corncrib. The toe sacks were heavy. Their burlap scratched his bare arms and Jack knew whelps would rise if he held on to them for too long. After shifting a couple of the sacks, Jack ran his hand down into the bin, feeling for anything different or unexpected. Smooth cotton, like the percale Mama used to make sheets, met his fingers. Jack shoved another sack away and lifted the fabric from its hiding place. When it cleared the edge of the bin, he shook out the fabric and dropped it.

A drift of smooth cotton, light in color except for a dark cross-shaped patch on its upper left settled over the pile of corncobs on the floor. Toward the top, the material narrowed into a cone that ended in a sharp, stiff point. The last time Jack had seen such a thing was during one of his few trips to Jacksonville. He had stood mesmerized as several hundred men in white robes and hoods marched through downtown to the river where they burned a gigantic cross. At the time, his father had called the group unChristian, but that was before times turned so hard and Daddy changed. Jack had no idea exactly when Daddy had become Klan.

Chapter 23

DeWitt paced the hotel lobby's black and white tiles, hand in his pants pocket jingling his keys and loose change. Through the restaurant's glass doors he caught sight of Meg entering the dining room with a loaded tray. The jingling in his pocket increased. One of the other girls said something to Meg and jerked her head toward the reception area. Meg glanced in DeWitt's direction, amusement lighting her eyes. After giving the tray to her coworker, she glided through the restaurant doors.

"You're still in your waitress get up. The boss hates it when any of us are late, especially to his election fundraisers."

Meg raised an eyebrow. "For somebody who feels the way you do about his boss, I would've thought being late didn't matter."

"Shh. I need my job."

Meg placed a finger against her lips and glanced around the lobby. "Not a soul in sight. Your secret's safe."

DeWitt grabbed her hand and pulled her into his arms. "In that case . . ." A deep kiss smothered the end of his sentence. When Meg began to squirm, he pulled back and grinned.

"DeWitt, I need my job too. Albert'll kill me if anybody tells him about us kissing in the lobby."

"No, he won't. You have him wrapped around your little finger and you know it."

"I know nothing of the kind." Meg pushed him away, a half pretend expression of exasperation turning her mouth into a thin line. "Go to the kitchen and get a Co'Cola. I'll be back in a minute."

"Don't make it too long a minute. I'm serious about not being late."

The road south shot straight through the pine forests to the edge of the Santa Fe River where Sheriff Ike Darnell's biggest supporter and benefactor, Carlton Smith, had a large farm. DeWitt pulled up beside Ike's Ford and sighed. Ike expected DeWitt and, by extension, Meg to earn their barbecue and Brunswick stew by helping with the setting up and by serving the crowds that would flock in for the free food later in the afternoon.

When the preparations were complete with a half hour to kill before the first guests arrived, DeWitt and Meg strolled hand-in-hand toward a swing hanging from the limb of a huge live oak. Once ensconced in the deep shade, DeWitt put his arm around Meg and kissed her temple.

"Thanks, Baby, for all of your help. Ike just takes it for granted that wives and sweethearts can be ordered around like us deputies."

"I can take him for one afternoon. Poor you. You have to put up with him every day."

DeWitt leaned down and turned her chin toward him. He kissed her lightly on the lips. "That's one of the things I love about you. You're a really goodhearted person."

Just being this close to Meg set his pulse racing. All he could think about was the day they would marry and his frustration would end. There were times when he thought he couldn't stand the self-denial another day. Other men found comfort in casual encounters bought for a few dollars. His pals, already married, urged a visit to a certain house just north of town. DeWitt sometimes wondered if one time would really hurt anything. The boys said that what Meg didn't know wouldn't hurt her.

Unable to sit still another minute, DeWitt grabbed Meg's hand and pulled her to her feet. "There's something in the barn I want to show you."

"DeWitt, do you really think that's smart? You know how we are when we're alone."

"It won't hurt anything if we just kiss a little. Come on. I just want to hold you."

Looking down into Meg's eyes, DeWitt was gratified to see that she seemed as frustrated as he felt.

The big barn was dusty and hot, but also private. DeWitt felt sure no one had seen them slip through the open end as he led Meg toward a tarp-covered piece of machinery at the back of the central hallway. Once behind the concealed machine, DeWitt took Meg in his arms. His desire soared when she melted against him in response. He groaned as he covered her mouth with his and heard her breathing increase to match the rapid pace of his own. They rocked in a passionate embrace until Meg pulled back and leaned against the tarp.

"You make me forget everything when you kiss me like that."

"That's the general idea." DeWitt put his hands on her shoulders. "I know I said I'd wait as long as it takes, but have you thought anymore about setting a date?"

"No, I haven't thought about it. I've dreamed about it, eaten my meals with it, taken my bath with it."

"And?"

DeWitt looked down into Meg's eyes. His love was as deep for her as ever, but it was mixed with insecurity and pain. She must have sensed his mixed emotions because something seemed to melt within her.

She placed her fingers against his cheek and caressed it. "DeWitt, I want you more than my independence, more than

I fear poverty. What we have is forever. I've been stupid to risk losing it."

"Yeah, but will you set a date?"

"I've always thought Christmas would be a good time to get married. We wouldn't have to spend money on decorations and all the relatives would be around."

DeWitt was silent for a moment as though he couldn't quite believe what he had heard, then he whooped and picked Meg up off her feet. He swung her around until they were both dizzy. She landed next to the tarp and stumbled into it. DeWitt grabbed her to keep her from falling and then froze. She followed his gaze.

The tarp covering the machine they had hidden behind was knocked askew revealing a rear bumper with a yellow automobile body above, a body missing its passenger side fenders.

"I'll be damned. This has got to be the same car Jack and Zeke saw at the Santa Fe sinkhole."

"You know, when Jack first told me about what he and Zeke saw, I prayed it was somebody who'd come from a long way off to dump his dirty work. Do you think Ike knows?"

"Before all the lynchings started this summer, I'd have said Ike Darnell might not be the best cop in the world, but at least he wasn't doing any harm. Now, I think he'd allow his own mother to be lynched if he thought it'd buy him another vote."

"You think our host is Klan?"

"Couldn't be anything else."

"Do you think Mr. Smith was the man they saw that night?"

DeWitt was silent while he thought about how much he should tell Meg. The barn's owner was a powerful man. For years, rumors and innuendo had flitted around him like flies hovering over rotten fruit, but never lit long enough to stick. If what he now suspected was true, Meg, Jack, and the Taylors were all in serious danger.

The face that looked up at him so trustingly owned him body and soul. He couldn't decide if the Klansmen were willing dupes of the power behind all the killing or if they were preparing themselves for a cut of the profits once the takeover was complete. For all their high talk over the years about rubbing out vice in the name of God, Klansmen seemed to have skipped the Sundays when the Sixth Commandment was taught. *Thou shalt not murder* had no meaning for them at all.

"Maybe. Of course, somebody else could have driven that night. There's no way to know for sure."

A voice coming from the front side of the Model T made both of them jump. "What night would you be talking about?"

The man who had silently joined them was backlit by sunlight pouring through the barn entrance, but DeWitt didn't need to see the face to know who it was.

"Nothing special, Ike. I was just telling Meg about how we found Dr. Latham's car abandoned out on the Valdosta highway last month."

"That so? How peculiar." The sheriff paused and DeWitt's heart rate increased. "Well, you two lovebirds can discuss missing cars another time. Right now, you're needed back at the tables. The first guests are arriving."

Relief flooded DeWitt. It seemed that Ike was irritated by their absence, but hadn't overheard everything they had said.

"Sorry, Boss. We just wanted to be alone a little."

Ike Darnell cocked his head and grinned when they came abreast. "I know it doesn't look like it, but I was young and in love once. I'll let it go this time. Just don't take advantage again today. This is an important rally for my campaign."

When the sheriff was out of earshot, Meg muttered, "You

taking advantage? He has some nerve. This was supposed to be your afternoon off."

"Don't say that so loud."

The rally went on for hours with speeches, food, music, and more speeches. When Meg and DeWitt were finally free to leave, they climbed into his truck and headed for town. DeWitt reached over and took Meg's hand, pulling her closer until she nestled against his side.

Kissing the top of her head, he said, "Thanks again for today. You're a real trooper. Ike and his wife said to tell you how much they appreciated your help."

"Yeah, I bet they did. It was for you, not them." Meg's voice sounded grumpy and tired.

"I'm sorry they had you waiting tables like some kind of servant."

"It's okay. I'm used to it."

"That'll stop after Christmas. Right?"

"We'll see. There's no reason for me to quit working just because we get married."

"You're one stubborn lady, but that's one of the things I love about you. You got gumption."

"And don't you forget it." Meg's voice sounded sleepy as she dropped her head on his shoulder.

DeWitt chuckled and hugged her. "As if you'd ever let me."

They drove in silence for several miles when Meg suddenly sat up and moved back. DeWitt sensed that she was trying to see his face. "Did you talk to Mr. Barnes about his editorials? One of the girls said she saw you coming out of the Tribune office not long after you dropped me off the other day."

"Yeah, but I don't think it did any good. I know you think he's just a harmless old man who only wants what's best for the community, but I'm not so sure. Some people can put on a really good front when they have a lot to hide. If Barnes is so concerned about morality, why won't he denounce the lynchings? A man who condones murder has a lot to answer for."

"I suspect he's afraid like most people."

"I think there's another reason."

"Like what?"

"With all of the vice kingpins dead, that leaves a big hole. I think somebody's getting ready to fill it by taking control and consolidating all the gambling, moonshining, and prostitution under one leadership. Why not the man who stirred up all the violence to begin with?"

"I just can't believe that."

DeWitt sensed Meg's distress even though he could only see the outline of her profile illuminated by the faint dashboard light. He pulled her under his arm again and kissed her temple. "Don't worry about Silas Barnes. He's a tough old bird. Did you know that he decided he didn't like the man who was sheriff before Ike? The sheriff had ideas about colored folk being equal in the eyes of the law. Barnes started a campaign against him and the man lost his next election. He's not the sainted do-gooder he likes to make out to be."

"No, I didn't know that. Ike's been sheriff as far back as I can remember. How do you know about the other sheriff?"

"The department's old colored janitor. He told me one day when he found me cussing and kicking stuff out behind the office. I was really mad at Ike. He heard some of the things I said."

"You're lucky he didn't report you to your boss."

"Yeah, but he's a good guy and he agrees with me. He wishes someone else was sheriff. It really is time for a change."

"No Republican's going to run. We haven't had a Republican in office in this county since Reconstruction. Is a Democrat willing to take him on?"

"No, Ike'll win again. He's got too much support across the county now, but he's not going to be in office forever. Someday, people will see him for who he is. When they do, I'm going to throw my hat in the ring."

"You'd be wonderful. Do you think the party would support you?"

"Probably not, but I can dream can't I?"

"Of course you can. And one day things will be different. People will have money again and it will be a better world."

"Now who's dreaming?"

"Don't be depressing. Things can't stay this way forever. They just can't."

DeWitt heard the edge of desperation in Meg's voice and a momentary clutch of fear gripped his heart. They had come so far as a couple and he wasn't sure how he would react to another disappointment. As much as he loved Meg, her past reluctance to commit to a wedding date had often left him confused, frustrated, and angry. He pretended not to listen when the other deputies teased him about being "that girl's toy," but secretly DeWitt sometimes felt like Meg's yoyo. As stupid as he knew it was to set tests for the person you loved, he couldn't help himself.

"Whether the world changes or not, it won't affect us, will it, Darlin'?"

He wasn't sure, but he thought he heard a slight hesitation in her voice when she answered, "It's like the song. I'll be loving you always."

Meg hummed the Irving Berlin tune all the way to the hotel curb. Somehow, it didn't make DeWitt feel better. He guessed there had been too many dashed hopes and too much frustration for him to be completely confident in a Christmas wedding.

It was past midnight by the time Meg was finally bathed and ready for bed. She stretched out on top of the sheet because it was too hot for more cover than her thin nightgown. Although she was dead tired, sleep didn't come immediately. For once, it wasn't trouble that kept her awake. Instead, she grinned into the darkness and hugged herself for sheer joy.

Now that she had finally put her fears aside and committed to a wedding date, she was at peace and happier than she had been in a long time. It felt profoundly, deeply joyous to know that she and DeWitt would be together no matter what came their way. Their love would carry them through the bad times and enrich the good times. Why she hadn't seen this before was something she would ask herself for a long time to come. DeWitt was the best of men and he loved her with his whole heart, of that she was sure. The outside world was a place of trepidation and uncertainty, but within the circle of their love, they were safe and secure. She had to be the luckiest girl alive.

The following morning Meg sang softly as she lay the restaurant tables in preparation for the before church breakfast seating. It saddened her to see how few people came in these days. The numbers had grown smaller each week since last October, but she knew everybody was afraid to spend the money they had left on eating in a restaurant. It somctimcs madc hcr afraid that Albert might be forced to let her and the other younger employees go, since they were the last hired.

As she put flatware, cups and saucers, and water glasses at each place, she felt eyes following her and turned with a big smile toward the source. She thought DeWitt must be early today, but instead of the love of her life, she found her boss observing her. He wore an expression that she couldn't quite put her finger on and his fingers tapped the spine of a ledger book pressed against his chest. She cocked her head at Albert and gave him "the look," the one that mothers and teachers have used for centuries to control unruly children without having to open their mouths.

Albert smiled sheepishly and went to his usual table. A few minutes later, Meg went to get his order and had to say his name twice before she had his attention.

"Sorry. Just the usual, please."

"You sure you want to disappoint Flossie? You know how she gets if any of her specials go to waste."

"Of course. I'd forgotten today is Sunday. Bring whatever she recommends."

Meg turned in the order and then carried a tray of clean glasses to the serving station where an older waitress was folding napkins.

"What's wrong with Albert? It's like he's on another planet."

"Don't know. He seemed fine when he arrived this morning."

Meg clicked her tongue. "I wish he'd just come out with whatever bee he's got in his bonnet. He's been acting strange for days now. It's getting on my nerves."

"Sorry. I haven't noticed anything. Maybe it's just you he's acting weird around."

"I can't imagine what I've done to upset him."

"Oh, I wouldn't worry. He thinks of you like one of his own daughters. He probably just has hotel business on his mind. The owner's accountant is coming tomorrow for the annual audit."

"Yeah, that must be it." Meg glanced again at Albert and saw him pouring over the hotel bookkeeping ledger. It seemed that Albert wasn't the only one not paying attention today. Meg had completely failed to notice the large book he must have carried into the restaurant with him. She smiled to herself. At least her reason for having her head in the clouds was a lot more exciting than a bookkeeping audit.

Meg performed her duties without another thought to Albert until she delivered his breakfast. As she lifted her empty tray from an adjoining table and turned to go, he called after her.

"Meg, could you please come to my office after the morning rush is over?"

She searched his face, trying to read what had prompted his request, but his expression was bland and composed. "Sure. I should be free about 10:00."

At ten, she knocked on Albert's office door. As she entered, Albert looked up from the ledger he was still poring over. His expression made it appear that he dreaded her arrival. She mentally reviewed her work performance, suddenly fearing that she was about to be fired for some fault of which she had no knowledge.

"Have a seat Meg. Can I get you some tea or a Co'Cola?"

Now Meg was really concerned. She was usually the one who stepped and fetched for Albert, not the other way around. When she shook her head, Albert sighed and sat back in his chair.

"Are you still seeing Deputy Williams?"

Meg couldn't have been more surprised. "Yes, Albert, you know I am. You've seen us coming and going together."

"Are you still serious about him?"

"Of course I am. We've set a wedding date for Christmas week. Why are you asking these questions?" For no reason that she could explain, a worm of fear began gnawing its way up from the pit of her stomach.

"Meg, I think you know that I look on you like my own child."

"Albert, you're scaring me. Has something happened to DeWitt?"

"No, sweet girl, but I have something to tell you that's going to hurt. I've talked it over with my wife and oldest girl. They both say you have to know."

"Know what?"

"Meg, DeWitt may not be the man you think he is."

"Albert! I know you don't like DeWitt because he's part Seminole, but this is really going too far."

"Hear what I have to say before you're so quick to judge my motives. It would be easier to cut out my tongue than hurt you, but I care about you enough to want what's best for you."

"Albert, tell me what's going on before you give me heart failure."

A pained expression crossed Albert's face. "Maybe you've heard about the house out north of Five Points? The one where there was a lynching?" Meg nodded. "Earlier this week Mrs. Menzies and I were coming back from visiting my cousin in Valdosta. When we passed that certain house, Deputy Williams was standing on the front porch. He and one of those girls had their arms around each other, all hugged up like."

Meg blinked and wondered if her hearing had suddenly played tricks on her. When she didn't respond, Albert continued. "Please believe me. I hate having to be the one to tell you this."

Frozen with pain, Meg didn't move or speak for several beats. When her tongue finally thawed, its tone was razor sharp. "I don't believe you. It must have been the other deputy you saw."

Albert looked at the ceiling and Meg could have sworn his lower lip trembled slightly. When he looked at her again, she saw only deep concern in his eyes.

Quietly, he continued, "I wouldn't have said anything if I wasn't very sure who it was we saw. As we passed, Deputy Williams turned toward the road. I saw his face clearly and I'm sure he saw mine."

Meg couldn't believe the implications of what Albert was saying. It didn't make sense for DeWitt to be with another woman when she knew beyond a doubt that he loved her. He wasn't that kind of man, but then the memory of all their arguments about getting married and their physical frustration flooded her mind. She had always been told that men's needs were great and hard to control, which was why some of them were unfaithful. She loved DeWitt deeply, but she wasn't prepared to share him with another woman for any reason. To her, that part of the wedding ceremony about "forsaking all others" applied equally to the groom. If a few months of physical denial could make him turn to a prostitute, then she doubted he could handle the hardships that came with marriage. To think she came so close to marrying a man who would hand out hard earned money for a momentary pleasure made Meg physically ill.

She stood up and put a hand on the desk for support. "Thank you, Albert. You may well have saved me from making a terrible mistake." With that, she turned and fled the room.

Chapter 24

Jack dangled his legs over the edge of the hayloft and pondered the argument that had gotten him sent away from the supper table in disgrace. Of course, argument wasn't exactly the right word because you didn't talk back to Daddy without risking a hiding with his razor strop, but Jack managed to speak his mind at the outset. Daddy's reason for not letting him work for Mr. Taylor didn't make sense. The two families had been neighbors for many years and used to help each other until last year when everything changed.

All of a sudden, Daddy stopped speaking to Mr. Taylor and forbade any of the family to see Zeke and his grandfather. When Jack asked why, all he got for an answer was that "Blevinses don't have no truck with niggers no more." That was plain stupid. Jack refused to stop hanging out with his best friend even though he had to sneak around to do it. He had gotten a couple of whippings, but he didn't care. He kept on going to Zeke's house no matter what Daddy said or did. For Jack, being disloyal to a friend would hurt a lot more than a beating.

Gentle head butting and low-throated rumbling made the thin line of Jack's lips curve upward in a half-hearted smile and he absentmindedly scratched behind the cat's ears and under her chin. With such encouragement, she placed her front paws on Jack's lap so that she could rub against his chest and face, marking him with her scent so that all other felines knew he was her kitten.

She was a good mama who placed dead birds and other prey on Jack's windowsill, lest her largest baby go hungry.

When the cat started grooming his bare arm, Jack's throat tightened. He wrapped his arms around the soft tabby body and buried his face in her fur as a quiet sob escaped his firmly clinched lips.

The back screen door slammed, momentarily silencing the crickets that sawed away in the early evening twilight. Jack swiped the tears from his cheeks and drew his legs up onto the loft's wide pine planks. Stretching out full length on his stomach, he made himself invisible to anyone on the barn's dirt floor below.

He had no intention of speaking to his father until he absolutely had to. Mama could beg all she wanted. Jack was fed up with Daddy's meanness. He acted like he was the only farmer getting threatening letters for unpaid debts. Everyone they knew owed money to the bank or the farm supply stores, usually both. Jack would love to ask what made Daddy think he was so special.

Seeing a shadow at the barn's entrance, Jack pushed the cat away and silently scooted behind the closest post. Peering over the loft's edge, he watched as his father strode to the corncrib and flung its door back. The seed bin's rusty hinges creaked and then all was silent again. When he emerged from the crib, Arnold Blevins carried his white hooded robe over his arm. The truck's starter ground loudly in the barn's hallway and the engine coughed to life. Jack watched as the truck backed out and turned toward the lane leading away from the house. He didn't know where his father was going, but he knew wherever it was, no good would come of it.

Curiosity aroused, Jack jumped out of the loft onto the packed sand floor. His feet went numb from the impact followed by tingling that spread from his toes up to his calves, but it didn't keep him from slipping into the cornfield beside the barn and secretly following his dad's truck toward the road that ran in front of the farm. Jack didn't have a clue what he thought he could accomplish by trying to follow his dad. He knew it wouldn't be possible to keep up once the truck reached the main road. He was running on pure emotion.

The truck reached firmer ground and sped up, forcing Jack to run hard in order to keep up. His pounding feet sent up little clouds of dust and his lungs burned. When the truck finally halted at the end of their lane, Jack leaned over and propped himself up with his hands on his knees. His chest heaved and sweat dripped from his face onto the field's tilled soil. It was futile to keep up the chase. Jack decided he might as well return to the house now that his dad wasn't there.

He stood up ready to start back down the lane, but something he couldn't explain made him stop and watch the truck. A clutch of fear gripped his midsection. Instead of turning right toward the state highway, the truck turned left toward the creek. In another moment, a line of cars and trucks appeared. All of them were headed in the same direction as his dad's truck.

Instinct set Jack's feet tearing through the cornfield toward the woods and the creek that ran through them. Once he entered the trees, he ignored the brambles and debris that snagged his overalls and jabbed his feet. Zeke and his grandfather had to be warned.

Terrified that he wouldn't reach them in time, Jack splashed into the creek without a thought to the occasional cottonmouth that slithered silently through the water. He didn't care that the sound of his pounding feet echoed in the forest surrounding the Taylor's back tobacco field. He didn't allow himself to slow down until he saw a strange glow in Zeke's backyard.

Stunned by the sight of so many torches, Jack stopped in his tracks and dropped down to his knees, trying to think what to do next. Going to the house was out of the question now. He wouldn't help anyone by getting caught. There was no telling what those men would do to him despite his dad being with them. As he crouched in the dirt, a screen door slammed and angry shouts came from the yard. Boiling rage sent bile surging from the pit of his stomach. He leaned to the side and lost his supper. He was too late to do anything but watch and pray.

Jack sat back on his heels, wrapped his arms around his knees, and rocked his body in the self-soothing manner he hadn't used since he was little. He didn't know what else to do, but he was determined not to desert his friends, even if he couldn't stop what was about to happen. And if he was going to be a secret witness to evil, he needed to be as close as he could get without being seen. Stretching out full length, he slithered along on his belly between the tobacco plants until he reached the pine thicket at the field's far side. He crawled into the cover and turned in the yard's direction.

A dark form crouching in the underbrush made his heart lurch. Jack froze and peered into the darkness. When he heard a small whimper, Jack knew who was hiding there watching the horror unfold. He slipped up behind his friend and grabbed him, clapping a hand over his mouth. Zeke squirmed with the strength of a tiger.

"It's me," Jack whispered. "Stop fighting. I come to help."

Zeke's thin shoulder slammed into Jack's chin, making him see stars. He'd never known so much energy to come from the skinny, undersized little body. The force knocked Jack off balance, sending him onto his back with Zeke on top of him. Jack felt his breath leave him with a jab to his mid-section, but he held onto Zeke for dear life. Jack kept his hand clamped over Zeke's mouth even when teeth sank into the webbing between his thumb and forefinger. Jack held firm when feet pummeled his legs and fingers clawed at his bare arms. When blood made his hand slippery, he threw his legs around Zeke's body and tightened an arm across his friend's mouth. Nothing could have broken his grip.

Chest heaving with his effort, Jack croaked into Zeke's ear, "Stop it. You cain't do nothing to help your granddad. And gettin' yourself lynched ain't gonna solve nothin'."

Zeke's body remained rigid, but his violent struggling ceased. Jack sat both of them up. He pulled Zeke closer and held him tighter. Finally, the tension went out of the younger boy's body.

"If I let you go, will you stay quiet?"

Zeke's head nodded as much as he could with Jack's arm still clapped over his mouth. Jack decided that releasing Zeke all at once might not be a good idea, so he let only his palm drop away.

Zeke slumped against Jack and whispered, "Let me go, you damned white boy."

"Not until you promise to keep quiet and out of sight. You gonna do it?"

"Yeah, just let me go."

Jack released Zeke, who rolled onto the ground. The two boys lay side-by-side breathing hard and listening to the shouts and the sounds of more vehicles arriving in the Taylor yard.

"I need to see what's happening."

"No, you don't. It ain't a sight you'll ever forget."

"You mean like when I watched my mama and daddy go back into our burning house?"

Jack felt deeply ashamed. How could he have forgotten that Zeke had already witnessed two deaths? "I forgot. I'm sorry."

Zeke started toward the source of the sounds and light, but Jack grabbed his arm. "I'm coming with you."

"Suit yourself. You can watch your damned coward of a daddy hiding under his sheet."

Jack's prayer had gone unanswered. "How do you know it's my daddy?"

"His truck was the first one that pulled into the yard. Me and Granddaddy thought something was wrong. Thought maybe he'd come for help until we saw the white robe."

Zeke tried to jerk free, but Jack held tight. "How'd you get away?"

The younger boy turned to face Jack. Despite the dimness of the dwindling twilight, Jack could see the hatred and rage in Zeke's eyes. "Granddaddy sent me to hide in the woods when he saw what was about to happen. He made me promise not to show myself no matter what happens. Your daddy was carrying a rope."

During the short time they argued, it seemed that Zeke suddenly became a completely different person. The shy little boy Jack had always known disappeared and a hard-eyed, much older stranger took his place.

Jack drew a sharp breath and whispered, "Zeke, I ain't my daddy."

Zeke stared into Jack's eyes and then turned away without reply. When he started inching forward, Jack felt he had no choice but to follow. They managed to crawl through the undergrowth without attracting the attention of the white robed figures that circled Isaiah Taylor. Zeke's elderly grandfather stood stiff backed and head held high despite his hands being tied behind him. A stout rope with a noose on one end hung draped over a nearby live oak limb. Next to the tree, a tall wooden cross reared up against the sky. Too many torches to count illuminated the whole sickening scene.

One of the Klansmen stepped out of the crowd. He held up what looked like fishing rods within a few inches from Mr. Taylor's face. "You been spying on Klan business, old man?"

"No, sir, I ain't been spying on nobody." Mr. Taylor's voice sounded surprisingly strong.

"We know it was you that bought this fishing gear.

Somebody found these down at the river near the sinkhole. How'd they get there?"

"Well, I do some fishing from time to time. That part of the river's a good spot. I been looking for my rods for a while now."

"You do any fishing there back in June?"

"Could have. What day in June you thinking of?"

"Wasn't day. It was night."

"Yes, I did some night fishing several times back in June."

"Anybody with you?"

"No. I don't take no one night fishing. I have secret places."

A voice called, "What about your grandson?"

Isaiah's eyes scanned the crowd until he located the voice's source. "I don't take my grandson out late at night. It's past his bedtime."

"So, it was you fishing with *two* rods?"

"That's right. I tie one to a stob and set it in the ground, then I hold onto the other one."

An angry voice called out, "That don't make no sense and you know it."

"Well, sense or no, that's what I do."

Jack felt physically ill as he recognized the next voice. There was no mistaking who it belonged to. "Taylor's telling the truth. I've seen him do it that way."

"You been fishing with a nigger, have you?"

"No, but I saw him one night when I was out fishing with my boy."

Zeke swiveled so that he looked straight into Jack's eyes. Jack shrugged and shook his head. His father had never taken him fishing, nighttime or otherwise. With deep bitterness, he wondered why his old man couldn't have tried to do the right thing before things got to this point. For the life of him, Jack would never understand his father, but it really didn't matter anymore. Jack had stopped trying.

"Peculiar fishing habits ain't a hanging offense, but immoral conduct is. You still making moonshine and selling to any nigger with a penny to his name?"

"I've stopped making and selling. I got the message."

"I doubt it. See, I don't believe that you were fishing alone anymore than I believe you've stopped making shine. When the Klan asks questions, we expect the truth. Of course, everybody knows the truth ain't in a nigger. String him up, boys."

One white robed figure pushed another one forward from the group. "We gonna give you the honor, seeing as how you'll benefit most from having this nigger gone from your backyard."

To his horror, Jack recognized his father's beaten up work boots below the soiled hem of the white sheet. His father stepped up to Isaiah and took the old man by the arm. The two men seemed to look briefly into each other's eyes before Arnold Blevins led his former friend to the tree and placed the noose around his neck. For a moment, Jack felt sure Mr. Taylor looked directly at the place where he and Zeke were hiding. Zeke must have thought so too because Jack heard his breath catch, then his body began shaking.

Four men walked behind Mr. Taylor and took the other end of the rope. Slowly, they hauled Isaiah Taylor up until his feet dangled a couple of inches above the ground, then they tied the rope to the tree. Isaiah's body bucked as air ceased traveling into his lungs. His eyes bulged. His mouth worked and made sucking sounds. It felt like an hour, but in reality it couldn't have been more than thirty seconds before the elderly body went slack.

After another five minutes or so, a Klansman stepped up to the body and felt for a pulse. "He's gone. Light it up and let's get out of here."

One by one, Klansmen filed by the cross and dropped their torches against its base. Within seconds, the night blazed.

Chapter 25

The junior college library clerk who had first shown Liz into the rare documents room now greeted her like an old friend whenever she arrived.

"Hi, Liz. *We been mighty lonesome here without you, but things'll be better frum now on.*"

She realized the young man probably thought he was being funny, but his off-key rendition of the country song sent an icy jab straight to her heart. He had no way of knowing that Jonathan sang it when her work schedule or his deployments had kept them apart for extended periods.

She plastered a smile on her face and responded, "Hi, yourself. You're a great librarian, but I'd leave the singing to the professionals."

"You wound me. You truly do. I guess you're here for research, not to see me."

Liz couldn't help but chuckle as the clerk flung a hand over his heart and his features drooped into a hangdog expression.

"I'm here to finish up my research, but seeing you is an added bonus."

His face came up in a flash and he wiggled his eyebrows at her Groucho style. "Well, in that case, how about meeting me at the student center after I get off work. Say around 10:00?"

"Sorry, I can't be responsible for keeping children up past their bedtime."

"Ouch. Well, since you're intent on hurting my feelings, just go on and spend your time with those old books."

"I will. Thank you for your permission."

"Any time, Fair Lady."

Liz laughed and blew the young man a kiss as she passed into the rare documents room. She enjoyed their innocent flirtations which both of them knew would never be more than that. She had met his boyfriend on a previous visit and they seemed very devoted to one another.

The 1930 volume still had her marker in place where she had left off last time. She flipped to the following week's pages expecting the same editorial diatribe, but that particular edition was devoid of Barnes's opinions. In place of his column, a brief notice appeared stating that Mr. Barnes had taken time off to be with his family and that his editorials would resume at a later date.

Liz wondered if he was giving up his campaign and was looking for a new subject. After months of ranting about local vice, there surely couldn't be much left to say. And Ethel had confirmed Liz's suspicions that the lynching victims were involved in vice, so it looked like Editor Barnes's mission, and possibly more importantly, his suspected sub rosa goal might be near completion. Nonetheless, Liz believed in being thorough.

The police column for that week had only one entry.

Isaiah Taylor, 80, Negro, was found hanging from a tree in the yard of his home in southern Columbia County. Members of the O'Leno Missionary Baptist Church reported being drawn to the home around one a.m. by flames that were visible for several miles. A large cross burned beside the body and the Taylor home was destroyed by fire.

Great concern was expressed over the disappearance of Taylor's eleven-year-old grandson, Ezekiel. The grandson had been Taylor's ward since the boy's parents died in a 1923 house fire said by some to have been set by a white man the boy claimed to have seen running from the scene. Church members speculated that the same man was responsible for the most recent events. Ezekiel Taylor is said to be small for his age and shy of strangers.

Any sightings of a boy meeting this description are to be reported to the Columbia County Sheriff's Department.

Liz read the report twice trying to decide why the Klan had targeted this particular old man and his grandson. There was the mention of O'Leno again. Perhaps the trouble centered on that area, but when she consulted a county map, it became clear that the lynchings had occurred in seemingly random locations. As terrible as the other lynchings had been to visualize, Isaiah Taylor's death touched Liz in a way none of the others had. In her mind's eye, she had a vivid picture of the elderly victim hanging from the tree and of a terrified child being forced to witness his grandfather's murder.

Doing a quick calculation, Liz realized that Ezekiel would be in his early nineties, if he had survived. She knew from her course work and reading that children were occasionally Klan victims. A horrible mental image formed.

Liz's breath caught as she choked back a rush of bile. Shoving her chair away from the table, she jumped to her feet and began pacing the small room. Capone had always been a fascinating research subject, but now Liz felt deeply repulsed by her main bad boy. If her suspicions were proven true, then he was ultimately the cause of all the death and violence wreaking havoc during the summer of 1930, including the probable death of this innocent child. It suddenly seemed appalling that she had always been so fascinated by risky, self-absorbed men.

That attraction had been the one area of her life that caused her parents some anxiety. In all else, Liz was the child who never set a foot wrong, who excelled as a parent and teacher pleaser. As an adolescent, she was an honor student who participated in service projects and volunteered at the local animal shelter. She was kind to the kids who were shunned by the popular ones. All that goodness was counterbalanced, however, by her choices in boyfriends.

A different Liz seemed trapped beneath the surface of her outwardly sedate facade. This other girl was a wild child who sought release in the company of males of whom her parents never approved. It had been as if she needed something untoward in her life to achieve . . . what? Balance, perhaps? She really didn't know even now why she was attracted to the risky guys, but they were definitely losing their luster.

Liz stopped pacing and stood by the window. The nearby pines swayed in the strong breeze being pushed by an advancing cold front due to descend in the wee hours of tomorrow morning. Liz shivered and pulled her sweatshirt closer around her body. The information she was gathering no longer felt like research from which she was at least one step removed.

It felt as though another kind of boy was calling to her personally, demanding that she shine light on the injustices he had suffered. A new, unfamiliar rage filled her. She suddenly wanted to know—needed to know—the fate of an eleven-year-old who wasn't even a footnote in history, a child who may have died long before she was born. Little Ezekiel Taylor deserved to have his story told.

Liz began turning pages, searching for anything related to the lynchings. The first thing she found was Silas Barnes's next editorial.

My Fellow Citizens,

If you are a regular reader of this column, you know this writer possesses a profound belief in the importance of moral conduct and opposes anything that threatens the sanctity of the family or besmirches the name Columbia. Since January of this year, this column has denounced the nefarious activities of those persons guilty on both counts.

Since June, private individuals, seeing public officials derelict in their duty, have carried out on the local criminal element acts of lethal vigilantism. Although there was no intent with this writer to incite violence, it cannot be denied that those private individuals have made significant progress toward ending the vice activities in this county, something the Columbia County Sheriff's Department has failed, some would say refused, to do.

Those who violate the laws of God and man should expect to be brought to justice, whether by officials sworn to enforce the laws or through other means when those authorities fail in their duty. Unfortunately, in acting where sworn peace officers have failed, it is believed that a line may have been crossed on Saturday night last. If true, this brings shame to the righteous work being carried out. Perhaps it is time for private individuals to stand down and to agitate until authorities finish the job that was begun by others.

Liz was more confused than ever about Silas Barnes's motives. Instinctively, she reached for her phone. She sometimes asked Jonathan's opinion in matters of the male psyche. She had her finger on the speed dial button when memory landed a blow to her solar plexus. Disgusted, she quickly deleted his number, but not before making a note of it in her spiral. Staring at the page, she shook her head and scratched out the number until she wore a hole in the paper. Evicting him from her head, heart, and life was her only option now.

Still, she wished there was someone she could discuss theories with. Roberta came to mind, but Liz had dodged her calls and had only replied to her increasingly angry voicemails with cryptic texts for a couple of months now. Liz didn't have the nerve to call her fiction editor to ask a favor. She would have to admit that she hadn't written a single word of her novel since they last spoke. In fact, she hadn't even thought about the damned thing. One of Roberta's dressing downs was not what her own psyche needed right now.

Liz sighed and resumed flipping newsprint pages. The following week provided no burning crosses or lynching victims, but one very unexpected item jumped off the page. Surprised, she sped read it, marked it, and flew to the next edition. In excitement, Liz skimmed and scanned all the way through to the end of the year, but incredibly, not a single word related to the murders or to vice activities appeared. With the same suddenness that the violence began, it disappeared without a whisper from the pages of the Columbia Tribune and apparently from the lives of the county's citizens. Save for that one final startling incident toward the end of July, there was nothing. No criminal investigations. No arrests or trials. No mention whatsoever of the lynchings or the KKK. It was simply as though 1930's summer of violence had never occurred.

Liz turned back to the article she had marked and began adding to her notes. The week after Barnes's call for an end to vigilantism, his column's space had a new byline. The editorial, written by the paper's only reporter, pled for any information on the whereabouts of his boss, Silas Barnes. Mrs. Barnes told police that her husband was last seen in the company of a late evening male visitor to their home.

After Mr. Barnes answered the door, he didn't invite the visitor in as was his custom, but went out onto the front porch. From the bedroom, she heard raised voices, then a car started and backed out of the driveway. Barnes had not returned home that or any other night since.

Liz flipped through the remainder of the year for a second time, reading more slowly this time. When she finished the last page, she closed the large cover and pushed the book away. It was all just so wrong.

She went to the shelves and hauled the volume for 1931 back to her table. January—weddings, funerals, traffic tickets, high school basketball scores—small town American life in any decade of the twentieth century. The ease with which the county had settled back into somnolence angered Liz. She flipped through February, her disgust growing with each page reporting the mundane. Then the first week of March threw her another tidbit.

A forester cruising timber for a logging company had made an unpleasant discovery resulting in Silas Barnes's car being pulled from a swamp near the state line. Although the body had suffered greatly from time in the water and from the attentions of the swamp's denizens, there was no doubt as to the identity. But after that, Barnes, like the other victims, might never have existed.

Liz slammed the volume and sighed heavily. It appeared, like Silas Barnes and the other unfortunates, she had come to a dead end.

Frustrated, she shoved the volumes back in place on their shelf and gathered her belongings. Her stomach growled loudly, reminding her that it must be well past her usual dinner hour. The 7 Lakes Café came to mind, but Liz didn't think she could handle any more rejection this week. Ethel had been less than willing to talk about Silas the last time they were together. She bade the clerk farewell and made her way to the library's front doors.

As she trudged to her car, Liz's mood matched that of the gloomy November evening. The wind had died and all was now still. The atmosphere waited quietly in anticipation of the change that was on its way. Heavy clouds covered the stars making the seventy-degree air so thick that the concrete sidewalk beaded over with sweat. Warm, humid, clammy November weather—she had no idea how much she would hate it.

It wasn't that she was unaccustomed to winter rains. She had grown up with them. By now, Seattle would be experiencing the first of its winter deluge, but the mountains so close to the city would also be getting snow. Liz hadn't realized how much she would miss snow skiing and four real seasons until they were now many hours away in the mountains of Georgia, North Carolina, and Tennessee. She scurried to her car and jumped in, using her sweatshirt to wipe the moisture from her face and hair. Peering at her reflection in the visor mirror didn't improve her outlook. Her hair, usually barely under control, was now a mass of wild frizz. How did people stand this damned climate?

She jammed her key in the ignition and reversed. No wonder colonial Florida had been reserved for exiles and castoffs from Georgia's Creek Nation. No sane person would want to live in this soupy swamp. Without warning, Hugh's face appeared in her thoughts. He had grown up in this part of Florida and didn't seem to mind the climate at all. He always appeared cool and unruffled regardless of the weather. It was enough to make her dislike him. He was irritatingly, maddeningly unflappable. Nothing ever upset him.

Liz grinned with guilty pleasure as she visualized Hugh in some predicament that sent him into a tailspin. But then the image of his face while he told her about his divorce unexpectedly surfaced and empathy for a kindred suffering soul replaced the impish glee.

A blaring horn and squealing tires snapped Liz out of her reverie. Almost too late, she realized that the traffic light at the main highway was red. Averting her gaze to avoid the angry glare of the other driver, Liz glanced in the rearview mirror and reversed out of the intersection.

She put her head on the steering wheel and breathed deeply. Damn, damn, damn. What a stupid thing to do. But it was just the latest in a long list that began late last summer when she impulsively decided to follow Jonathan to Florida. It was time for an honest review of where her decisions had brought her. She sighed and began a mental list. At the top was the need to take a good long look at herself and the way she had lived her life for the past three years.

In all honesty, she would have to admit that coming to Florida was the best thing that could have happened to her professionally. She had a great job with huge potential at a big time university. But most importantly, she had a research subject who had grabbed her heart and soul.

Her personal life might be a mess, but she knew in her bones that she was onto something important where Ezekiel Taylor was concerned. Images of a little boy being forced to watch his grandfather's murder kept mingling with her personal ruminations and she did nothing to stop them.

A horn blast from behind made her nearly jump out of her skin and propelled the Prius onto the highway. The traffic on I-75 south was light for a change, allowing Liz to think. Life hadn't turned out the way she had visualized last fall. It would feel really good to lay all of the blame on Jonathan, but a small cry from her conscience demanded that she, for once, take an in-depth look at the relationship.

Liz mulled it over for several miles before she was forced to conclude that Jonathan wasn't the sole author of her unhappiness. She had willingly put on blinders by unquestioningly accepting his refusal to express his feelings for her. She had never once asked him how he felt about her or if he was committed enough to their relationship to make moving to Florida worth the disruption to her life.

In all honesty, unlike little Ezekiel, she had a starring role in creating her own misery. Her willing acceptance of whatever a man offered had played a major part in the failure of yet another relationship. And while she was taking stock, it became clear that an assessment of what she really wanted in life must become a priority as well. After a few minutes of painful analysis, Liz realized she could accomplish that goal better without male encumbrances. Absolutely no more romantic entanglements until she had herself figured out.

Since her professional life was the only thing she felt was fully under her control, that was where she would start. She could opt to throw herself solely into her job related duties, but that wasn't enough. It wasn't where her only passion lay. Though she would work hard and meet all of her responsibilities at the university just as she always had done, research was her real love. And she now had a subject who deserved every ounce of her intelligence and skill. Wherever the trail led, she was going to find Ezekiel Taylor. His story would now be the filter through which Capone's connection with the area was viewed.

Chapter 26

When dust from the last departing vehicle settled, Jack rose to his feet. The cross next to the hanging tree blazed high into the sky, creating an eerie night and day effect. The yard beneath the cross's fiery halo was as bright as noon, but beyond it, the moonless night settled over the land like a thick, wet blanket. Smoke filled Jack's lungs and flying ash stung his eyes. The fire was so intense it made Jack's bare skin tingle from several yards away.

Feeling movement at his side, Jack glanced down at Zeke as he came up to a sitting position. Sweat poured down his face and dripped from his chin. Jack wasn't sure if the cause was the heat or the sight of his grandfather swaying ever so slightly in the light breeze that stirred the acrid atmosphere.

Without warning, the front of the house exploded, shooting flames high into the sky. Jack threw himself on top of Zeke and pushed both of them flat against the earth. When he raised his head, the old wood structure was completely engulfed in flames. Zeke groaned and struggled beneath him.

"Get off of me."

Jack rolled over and both boys sat up. Zeke looked at the tree and at the fire and then put his head on his knees.

"Did I hurt you?" Jack tried to put his arm around his friend, but Zeke jerked away.

"Nobody cain't hurt me no more and you cain't make it better. You cain't do nothing."

Zeke's words landed like a hard slap across the face, but Jack didn't retaliate. Instead, he reached out again only to be punched in the chest. Fighting the urge to hit back, Jack said,

"Get up. I don't think those men believed your grandfather about the river." Jack grabbed Zeke's overall strap and hauled him to his feet. "We got to get you away from here."

"I ain't going nowhere with a murdering white son of a bitch." Zeke's eyes blazed as brightly as the fire that scorched their skins.

Under normal circumstances, the words might have made Jack laugh, but Zeke's eyes were wild, like a small animal with its leg caught in the teeth of a trap. When he began swaying, Jack threw his arms around Zeke to keep him from falling. His whole body was trembling and then the wailing began. Fists pummeled Jack, but he refused to let go. For several minutes, the younger boy was a fury of screams, sobs, and punches. When the raging finally slowed, Jack eased his grip and allowed Zeke to wrench himself away.

"You're right. I cain't make anything better, but we can get you where you'll be safe."

A snarl curled Zeke's upper lip. "Don't you get it? Ain't no place safe for colored folk."

The intensity in his friend's voice made Jack stare. A new quality radiated from Zeke and it seared Jack to his core. He thought for a moment and then asked, "Well then, who do you trust the most?"

The question seemed to puncture the energy Zeke garnered from his rage. His body shook like it was midnight in January instead of sultry July. Zeke drew a ragged breath as his gaze dropped to the ground. He shook his head. "I ain't got nobody."

"There's got to be somebody."

Zeke's head moved from side to side.

Jack chewed on his lower lip. Finally, he said, "What about Preacher Jackson?"

"What about him?"

"I bet he'll help."

"So? Klan's gonna get me in the end. You know it. I know it."

"No they ain't."

Pure cussed determination propelled Jack to his feet. He grabbed Zeke's arm and dragged him across the yard toward the road.

"Let me go." Zeke jerked away and shoved Jack hard with both hands. "I told you I ain't going nowheres with you."

"You can hate me all you want, but you're coming. Give me trouble and I'll cold cock you where you stand." Jack clinched his fists and stared down at his friend with every ounce of conviction he could muster. "And you know I can do it."

The boys glared at one another until the hate in Zeke's eyes died. Breaking eye contact, he looked back at his blazing home. His head sagged and he took Jack's hand. Once again, Zeke became the kid Jack loved like a little brother and would go to the ends of the earth to protect.

At the edge of the woods, Zeke stopped walking. Jack tugged on his hand, but Zeke stubbornly refused to move. When Jack turned around, Zeke asked in a voice colored with both anger and desperation, "Jack, why're you my friend?"

The question surprised Jack. He had always been so busy not caring what other people thought, he'd never really considered his reasons for continuing a friendship that was damned by nearly everyone he knew. Under normal circumstances, he would have laughed at Zeke and wrestled him to the ground, tickling him until he cried "give." After all that had happened on this awful night, though, Jack felt that Zeke deserved an answer.

Several seconds passed before he replied. "We've been friends all our lives. People who been with you that long are important. You got to hang on to them. It don't matter who their folks are or what they look like. I guess the answer is that you just too important not to be friends with."

Zeke appeared to think about the explanation and then stepped forward, pulling Jack along. The boys walked away from the scene of devastation without saying anything more.

The light was on in Preacher Jackson's kitchen when the boys slipped out of the woods and onto the back porch. Jack knocked softly at first and then louder when the room suddenly went dark.

"Preacher, it's Zeke Taylor and Jack Blevins. Let us in. Please."

The back door cracked open an inch. "What are you boys doing out on a night like this?"

"Zeke's granddaddy's been lynched. You got to help us."

The door opened wide enough for the boys to pass into the house. Once they were inside, the door clicked shut and a bar was dropped across it.

Kerosene lamplight slowly came up, covering the room in a soft amber glow. Mrs. Jackson returned to her place beside her husband's empty chair. It was long past suppertime so no food was laid on the scrubbed pine table. Instead, the big family Bible lay open. Jack caught the first lines of a familiar Psalm. *I will lift up mine eyes unto the hills . . .*

It only took a minute to explain why Zeke needed refuge. Preacher and Mrs. Jackson listened intently until Jack finished.

"We saw the line of vehicles, and later the fire. We feared the worst." The preacher shook his head and his eyes welled with tears. "You did right in bringing Zeke to us. Brother Taylor's been a deacon in our church for many years. Mrs. Jackson and I will find a way to hide him from the Klan, no matter what it takes."

Jack searched the preacher's face. Fear mixed with angry determination shone from the elderly eyes. Jack guessed it was the best he could hope for.

He turned to Zeke and play punched him on the shoulder the way he always did when he wanted to express friendship and caring. "Well, I better be going. I got stuff to do before morning."

Zeke's head snapped up. "Where you headed?"

The look in the younger boy's eyes broke Jack's heart and he threw his arms around Zeke, hugging him fiercely. "You stay safe. Do what Preacher and Mrs. Jackson say."

"I want to go with you. You and me's always stuck together." Jack heard the panic in Zeke's voice, but there was nothing he could do about it anymore.

"I'm sorry little buddy, but you gotta stay here with folks who can take care of you. I cain't do that as good as Preacher and Mrs. Jackson. It's gonna be awhile before you and me can see each other again."

"But where are you going?"

Jack pushed Zeke into Mrs. Jackson's outstretched arms and walked quickly to the back door. With his hand on the knob, he turned toward his friend and called out a single word.

"Town."

Jack could hear Zeke yelling for him to come back all the way to the road that ran in front of the house.

The state highway didn't have much traffic, but Jack got lucky. A tractor-trailer driver saw his thumb and pulled over in a shower of gravel and sand. Jack guessed the driver must see folks hitching rides all the time because, other than telling him to hop in and asking how far he wanted to go, the man didn't question why a twelve-year-old boy was on the road alone. And he didn't seem to think it odd that a kid needed a ride to the Blanche Hotel in the middle of the night.

Jack slipped into the alley at the back of the hotel and ran to one of two metal structures hanging from the building's wall. Grabbing the bottom rung, he heaved himself up onto the ladder. As he crept up the fire escape, he hoped he had guessed right. Since there were only two, he was pretty sure he had chosen the one leading to Meg's bedroom window. If not, he'd try to sneak back down without creating a scene and climb the other one. When he reached the third floor, he peered through the open window and called softly to the woman stretched out on the narrow single bed.

"Meg."

The woman stirred and Jack said a quick prayer that he had chosen correctly. "Meg. Wake up. I need to talk to you."

The sheet flew back and Meg sat up, staring at the window with big frightened eyes.

"It's me, Jack."

She was at the window in an instant. "What on earth are you doing here? You nearly gave me heart failure. Get inside before someone sees you."

Jack landed on the bedroom floor with a thump.

"Shh. I can't get caught with a male in my room even if you are my brother. Now tell me what's going on."

"I'm leaving and I wanted to tell you goodbye."

"Leaving? Where on earth would you be going in the middle of the night?"

Until that moment, Jack hadn't really considered an actual destination. He chuckled and answered, "I don't know. California, maybe."

Meg sat down on the bed and put a hand on each of Jack's shoulders. After giving him a quick shake, she said, "Jack, this isn't funny. Stop joking around and tell me why you aren't at home in bed."

"I gotta leave. I can't take it no more."

"You don't got to do anything until you tell me what's happened."

Jack's head started swimming and he sat down on the floor. With the rush of memory, it suddenly felt like the whole world toppled in on him, crushing him beneath its terrible weight. His heart raced and his breath came in gasps. Between sobs, he told his sister everything that had happened that night. He described following their father, the words that were spoken, the hanging tree, and the fire. But most especially, he told of their father's part in Isaiah Taylor's murder, every gut wrenching, lurid detail of it.

"Now do you see? I ain't never going near that old bastard again."

"But what about Mama? It'll kill her if you just disappear."

"Wait a couple of days and call home for me. You tell Mama that I'm okay and I'll write to both of you as soon as I can. Tell her not to worry. I can take care of myself."

"Jack, listen to me." Meg's voice sounded panicky. "You're twelve-years-old. You've never been more than fifty miles from home in your life. You can't do this."

"Meg, I'm hopping the westbound train that leaves at 4:00. By full daylight, I'll probably be somewhere about Tallahassee. I can't stay here arguing with you."

Jack stood and quickly embraced his sister. Before she could get her arms around him, he was through the window and onto the fire escape. He could hear her frantically whispering his name while he jumped from step to step. When his feet hit gravel, he stopped and looked up, trying to drink in every inch of his beloved older sister.

A train whistle blew in the distance, making both of them jump and stare in the direction of the depot. Sound carried so much farther in the dead of night. Jack cocked his head and listened intently. He could just make out the squealing of metal on metal as the train's wheels responded to the brakeman's commands. There was no more time to waste. Jack threw up his hand and called, "I love you and Mama. Take care of her and don't worry. I promise I'll be all right."

The whistle sounded again and Jack started running.

Chapter 27

After returning from Lake City, Liz spent the remainder of her weekend pouring over the research notes she had gathered thus far. The names of the long dead swirled around in her mind like faceless wraiths, all except one. For no reason Liz could put her finger on, she had conjured a strong visual of Ezekiel Taylor. His features were softly rounded—childish with the unconscious innocence of the prepubescent. When she closed her eyes, she saw smooth dark skin not yet marred by the bane of adolescence. Close-cropped curls covered his well-formed head. He was a handsome child with a cherubic face, but his eyes haunted her.

They were deep midnight pools of terror and pain. Common sense dictated that she had superimposed her imagination on the figure of some child she had seen recently, but she didn't care. Being able to put a face with the name made Ezekiel all the more alive. In 1930, a very real little boy had experienced horror and Liz was determined to uncover who was responsible.

But the more she reorganized the information, the more frustrated she became. She didn't have nearly enough data to support any of the nebulous conclusions forming. It looked as though she would need to spend many additional hours going through county records and chasing down anyone connected with the violent summer of 1930, provided people were still alive who knew anything, even second hand.

It would help so much if she had someone with whom she could discuss her research. Jonathan and Roberta were the first names that presented themselves, but they were immediately rejected for obvious reasons. And then it came to her. She worked with one of the finest historians in the region. It was ridiculous not to seek his advice.

On Monday, Liz checked his schedule with Maria, the departmental secretary, and made an appointment, something that made the girl shake her head in surprise. When the late afternoon time arrived, Liz made her way down the hall to Hugh's corner office and knocked on his door.

"Come."

Liz opened the door and poked her head inside. Hugh was pounding away on his desktop keyboard. "If you're busy, I can come back."

Hugh turned away from his computer and grinned. "Not on your life. Nobody makes appointments in this department, so this has got to be serious."

Liz felt the blush creeping up from her throat onto her cheeks. "If you're involved in something important, this can wait."

"Liz, come in and sit down. My door is always open to colleagues. You don't have to apologize for wanting to talk."

"Thanks. I need a second pair of eyes."

"The new courses' syllabi?" Hugh's smile brightened. "I didn't expect anything on that until after Thanksgiving."

"I'm sorry, but I'm afraid not. I've run into a problem with my Capone research."

"Oh."

Liz sensed his disappointment. It made her self-conscience. To compensate, she babbled. "You'll have the course descriptions on time as promised. I won't let you down. I haven't shown you anything yet because I want to tie up a few final details."

That was the truth. So why did she feel so guilty?

She mentally gave herself a shake and smiled. "I really need someone to bounce my ideas off and you were first on my list."

Now that *was* a lie.

Liz hoped Hugh didn't detect it and searched for something to say for cover. Finding nothing particularly brilliant, she spluttered on. "You've been at this so much longer than I have. That didn't come out right. You're not that much older than me. But you do have vastly more experience. I mean . . ." Liz knew her face must now be as bright as a boiled lobster.

She swallowed hard and forced some constraint onto her tongue. "I mean I respect your opinion and would appreciate any insights you care to offer."

Watching Hugh's expression brighten with pleasure launched another stab of guilt. Or was that humor she saw dancing in his eyes? Liz winced internally and broke eye contact. She feigned interest in the view from his window. It irritated her that she sometimes found her boss so unnerving. Never knowing quite what he was thinking put her on edge.

"Well, don't just stand there. I can't give you the benefit of my vast knowledge and experience if you don't sit down and talk to me about the problem." Hugh's ironic grin told her it was humor she had detected before and at her expense.

As she crossed the office to a visitor's chair, it occurred to her that she might be taking herself just a little too seriously. She shook her head and smiled sheepishly. "Please forgive my rattling on like that. I guess I'm a little frazzled. I haven't been sleeping so well lately."

The humor in Hugh's eyes died immediately. "Hope we aren't working you too hard." He leaned on his desk and made a bridge of his fingers as he searched her face. "Liz, if you need more time for the new course proposals, all you have to do is ask. I don't really need to see anything until after the Christmas break. I realize this semester has been something of a whirlwind for you."

"Thank you, but it's nothing that I can't handle."

Liz bit the inside of her lower lip to prevent tears rolling down her cheeks. Not only were his kindness and solicitude unexpected, even the dimmest bulb could sense the depth of his sincerity. She didn't want or need an emotional scene where she poured her heart out about Jonathan. It would be humiliating and unprofessional. Determined not to disgrace herself in front of her boss, she opened her spiral and began flipping pages before he could ask more personal questions, like why she wasn't sleeping well.

She shoved the notebook across his desk. "Here's a chart of the information I've collected."

If he thought her curt or abrupt, Hugh didn't show it. He inspected the pages and then looked at Liz. "It was certainly a violent summer. Any theories?"

With the conversation back on safer footing, Liz's professional demeanor kicked in. "Since a reliable source has confirmed that the first six lynching victims controlled vice in the county, I think there are some likely possibilities." Liz held out her left hand and used her fingers to tick off the options as she spoke. "A) Silas Barnes wanted to take control of vice in the county and used his column and the Klan as tools toward that end. Someone then cut him out of the action or took revenge for all the horror he had created. B) Capone was trying to take control of north Florida vice and Barnes may have been his proxy with the Klan. Barnes became Capone's last victim for some reason yet to be established. C) Someone else was the mastermind and Barnes was his tool, either knowingly or unwittingly. Perhaps Barnes discovered how he had been used, confronted the man behind the violence, and paid for it with his life. D) It was all just coincidence. No one was trying to consolidate vice operations. Capone acted out of character for some unknown, unrelated reason. Silas Barnes's disappearance was unrelated to the violent events of the summer of 1930."

"Are you leaning toward one theory over the others?"

"I'm trying very hard not to be swayed by my dislike of Editor Barnes. He comes across in his column as a pompous, bigoted hypocrite. On the one hand, he is all about morality and the sanctity of the family. On the other, he apparently had no problem at all with murder. How could he not see the dichotomy?"

Hugh's mouth curved up in a tight smile. "As a historian, I think you know the answer."

"Of course he was a product of his time and place, but for God's sake. What happened to thou shalt not commit murder?"

Instead of answering her question, Hugh pointed to a name on the chart. "Why is Ezekiel Taylor circled and underlined? Was he a major player?"

Liz let a disgusted grunt escape as she shook her head. "He was an eleven-year-old child who disappeared the night his grandfather was lynched. Can you imagine what that must have been like? Forced to watch as your grandfather was strung up? He deserves to have his story told."

Hugh's eyes widened ever so slightly. "Are you changing the focus of your research?"

"Not changing it completely. More like enlarging its scope and adding another filter through which to evaluate the facts. When I read about the grandfather's murder, it was as though Ezekiel reached up from the page and grabbed me. This sounds fanciful, but it felt like he was calling my name, begging for justice."

"Seems like you've really connected with this kid. What happened to him after the lynching?"

"I don't know, but I'm going to find out. I'm going to chase a good boy for a change." Liz regretted the words as soon as they were out of her mouth. Angry with herself, she reached for the spiral and slapped it shut.

Hugh's expression shifted from amused to perplexed. "Liz, has something happened? You just haven't seemed yourself the last day or so."

This time, she couldn't stop the tears. They rolled down her cheeks before she could turn away from Hugh. In mortification, she jerked a tissue from the box on his desk and swiped at her face and eyes.

Smiling weakly, she replied, "I can't fool you, can I? Something has definitely happened, but I'm not going to burden you with my personal problems. It's a sorry tale not worth the telling."

Hugh's mouth became a straight line as his eyebrows rose. He cocked his head to one side and gazed into Liz's eyes. "After I spent an evening giving you a blow-by-blow of my divorce, I think I can spare you a minute or two."

When Liz didn't speak, his expression became rueful. "I don't mean to pry and you can tell me to mind my own business, but I'm sensing your Navy pilot has perhaps been a disappointment?"

To her chagrin, Liz hiccoughed. It took all of the energy she could muster not to break down completely and sob like a baby. Cogent utterances were impossible. Feeling an abject fool, she nodded and swiped at her eyes again.

Hugh leaned back in his chair. "Liz, I don't know what he did to hurt you, although I think I can probably guess. My opinion may not be worth much at the moment, but I'm going to share it with you anyway. Any man who would be stupid enough to mistreat a woman like you should have the holy living shit beaten out of him."

Out of nowhere a whoop of laughter bubbled up. It erupted and bounced off the room's wainscoting. Hugh's reputation among their departmental colleagues was that of a somewhat dour workaholic. Her boss giving Jonathan a walloping was something Liz would not have imagined in her wildest dreams. The longer she laughed, the harder she laughed until hysterics threatened. When she finally managed some control, her cheeks were wet, but with tears of mirth. It felt strange, but really good too.

Liz glanced sheepishly at Hugh who smiled gently and asked, "Better?"

"Yeah, but about now I'm sure you're regretting giving me a job. Please believe me. I can't ever remember howling like that. I'm so embarrassed."

"You shouldn't be. Friends understand. They don't judge."

"Thanks." Liz dabbed at her eyes and chuckled. "After that display, I think I owe you an apology and an explanation."

"Apology not necessary but accepted. Explanation? Only if you want to give it."

"I do. Maybe talking about it will be a good thing. And when I'm finished, remember—you asked."

Hugh listened intently as though he was absorbing every word she said and saw each scene as she described it. He didn't make comments and he didn't appear disgusted by what Liz now thought of as her stupidly impulsive decision to follow Jonathan. The fact that she fell into a better job as a result hardly seemed a good trade for one's self respect. When she wound down to the end, the tightness in her chest eased.

It was as though the iron bands of some medieval torture device had been pulled ever tighter until she was in danger of being crushed by the pressure. Then suddenly, they were set loose. Months of built up tension simply evaporated. This must be what catharsis felt like. Liz realized that she had stopped speaking and that she was actually smiling. The silence was peaceful and Hugh's presence was comforting.

"Thank you for listening and for not telling me what a fool I've been."

His mouth curved into a crooked grin. "We're all fools in love. I think my marriage bears witness to that particular verity."

"It isn't foolish to love someone and to honor your vows."

"Perhaps. I would like to think so at any rate." Hugh tilted his head to one side and raised his eyebrows almost to his hairline. "You know, I really hate people who point out the bright side of every tragedy. Don't you?"

He looked so comically pensive Liz couldn't help laughing again. "Yeah, just hate 'em, but somehow I think you're building up to being one."

"I am. It goes something like this. As much as you're hurting now, think what would it have been like if you'd married the SOB only to find out who he really was afterward. Some people might say you've had a lucky escape."

"My head says you're right. My heart may take a little longer."

"The heart usually does."

After talking so much, Liz suddenly felt pangs of uncertainty, afraid she had shared far too much with the man who was first and foremost her boss. She also recalled how abrupt and curt she had been with him recently.

"Hugh, you said I hadn't been myself lately. Thank you for seeing it that way and I hope you'll accept another apology. This one for my being rude the other day. Please tell me that I'm not usually like that."

"You aren't. You've had a lot on your mind."

"Thanks for understanding."

"Anytime, as long as you return the favor."

Liz nodded. "You got it, boss."

Hugh's face fell. Damn it. In her desire to keep him at arm's length, she had done it again. She made a mental note to be more careful, more conscience of his feelings in the future. She certainly didn't want to encourage him to expect more than she could give, but she respected him as a colleague and valued their growing friendship. He really seemed like a sweet guy, not her type, but a nice catch for someone when he was finally over his ex.

Hugh cleared his throat and said, "Let me take another look at that chart."

He didn't meet her eyes as she slid it back across the desk. He opened the chart and studied it for a minute.

"You're going to need a lot more than Capone's being in town to link him to the lynchings. I can understand the allure of that particular theory, but remember that gathering facts comes first. You've still got a lot of work to do before you form theories."

Although she had a pretty good idea where it came from, Hugh's sudden switch to professorial mode still felt like a slap in the face. He spoke to her as if she was one of his students. She reached for the notebook.

"Yes, of course. I've only scratched the surface. I plan to spend a lot of time on research before I attempt an article."

"Very wise, as long as your university work doesn't suffer."

Liz wondered if her eyes were bulging because she was sure her blood pressure had just soared into the stratosphere. The man's effrontery was astounding. Just who did he think he was talking to? Simply because she couldn't be more than a colleague, wasn't ready to have her heart trampled on by any man just yet, gave him no reason to doubt her professionalism.

Liz did not even try to keep the edge out of her voice. "That will not be a problem. Now if you will excuse me, I won't take any more of your time."

She didn't wait for a reply. As Liz strode back to her office, annoyance turned to full blown temper. She closed her door harder than intended and flung her notebook on her desk. Just when she thought she and Hugh understood each other, he threw her another curve. The man really was insufferable.

Chapter 28

The depot and rail yard were deserted except for a Seaboard Line freight train chuffing beside the water tower. Jack hid behind some bushes across the road and watched as the brakeman strode up and down the line, checking the couplings and the boxcars' doors. Everybody knew that hobos rode the rails all over the country and that they had to be especially careful to avoid the railroad companies' bulls and their billy clubs.

Jack had no intention of having his head busted open before he even got his first ride, so he decided to move a little farther down the tracks beyond the depot to a place where he thought he could jump a car without being seen. When the bull went to the far side of the train, Jack left his hiding place and crept along the edge of the street, keeping well away from the pools of light created by street lamps. The curbing stopped at the end of the block and so did the lights. From there on, only the feeble light of a new moon lighted the way.

When he was absolutely sure that he would not be seen, Jack slipped across the road and into the brush lining the tracks. As he crouched, waiting for the train to begin its westward crawl, he tried to visualize just how you went about jumping into a moving boxcar. The story back in March, of a vagrant who missed and lost his legs, took on personal meaning.

A whistle blast and the rumble of turning wheels ended Jack's ruminations. His muscles tensed as he watched the light from the engine's headlamp grow brighter. When the smokestack drew even with his hiding place, Jack leapt up and trotted forward. His idea was to pace his gait to that of the train for a few feet and then jump into an open car. What he hadn't counted on was how many of the cars were sealed. As the train picked up speed, Jack's lungs were on fire. Trying to keep pace wasn't getting him anywhere, so he stopped and scanned back down the line.

Only one door was open way back near the caboose. Heart thumping, he put his hands on his knees and panted, waiting for that car to reach him. He would start running again when it was closer and then make his jump when it drew up beside him, kind of like getting on the farm wagon as it moved along at the ends of the field, only faster.

The dark shadow of the open boxcar door loomed a few feet away when Jack began running again. He had always been the best sprinter in his class even if he was one of the smallest boys. His legs were long in proportion to the rest of his body and his muscles were strong from all the farm work and roaming around the countryside he had done since he was a little kid.

His knees churned harder as the car came abreast, but the train was gaining speed with every westward inch it made. The rough ground made him keep one eye on where his flying feet landed while he watched for any handhold that he could reach. Surely his momentum would let him swing up into the car.

The revolving wheels' clickity-clack increased alarmingly and Jack knew it was now or never. He stretched out his arm and grabbed metal and wood. He threw his opposite arm up and over. Now both hands gripped the back end of the opening. His feet left the ground in one mighty push. The upper half of his body landed inside the opening, but he teetered terrifyingly on the car's edge. He tried dragging the rest of his lower half into the car with a forearm over forearm crawl, but his skin was slick with sweat. His heart leapt into his throat. He was stuck. He couldn't drop back to the ground and he couldn't go forward into the car.

Jack wasn't sure whether he prayed inside his head or shouted into the black, but the words please and God were repeated over and over. Tears poured down his face as the train's increasing speed tossed his legs this way and that. His arms quivered with the effort of not being thrown under the train to certain dismemberment. With his strength ebbing, Jack prayed that death would be quick and painless, but that would take a huge miracle and it seemed like the world was out of those just now.

In the next moment, it felt as though Jack's arms were being jerked right out of their shoulder sockets. He was dragged up and over the car's outer edge, leaving several pieces of skin on its rough metal and replacing them with splinters from the car's wooden floor. In the scramble to gain purchase, he skidded forward and banged his head hard against the opposite wall of the car. The collision sent him rolling.

The lower half of him rested on solid wood, but his head and shoulders were suspended in space, whipped and stung by the force of the passing wind. Iron bands wrapped around his ankles and dragged him backwards. As his chin bounced along wood, Jack's mouth filled with a funny metallic taste. Strangely, he felt like he was falling down a well.

Jack awoke with a throbbing head. At first he couldn't figure out where he was, then his near death experience came back in a rush. Someone had saved him, but he had no idea who. He rolled onto his side, but it hurt too much to open his eyes. Sunlight turned the backs of his eyelids red and warm humid air bathed his sweaty face.

The pile of croaker sacks he was lying on made his neck itch something fierce and the dust coming off them made him sneeze. As his eyes tried to adjust to the flashing patches of light coming through the open boxcar door, rough voices in the vicinity of the front wall filtered through the roar of wind and racing wheels.

"Looks like the kid's come to. Guess he's gonna live."

"Yeah, but bet he's got one hellova headache. That were a nasty spill he took. You shouldn't a jerked him so hard."

"So I shoulda let him fall under the wheels?"

"Guess not. Glad it were him and not me you was yanking on."

Jack leaned up on one elbow and groaned involuntarily. He opened his eyes and looked in the direction of the voices. Two men sat at one end of the boxcar watching him. Their faces, hands, and clothes were filthy and the smell coming off them turned Jack's stomach.

"Good mornin', young feller. Thought you was gonna sleep the day away. Want something to eat?"

Dizziness engulfed Jack when he tried to sit up. He leaned through the open car door and wretched. Not a whole lot flew back to splatter against the boxcar's side, but he felt better for getting rid of it.

"Glad you did that out the door. Hate it when somebody fouls his own nest." A scraggly beard surrounded the speaker's mouth. When the beard parted in a grin, there were several gaps where teeth should have been. It was hard to judge the beard wearer's age under all the grime and salt and pepper hair. Although he could have been anywhere between forty and sixty, Jack judged him to be around his father's age of forty-five. A halo of laugh lines surrounded his eyes, but otherwise, his face didn't have the wrinkles or papery skin of the truly elderly.

His companion was much younger and his face had come in contact with a razor much more recently. Neither man was physically imposing for both of them looked like they could do with a good meal. They were using teaspoons to share the contents of a tin can. Jack couldn't make out exactly what they ate, but it appeared solid like it might have some meat in it.

The older man saw Jack eyeing their breakfast. He nodded at the can and said, "It ain't much, but we'll share if you're of mind to eat." When he held out the can, the words Ken-L-Ration made Jack draw back in disgust.

"Folks cain't be too proud when they're hungry and ain't got no money. You ride the rails long enough and you'll learn that for yourself."

"I'm sorry. I didn't mean to seem ungrateful. I just don't think I can keep anything down right now except maybe some water." Jack's voice came out as a croak from his parched throat.

The younger man passed Jack a canteen. He unscrewed the lid with shaking fingers and let it drop to the side, dangling by a rough chain. The water tasted surprisingly sweet. Jack gulped greedily until a hand pulled the can away from his lips.

"Whoa. Slow down or you'll be sick all over again. No need in wasting good water."

"Thanks. I didn't know how thirsty I was. Who helped me into the boxcar last night?"

The older man jerked his head toward his companion. "Bud here pulled you into the car and then grabbed your feet when it looked like you was going to fly out through the other door."

Jack nodded. "Thank you. I'm much obliged. You took a chance. You might of gone through that door with me."

"Naw, I done that trick before. You might be surprised how many times. But you're welcome all the same."

The older man ate another spoonful from the can while he looked Jack over. "Now where would a boy like you be headed wearing mostly clean clothes that somebody ironed not too long ago? You look like you got a home to go to."

"I did, but I cain't go back there."

"Son, you ain't old enough to have done anything that your ma and pa won't forgive. Why don't you get off at the next stop and hitch a ride back to where you come from?"

The gentleness in the man's eyes and voice nearly brought Jack to tears. "It ain't me that did wrong. I cain't live with my old man no more."

The two hobos exchanged glances and the younger one said, "Look, my old man ran me off when I turned fifteen. Said he and my mama needed my bed and the food I ate for the new baby that was coming. They just couldn't keep me no more. Been ridin' the rails ever since. If I had a home to go back to, believe me, that's where I'd be."

"What if your old man killed your best friend?" It wasn't exactly the truth, of course, but it felt as though it was. Zeke might as well be dead for all Jack would ever see of him again. And if the worst happened and the Klan found him, then Zeke didn't stand a chance.

"Well, terrible accidents happen every day. People make mistakes and we have to find a way to forgive them. Cain't you make it up with your father?"

"It wasn't no accident. He meant to do it. He put the noose around his neck and watched while his buddies pulled on the rope. He's a mean, hardhearted, murdering son-of-a-bitch."

The men cut their eyes at one another again and the older one asked, "Was your friend a colored boy?"

Jack felt the blood rush to his face. "What if he was? What's it to you?"

"Now don't go gettin' all riled up. Ain't nothing to us. Considering the part of the country we're in, it just took us by surprise. That's all."

"Yeah, like Mac said, a feller's color ain't nothin' to us. Why in the jungles, you're likely to run into all manner of folk. Nobody thinks nothin' of it."

It took Jack a second or two to realize that the jungles being spoken of were the camps where hobos gathered for shelter and companionship between train rides. He knew that most communities, Lake City included, did what they could to keep the riffraff away from their towns. Then it occurred to him. He was now part of the riffraff.

Although he had never cared what other people thought about his friendship with Zeke, Jack felt like he needed to say something by way of explanation. "Zeke lived on the farm next to ours after his parents got killed. My old man and his grandfather used to be friends before Daddy turned so sour and mean. Me and Zeke knew each other our whole lives. We looked out for each other. We was friends no matter what anybody thought and I ain't living under the same roof with the son-of-a-bitch who murdered him."

"What about your mama? Won't she be missing you?"

"Mama's just gonna have to understand. Besides, she's got my sister to look after her. I'm going to write to 'em when I can." Jack's jaw clenched. "Besides, if I was to go home, I'd kill the old bastard or he'd kill me. When he dies, I hope he burns in hell for what he's done." Jack's boiling rage echoed in the empty car.

Mac's eyes darkened. "Yeah, I guess I wouldn't go home under the circumstances neither." A spoon rattled against tin as he held out the can. "Here. There's some left. Why don't you eat it?"

Jack shook his head. Feeling dizzy again, he stretched out on his back. The rhythm of the rails was surprisingly soothing.

"Well, if you ain't gonna eat nothing, you best rest until we get to the gettin' off place."

An uneasy feeling engulfed Jack and he rose up on an elbow again. "How far is this train going?"

"Depends on how far you want to go."

"I'm thinking California would be a good place."

Mac and Bud chuckled and then Mac said, "You and every other mother's son. What's so special about California?"

"Don't know. I guess it's as far from Florida as I can get."

"Well, you're gonna have to change trains lots of times before you get there."

Jack thought about this for a moment and then asked, "Where are y'all going?"

The two hobos looked at each other and the older one shook his head, but Bud said, "Oh come on Mac, he's just a kid. He ain't gonna eat that much. What'll it hurt to let him tag along with us?"

"Hell, Bud, we hardly get enough to eat ourselves."

For the first time since leaving Meg, Jack thought he might have made a mistake. The realization of what he had taken on began to feel overwhelming, but going home wasn't an option. He tried to keep his voice steady as he said, "Y'all don't have to worry about me. I can take care of myself. Just tell me which train to get on in Mobile."

Mac laughed. "Mobile? This train ain't going that far. We'll have to get off at Tallahassee."

"Oh. Will you help me find the right train at Tallahassee? I promise I won't try to follow y'all."

Bud snorted. "You see Mac? This kid ain't ever gonna make it on his own. I didn't save him from falling under the wheels just so some bull can split his head open."

Mac glared at Bud. "You ain't gonna let this go are you?"

It could have been Jack's imagination, but he could have sworn Bud winked at him before answering, "No, I ain't."

"Shit, I guess I ain't got no choice then. We're heading

for the San Joaquin Valley. Just about every kind of fruit or vegetable there is grows there. You got a mind to pick fruit?"

"Thought I'd join the Navy. I'll have to lie about my age, but I want to go to sea."

Both men howled. Mac could hardly speak for laughing so hard. "Son, there's no way you'll pass for eighteen. If you're determined to do this, you best come with us."

As much as it pained Jack to admit they were right, he saw the sense of what Mac said. "I guess picking fruit sounds pretty good. Thanks for letting me tag along with you."

"Probably be best if we pass you off as Bud or mine's kid. You want him?"

"Naw, I think we'd better tell folks he's yours."

Jack was quiet for a while and then asked, "Does that mean I have to change my name?" It surprised him how much that really mattered to him.

"Call yourself whatever you want when the bosses ain't around, but you'll have to use Johnson when we're working. That's me. Mac Johnson."

"Could you be my uncle instead? That way I won't ever slip up about my name."

Mac looked at Bud who shrugged and nodded. "That'll work just as well. By the way, what is your name, kid?"

Jack answered and then asked the question that had been gnawing at him. "I don't mean to sound ungrateful, but why are y'all willing to do all this for a stranger?"

Mac's mouth turned up in a crooked smile. "Son, we're all strangers one way or another, but we don't let that get in the way of helping out a fellow traveler. It's the hobo code and the first thing you got to learn is how to read the signs."

"Signs?"

"Yeah, the signs, the markings we leave for each other on trees and buildings. It's the way we know what places are safe and which ones to stay away from. Now you best try to rest. You're going to need to be fit when we reach Tallahassee."

Jack lay down on the pile of sacks and threw an arm over his eyes. Only time would tell how the new life he had chosen would play out. Mac and Bud had saved his life. They seemed like nice guys and they certainly knew how to survive riding the rails, but they must not have had a bath in weeks and their clothes were raggedy. Baths hadn't been too high on Jack's list of favorite things to do until he had no idea when he would next be able to wash.

How long would it take for his clothes to look like theirs—holes in the knees, rips in the sleeves, frayed cuffs, newspaper showing through the soles of his shoes? He'd left home with nothing, not even a sweater or winter coat. It might be the dead of summer now and he knew winter in California was supposed to be mild, but what if he got stuck in some place like Nebraska or Kansas where winters were brutal?

His stomach growled reminding him that he hadn't eaten since supper the night before. He wasn't sure he could put dog food in his mouth no matter how hungry he got. Of course, he had never really been hungry in his life. They might have been poor, but Mama always put good meals on the table. He had promised to write to Meg and Mama, but where he was going to get paper and a stamp was a mystery. Maybe Mac and Bud were right. Maybe he should go home.

Visions of Zeke's grandfather hanging from that tree and his blazing house lighting up the night sky rushed back. When he closed his eyes, the memory of his father putting the rope around Mr. Taylor's neck burned like it was happening right there in the boxcar. Hot anger surged up from deep within him, shoving aside his fear. No matter how dirty or hungry he got, anything would be better than living with that sorry murdering son-of-a-bitch Arnold Blevins.

Chapter 29

DeWitt shifted his weight from one foot to the other while wiping his face with an already damp handkerchief. An oscillating tabletop fan whirred valiantly, but its feeble breeze didn't reach beyond the edge of his boss's desk.

DeWitt cleared his throat. "I talked to Mrs. Barnes, Ike."

Sheriff Darnell's chair creaked loudly as he leaned back to meet his deputy's gaze. "Got to oil this damned thing, but I can't remember to buy the machine oil. Guess I'm gettin' old."

DeWitt ignored the bid for a compliment. "I'm afraid she wasn't much help."

Ike rocked back a little farther creating another round of creaking similar to nails scraping across a chalkboard. "Who's that now?"

"Mrs. Barnes." DeWitt tried to keep the irritation out of his voice. When Ike was evasive, it meant he could also be stubborn. "She thinks the man must have come on foot because she didn't hear a car arrive. Unfortunately, she didn't recognize his voice. She didn't get a look at him either because she stayed in the bedroom. The neighbors were even less help. But whoever he was, I'm betting on a local." Every instinct warned against naming the Klan directly.

Ike's brows drew together in a frown. "Can't imagine that anybody from around here would of meant ole Silas any harm. He spoke his mind, but everybody knew that was just his way. I ran some bums out of the IGA a couple of days ago. As sorry a pair as ever was. Find out if they're still around. They had the look of natural born killers about 'em. Why don't you get on that right now?"

"Will do."

DeWitt turned on his heel and got out of the office before he said something he would regret. He had worked for Ike long enough to recognize when it was futile to argue or even express a differing opinion. With Ike, it could be easier to beg forgiveness than to ask permission, which was exactly what DeWitt planned to do when his boss discovered that he hadn't exactly followed orders.

He was headed for the front door when Ginger, the department's secretary, whispered to him. "DeWitt, did he tell you?"

"About the vagrants? Yeah, thanks," DeWitt answered offhandedly. His mind was already on what he believed to be the truth behind all of the violence, but how he was going to prove it was another matter altogether.

"No. About the Blevins boy."

She now had his full attention. "What about him?"

"We got a call from Mrs. Blevins. Seems her boy hasn't been seen since old man Taylor was strung up. She sounded like she'd just about lost her mind with worry."

DeWitt nodded and strode through the open door. The Blanche was a ten minute walk from the sheriff's office. He made it in five. Breathing hard, DeWitt went into the restaurant and scanned the room for Meg. He found her at the big table near the kitchen door setting plates before a group of local businessmen who met there once a week and always sat in Meg's area. Since her back was to him, he called to her. A warning look over her shoulder and a slight shake of her head sent him to the closest empty table where he yanked out a chair and dropped down.

Fingers drumming a soft tattoo on the white linen cloth, he watched the scene playing out between Meg and the men while he waited. It infuriated him that those old farts kept her tied to their table for an eternity with small talk and what passed with them as innocent flirting. That was something that would stop once he and Meg were married.

When she finally sat in the chair opposite him, he couldn't keep the edge out of his voice. "Why didn't you tell me Jack is missing? I had to hear it from Ginger."

"Ssh! Not so loud. Albert won't like it if we disturb the customers."

"To hell with Albert. What's happened to Jack?"

Forks halted midair, the businessmen turned to stare at DeWitt. He nodded in their direction while the manager of the five and dime leaned across the table toward the farm equipment dealer. All four men then glanced at DeWitt and Meg as they continued to whisper among themselves.

Meg glanced at their observers and then turned back to DeWitt. "We can't talk in here. I'm due for a break. Meet me in the alley."

Before he could respond, Meg was out of her chair and half way to the kitchen. DeWitt slammed his chair under the table and left by the front door. As he trotted around to the back of the hotel, he wondered what was wrong with Meg. She had sounded like she was angry with him, but that made no sense unless she was upset that he had been working so much overtime lately. That didn't make sense either considering her devotion to financial security.

She had always been so protective of Jack, but he had found her calmly going about her job as if her little brother had gone fishing instead of being in danger from the Klan or worse. Something was really wrong, but explanations would have to wait until the boy was safe at home.

Meg stood on the hotel's back stoop, arms crossed and frowning when DeWitt rounded the corner. Even upset, she was still the prettiest girl he had ever seen and his heart swelled with love and the desire to protect her. If he found that somebody had harmed Jack, he would gladly kill him on the spot for causing Meg pain.

"DeWitt, it's not what you think."

Stunned, he shouted, "Then what the hell is it?"

As she relayed Jack's description of the night Isaiah Taylor died, DeWitt could hardly believe what she was saying. "Why haven't you told me about your dad? Him being Klan explains a lot."

"I didn't know until Jack told me. He found Daddy's robe not long ago."

"How on earth could you not know about your dad? Those bastards have been dressing up and lynching folks nearly every Saturday since the beginning of June."

Meg didn't meet his eyes, but her voice took on a hardness that he had never heard before. "Don't you dare accuse me of doing wrong, DeWitt Williams. Daddy's always come and gone without explaining why to any of us."

"And when were you planning to let your mother know about Jack?"

"I can't face going home, not even to see Mama. And I'm afraid to call. Daddy always insists on answering the telephone if he's in the house. I won't talk to him, DeWitt, I just will not do it."

Meg's lower lip trembled slightly and her eyes were bright with unshed tears. DeWitt's first impulse was to wrap his arms around her, but when he reached out, she stepped back, glaring at him. Puzzled, he tried to take her hand. In response, she shook her head. She must be trying very hard not to return to work with a tear stained face. As much as he wanted to avoid causing her more distress, he couldn't walk away without asking a few more questions.

"Was your dad there when Isaiah was lynched?"

"Why do you think Jack ran away? Why do you think I can't bear going home? Jack followed Daddy that night when he drove off and turned toward Mr. Taylor's."

DeWitt hesitated, fearing what her answer to his next question might mean for their relationship. “Did Jack see who actually strung Isaiah up?”

“I . . . I don’t know. He didn’t say.”

DeWitt sensed that Meg wasn’t telling him the truth, but he couldn’t bring himself to admit it outwardly. “Have you heard from Jack?”

“Not yet, but he’s only been gone a little over a day.”

“What about Zeke?”

“I don’t know. Jack left him with his preacher.” Her voice was now as even and expressionless as if she was talking about strangers.

“Meg, what’s the matter with you? Aren’t you worried about those boys?”

Meg’s eyes narrowed and a flush spread across her cheeks. “My twelve-year-old brother took off across the country without so much as a change of clothes. The Klan is probably hunting Zeke right now. I’m scared witless for them. How can you even ask that?” Her breathing became rapid, as though she had run a race. Her eyes glittered while she barked, “I’ve got to go back to work before Albert docks me for taking too long.”

Meg turned toward the back entrance, but DeWitt grabbed her hand before she could disappear. “Albert’s all hot air and you know it. Stay out here with me a few more minutes.”

He stepped up on the stoop beside her, but when he tried to put his arms around her, she pulled away for the second time and looked at him with an expression he had never seen before.

“I’ve got to go, but we need to talk. Soon.”

Meg fairly snatched her hand from his and dashed through the door before he could tell her he was sorry. He could have kicked himself for being so thoughtless. He especially regretted having practically accused her of not caring about Jack and Zeke.

Clearly, she was so worried that her normal loving sweetness had disappeared. Following her into the kitchen wouldn't make her feel any better. If he couldn't bring her brother back, the next best thing would be to find out if Zeke was safe and to figure out who to arrest for Isaiah Taylor's murder.

The sound of DeWitt's truck tires crunching on the driveway's sandy tracks must have reached Arnold Blevins's back field long before the truck came to a halt because he was half way across his backyard when DeWitt rounded the corner of the house. Catching sight of his future son-in-law, Arnold scowled and turned back toward the plow mule tied to a sapling at the edge of the field. He would have taken up the reigns again if DeWitt hadn't grabbed him by the arm and swung him around so that they stood nose-to-nose.

"Don't turn your back on me, old man. I know you for what you are."

"And just what would that be, you good for nothing half-breed?"

"You're a murdering son-of-a-bitch just like all Klan trash."

As they glared into one another's eyes, DeWitt wondered that Arnold didn't try to pull free of his grasp. His fingernails dug deep into the tender flesh on the underside of Arnold's upper arm but DeWitt didn't care. Any discomfort Arnold might be feeling paled in comparison to all the sorrow that he and his Klan cronies had wrought.

"I came here for some answers and you're gonna give them to me."

"Answers to what?"

"Like who put the rope around Isaiah Taylor's neck and what's happened to Zeke?"

"I don't know what you're talking about."

"Look, I know you were there when Isaiah was lynched. Tell me who did the actual hanging and it will go easier for you in the long run."

Arnold's lips twisted into a grin, but one without warmth or humor. "If you think anybody's ever gonna be arrested for lynching nigger scum, you got another thing coming. Nobody cares what happens to bootleggers, gamblers, and whores."

"Maybe, but people can surprise you. Look at Silas Barnes's last editorial."

Arnold emitted an ugly sound that might have been a chuckle. "Ain't you heard? Barnes has disappeared."

"And I'm wondering how much you know about that too. Who's behind Barnes's disappearance?"

"I think you've already give that answer yourself."

"The Klan does the dirty work, but it looks to me like someone else pulls the strings? Make it easy on yourself and tell who it is."

Arnold's eyes widened, then his mouth twisted into an ugly smirk. He winced as DeWitt increased the pressure on his arm and shook him hard. "If you don't care about anything else, at least have the decency to think about how what you do affects your wife and children. Jack's gone and not likely to come back. Your wife is worried sick. Think what it would be like for her to lose both children." DeWitt's mouth became a thin line and his voice grew harsher. "If you ever hope to see Meg after we're married, tell me now who's behind the killings."

Arnold didn't answer straight away, but it was clear that DeWitt's threat had struck home. He bit his lower lip and searched DeWitt's face as if he needed the answer to a question that hadn't been asked. Finally, he seemed to come to a decision.

"I never made it a secret that I don't think you're good enough for my daughter, but she's a stubborn girl. Looks like she's set on you no matter what I say."

"Glad you finally see it."

Arnold shook his head slowly and sighed. "It'd be more than my life's worth if it was to get about that I'd talked, so at least have the decency to keep your mouth shut."

"When the time comes, I'll do what I can for you."

"That ain't nearly good enough, but I guess it's the best I can expect." Arnold's voice became so quiet that DeWitt had to strain to hear. "If I was you, boy, I'd look closer to home for where all the trouble started. That's all I'm going to say. Now get off my land."

DeWitt's feet felt encased in lead. Arnold's words caught him off guard, creating a nameless fear that boiled up inside him. When Arnold's meaning finally sank in, the pieces began to fall into place. In desperation, DeWitt cast about for alternative explanations. There was a distinct possibility that Arnold was lying to protect a Klansman. Sending DeWitt on a wild goose chase would give him time to warn the real culprit.

DeWitt didn't trust Arnold any farther than he could throw him. Or perhaps the old man didn't really know anything and was just trying to get rid of him. DeWitt glared though narrowed eyes, silently willing his future father-in-law to crumble under pressure and retract what he had said. Arnold met DeWitt's gaze as firmly as a man who believed he had God on his side.

DeWitt silently cursed himself. How could he have been so blind to what was right under his nose all the time? He was usually the first to make sense of random facts gathered during investigations. Perhaps he hadn't wanted to see it. In all honesty, part of him prayed he had misunderstood, but prayers weren't going to change what he could now see so clearly.

Releasing Arnold, DeWitt turned on his heal and marched toward his truck without looking back. A big barn a little farther south near the county line was his next destination. He had no idea what he would find, but it was a place to start and it was nearby. It would take sound evidence to convict the man he now suspected was responsible for the summer of violence and death.

Chapter 30

On the fourth Wednesday of November, Liz stared out onto the rectangle of grass below her office window and thought how depressing the almost empty campus felt. Every major holiday of her life she had been with her parents and extended family. They had been within driving distance, but this year she guessed she would have a deli turkey sandwich in her apartment.

She couldn't afford to fly to Washington State for both Thanksgiving and Christmas. Maybe not having distractions would turn out to be a good thing. She could work on the new course proposals and make her final text selections for their bibliographies. It would be a productive weekend, albeit a lonely one.

She sighed and turned back to her desk. As long as she was going to tie up loose ends, she might as well call Roberta, her fiction editor whom she had been dodging for almost a month now. Roberta's last message had been angry and blunt. With luck, she could take the coward's way out and leave a message. Luck, however, had plans of its own.

"Hi, Roberta. It's me, Liz. Sorry I've been so unavailable."

Roberta was silent for a heartbeat and then she let loose. Liz got up quickly and went to peek into the hall. Any of her colleagues still around would certainly be able to hear considering Roberta's volume. Seeing the other office doors closed and their old-fashioned glass panes dark, she returned to her desk chair confident that she was the only one remaining in the area. She glanced at the open door one more time and then resumed her position facing the window.

"I'm really very sorry that I've broken so many promises. I know I've let you down."

The diatribe pouring through the earpiece increased in both volume and invective. Normally Liz took Roberta's scoldings without retaliating, but she felt herself getting angry now. It wasn't as though she had a contract for the novel lying neglected in her laptop. Roberta felt like it would sell quickly and when she wanted something, Roberta had no problem pushing for it.

Liz realized she had been pushed as far as she was willing to go. She was tired of feeling like she was disappointing people at every turn. Hugh hadn't mentioned the course proposals again, but she knew he needed them sooner rather than later. And her parents had said they understood about Thanksgiving, but she heard the disappointment in her mother's voice.

With her mother's words replaying in her mind, she responded, "Look, it's not like this is the first time you've had an author miss a couple of deadlines. And it's not like we had a Christmas release date set. Surely you can understand how difficult this fall has been for me."

More shouting flew through the ether.

"Yes, Roberta, as usual, I know you're probably right." It was taking all of her self-control to remain civil. Another angry jab from her editor and Liz snapped. "You're absolutely right, Roberta. I do not want a career in fiction. I'm focusing on my academic research. I hope enough will come from it for a book, not just an article as I had originally planned. It won't sell a million copies, but it *will* be something I'll be proud to put my name on. I appreciate everything you've done for me. I hope we can still be friends."

The ensuing silence lasted so long Liz wondered if the connection was broken. When Roberta finally spoke, her voice had lost its vinegar.

"Roberta, I know you think the novel will do well, but my heart just isn't in it right now. Not to mention that I can't afford the time it will take to get it into publishable shape."

As Liz listened to Roberta's cajoling response, she found her own anger ebbing. "Of course. If I ever finish it, you'll be the first person I call."

One more plea to Liz's common sense and Roberta gave in. "Yeah, I care about you too. Let's keep in touch as friends, okay? And when my first monograph is in print, I promise to send you an autographed copy."

Liz shoved her phone into her purse and wondered if she had just made a monumental mistake. Throwing away a perfectly good career in fiction in favor of searching for a child whom she might never track down could be the height of folly. But as she mulled it over, she realized what she had said to Roberta in frustration and anger was absolutely true. Her research was more important to her right now than anything else in her professional life. The need to find Ezekiel Taylor, little Zeke as she now thought of him, had grown into a palpable ache, one that would not go away until she knew the truth, however horrible it might be.

Something in that young boy called out to her. If she could bring him some justice, however late, then maybe she could come to grips with the problems in her own life. In changing the focus of her research from Capone to Zeke, perhaps she could alter the way she formed her relationships with men in general.

A light rapping at her door made Liz jump. Heart thumping, she whirled around to see Hugh smiling sheepishly. "Sorry I startled you."

"No need to apologize. I was a thousand miles away."

"Not going home to Seattle, I take it?"

"No. Too far and too expensive for a three day visit."

"I was surprised to see your door open. I thought I was the last one to leave."

"I'm just tying up some loose ends. I think better when it's quiet."

"Well, have a good Thanksgiving." Hugh took a couple of steps then stopped and turned back. A thoughtful expression crossed his face. "Liz, are you going to be alone tomorrow?"

As much as she hated to admit it, she nodded.

"I know this is short notice, but we would be delighted if you'd join us for dinner."

"We?"

Hugh grinned. "Sorry again. My sister and her family come up from Miami for the major holidays. I hope the prospect of dinner with four teenagers won't be too daunting. They're really terrific kids."

The way Hugh's eyes lit up when he spoke of his sister's children made Liz wonder if he wished he had kids of his own.

"So how about it? Nothing fancy or formal, just jeans and t-shirts. About two at the Cross Creek farm?"

Liz's first impulse was to decline, but the vision of a cold sandwich eaten alone in her apartment depressed her. She smiled sincerely and said, "How kind. I would love to. What may I bring?"

"What's your specialty?"

Liz had not done much cooking. She cast about for something her mother had made that wouldn't take too much talent. "Well, I'm not much in the kitchen, but I can make a mean cranberry sauce. I use orange juice instead of water when I cook the berries."

"Sounds terrific. Do you remember the way?"

"I'm sure I can find it. As I recall, there aren't any other houses on that stretch of road."

"That's right." Hugh paused for a heartbeat and then continued, "Come hungry. There's always enough to feed a small army."

"Will do. 'Til tomorrow then."

With a half salute, half wave, Hugh disappeared. The outer door to the department opened and clicked shut almost immediately, making Liz smile. She wondered if Hugh's haste was based on the belief that she would change her mind if he stayed around. Since their dinner in Cross Creek, she had made a point of being unavailable for a repeat, even a casual, business meal.

At this point, instinct told her that Hugh was probably interested in more than being mere colleagues. He no longer made her as edgy as he had at the beginning of the semester, but she wasn't ready for anything even remotely like an office romance. Entanglements of that sort could be complicated and messy. Sadly, that left her pretty much alone.

With Jonathan's exit from her life, she had no other close personal connections in Florida. She had been so focused on her new job, her research, and their relationship that she hadn't formed any real friendships. It was a testament to the strength of Jonathan's influence that a rather extensive tally of things and people she had let go or never pursued now haunted her. She had willingly sacrificed all on the altar of Jonathan's whims and selfishness.

What she needed was a circle of girlfriends like the one she left behind in Seattle. Of course, the pickings were somewhat slim within the male dominated history department. If she were going to acquire girlfriends, she would have to make the effort to go to more social functions at the university and at her apartment complex. As far as romance was concerned, until she could trust herself not to repeat old patterns, she was determined to keep all men at arm's length.

After a night of thunder and lightning, Thanksgiving Day dawned washed and shiny clean. The previous week's mugginess with its high humidity and temps in the low seventies had blown away with an advancing cold front leaving the air crisp, something Liz feared she might never experience again after her first Florida summer.

As she made her way south onto the two-lane road leading through the conservation area, a sensation so long absent she had forgotten how it felt settled over her. Neck and shoulder muscles became supple and relaxed. Stress she hadn't even been aware of melted away and Liz found herself singing along with the radio. For the first time since the breakup with Jonathan she actually felt something akin to happy and carefree. Getting out into nature was having a restorative effect.

Liz was enjoying the drive so much that she was on top of Hugh's driveway before she realized it. At the screech of tires, four teenaged heads, two of each gender, looked up from a game of touch football and observed her negotiating the turn into the sandy driveway. What looked to be the eldest boy loped to the front steps and yelled through the screen, then all four young people descended on the car.

"Hey. You must be Liz. Welcome to Cross Creek." The elder boy looked to be about seventeen. The other kids followed close on his heels in age.

"Thank you. You must be the nieces and nephews Hugh is so fond of."

The youngest, a girl of around thirteen, giggled and chimed in, "He's talked a lot about you too. We watched *The Untouchables* on TV last night. Did that thing with the baby carriage on the steps really happen?"

Liz realized that Hugh must have talked about her interest in Capone. "Well, I don't know for sure, but I suspect it was made up just for the movie."

"Oh." Disappointment crossed the girl's face, but then she brightened. "Well, it was good for an old movie anyway."

The screen door slammed and Hugh strolled over to the little group now bombarding Liz with questions about gangsters and shootouts.

"Okay, you four. Give the woman time to catch her breath before you start grilling her." Hugh put his arm lightly around Liz's shoulder and gave her a peck on the cheek, setting the two younger kids sniggering. He looked at the kids in mock anger and said, "I think I hear your mother calling you."

The youngest grinned and replied, "Uncle Hugh, you're so lame sometimes."

"Go. Now. The table needs to be set."

Liz watched the youngsters scamper to the door, laughing and pushing each other as they went.

After they disappeared into the house, Hugh squeezed her shoulder then let his arm drop. "They actually are rather excited you're here. They're getting bored with us old fogeys and are looking forward to tales of blood and gore from the crime expert."

Liz glanced at Hugh. In stylish jeans, v-neck sweater, and plaid shirt, he looked like an ad for Ralph Lauren. "You should give yourself more credit. I'd hardly call you an old fogey in that outfit."

"It all depends on who's doing the talking."

Liz hadn't intended to be so personal with Hugh, but she could tell he was pleased with the compliment. His hug and kiss had caught her off guard, setting a more familiar tone than they had ever shared before. Although the gestures had surprised her, she realized the casual affection wasn't at all unpleasant.

What unsettled her though, was what it might actually mean. Perhaps he greeted all of his women friends in that manner, but somehow it seemed out of character with the side of him she saw at the university. It certainly gave her something to think about.

Dinner was excellent and plentiful as promised. The long farmhouse table was completely covered by serving bowls and platters, including some Southern specialties Liz hadn't tasted before. When it was time to clear the table, Liz started gathering plates and was promptly directed to leave them.

Hugh and his sister had prepared the meal, so it was the kids and their father's job to clean up. Guests were exempt from all chores. His sister next announced that she was going to have a nap and perhaps Hugh might take Liz for a walk around the lake. Eying his middle, she opined the exercise would do him good.

As they started their circumnavigation of the lake, the sun hung suspended over the tops of tall cypresses on the western side. Its fading light burnished everything with autumn gold and cast long shadows, creating the kind of mood that one saw in movies where the main characters had come to a pivotal moment in their relationship.

"You have a wonderful family. Your sister and brother-in-law are so gracious and warm. And the kids are adorable."

"Thanks. I think so, but I realize I'm prejudiced."

They walked a quarter of the lakeshore in companionable silence. When a silvery weathered bench came into view, Hugh led her over to it. Liz sat down beside him and admired the scene laid out before them. Late afternoon sun diamonds danced on the lake's crystal water, adding to the cinematic effect.

"Liz, I hope you're enjoying being here as much as we . . . I am enjoying having you."

"It's a beautiful place. Thanks for inviting me."

"I hope you'll come again."

Liz hesitated, then didn't respond and the ensuing silence became awkward. She sensed Hugh wanted to say something more but was reluctant to do so. With his deep intake of breath, she became a little apprehensive. She just wasn't ready for a personal entanglement or romantic relationship yet.

"Liz, I need to know where you are on the new course proposals. If we're going to get them into next year's fall catalogue, I've got to have them finalized no later than the end of January."

Chagrined by her incorrect flight of romantic presumption, she replied quickly, "I'm afraid I have a confession. I'm not as far as I had hoped to be at this point. The good news is I'm sure I can have them finished and to you when we return from Christmas Break."

"Are you really sure you want to take on this much responsibility? You've seemed somewhat distracted lately and I've wondered if maybe you're thinking about leaving us."

Surprise followed by a feeling that might have been fear made Liz face Hugh with a hard stare. Despite the breakup with Jonathan, it had never once occurred to her to abandon her job and return to the West Coast. It chilled her that Hugh thought she would tuck tail and run back to her home territory. Perhaps she *had* spent too much time on research for her book, but she was consumed by it and she wasn't going to give it up. At the thought that Hugh might be about to suggest such, white-hot anger surged.

"I have never once thought about leaving and I'm shocked that you even mention it. When I take on a job, I give one hundred percent. Just because I haven't rushed the course descriptions doesn't mean you won't get them on time. And another thing, I have no intention of giving up my research."

Jolted by the strength of her reaction, Liz broke eye contact and let her gaze drift to an obliging Canada goose who had swooped down onto the lake while she was losing her temper.

"Whoa! I haven't asked you to stop working on your Capone article and I'm ecstatic you're staying. I've been afraid that maybe I'm putting too much pressure on you. That's all. You've moved across the country, taken a new job in a much bigger school, lost an important relationship. It's a lot to deal with. If you want to wait a year before designing new courses, I'll certainly understand and will think no less of you."

"Not on your life. I love teaching at Florida and the new courses are a career dream come true. You're right that this has been a hard semester, but my research is keeping me sane." Liz felt her anger ebbing. She reached out and placed a hand on his arm. "I want you to know I'm not going to let you down."

Hugh smiled and took her hand in his. "And I want you to know that I would never intentionally do anything that might hurt you or cause you distress."

It took a moment for Liz to be able to return Hugh's gaze. As the full meaning of his words settled in, something hard in Liz's heart cracked just a little. Hugh really was a kind, thoughtful man.

"Thanks for understanding. It's refreshing to find sympathy in a guy."

Hugh's gaze drifted out over the lake. "Liz, not all men are bastards. Some of us are actually capable of being caring and trustworthy."

To her horror, Liz felt tears well up. "I'm sorry for getting so angry. You're right about my feeling the pressure, but I'm a big girl. I can handle it."

He stood up and pulled her to her feet. "But that's just it. You don't have to if you don't want to. Above all else, I want you to be happy."

Her gaze followed his to the crystalline water. She didn't reply for a while. When she finally spoke, her words were without artifice or dissimulation.

"You know, I'm not sure I'm exactly happy yet, but

I think I'm getting there. It's been a wonderful day. I'm involved in research that I can put my heart and soul into. And I have a great boss who's also a pretty terrific friend. All in all, I'd say things are looking up."

Liz glanced up quickly when she felt Hugh pull back slightly. His expression had shifted from casual and open to unreadable.

Chapter 31

DeWitt steered his truck through the woods and parked in an opening where it wouldn't be seen from the road or the farmyard where he was headed. The engine went quiet, but he didn't make a move to leave the truck. Instead, he sat for a moment thinking about what he was planning to do and asked himself if he had anticipated all of the possible consequences. Once he started on this path, there would be no turning back. His conscience wouldn't let him quit if he found what he was looking for.

He'd rocked along all summer knowing things hadn't felt right, trying very hard to ignore the mounting pile of details and the logical conclusion they pointed to. Guilt dogged his steps these days. It floated just beneath the surface until some seemingly unrelated comment or small event reminded him of his failure to act. Then, the guilt roared to the forefront.

If he had done something sooner, did it follow that the later lynchings might have been prevented? He had no way of knowing at this point in his investigation, but he was very afraid the answer was yes. Of course, there was the opposite possibility. He might never know with any certainty if he could have changed things. He wasn't sure which depressed him more. Either way, one of the options was something he would have to live with for the rest of his life.

The palm of his hand slammed against the steering wheel. He had to get a grip. Beating himself up wasn't going to help anybody. It couldn't change the past. Worst case, it would only serve to distract him and distractions could prove dangerous.

Before he could change his mind, he jammed his flashlight into the waistband of his pants and yanked the driver's door open. Brittle pine needles crunched softly beneath his feet. After only a few yards, sweat rolled down his back and damp rings formed on his shirt under his armpits. There was nothing hotter than an airless pine forest in the Deep South during high summer.

Approaching undetected was his best hope of finding what he was after. Direct confrontation would only produce a surly denial and alert the suspect that he was under surveillance. Besides, DeWitt knew getting into the farmhouse without a warrant was impossible. His destination was the large structure at the edge of the farmyard.

The barn could be approached from the woods out of sight of the house and fields beyond. With any luck at all, the battered yellow Model T still rested under its tarp. If he could tie Carlton Smith to the lynchings, then he was one step closer to nailing the man he now believed was behind all the murders.

DeWitt paused and looked over the mule lot separating the woods from the back of the barn. If he moved along the wooden fence in a crouched position, he would pretty much be camouflaged should anyone happen to approach the barn from the house. Without further hesitation, he crept along the enclosure and slipped through the barn's wide rear entrance.

It took a couple of seconds for his eyes to make the transition between bright daylight and the barn's dusty gloom, but even so, he detected a mound in the middle of the hall that looked right for the auto.

He glanced through the barn's front entrance. The farmyard was empty of people and vehicles, but in the distance, men bent over their work. A tractor creeping along the top of a hill drew his attention. The field was a long way from the house. If the farmer had gone out to check up on his field hands, he had probably driven there.

DeWitt moved over to the tarp and lifted one corner, revealing a patch of battered yellow metal. Dust flying up into his face made him pinch his nose. It would be a sorry joke to have come this far and then give himself away with something so stupid as a sneeze.

When the sensation passed, DeWitt drew the tarp covering the passenger side back and took his flashlight from his waistband. Other than dust, sand, and bits of natural debris, the car appeared devoid of anything remotely like evidence. Shining the light under the front seat and running his arm around the space did nothing but smear his hand with dirt. When he had searched every inch of the front, including the glove box with its rusted out bottom, he turned his attention to the back.

The second seat had been removed and the floor covered with boards cut to fit, perfect for hauling sacks of seed and small farm implements. Dust motes swirled in the faint light coming through a hole in the leather drop down roof. Seeds, bits of hay, and kernels of corn were scattered over the rough sawn surface. Nothing out of the ordinary for an old auto converted for farm use. DeWitt dropped the tarp back into place and went around to inspect the other side. Nothing. He slumped down onto the running board. Disappointment rose bitter as gall.

The growl of gears shifting startled DeWitt. He'd been so focused on deciding what to do next that he had failed to remain alert. Truck doors slammed and male voices drifted across the farmyard. One voice was all too familiar and it was headed for the barn.

Despite the need to get away unseen, DeWitt didn't leave the barn. Instead, he jumped up and threw the tarp back into place. Then climbing onto the top crossbar of the closest stall, he swung himself up into the hayloft. The opportunity to eavesdrop couldn't be wasted.

"I got one more job for you, Carlton."

"You mean for me and the boys."

"No. I mean just for you. It's more, shall we say, delicate than the others."

"Okay. What do I need to do?"

"My deputy, that girlfriend of his, and the Taylor picaninny. Get rid of 'em tonight."

DeWitt's heart stopped, skipped a couple of beats, and hammered back into action. He leaned against a hay bale and willed himself to be still and silent.

The lull in the conversation below him seemed to last a lifetime. When he finally spoke, the Klansman's voice was hesitant.

"I already got the boys looking for the kid, but it don't seem like the girl would cause trouble."

"The girl, dumbass, spends every free second with Williams. You really think that half breed son-of-a-bitch hasn't talked to her?"

"But she's Arnold's kid. He's one of us."

"So what? She ain't nothing to you or me. Get rid of her along with the other two. If even one of them talks, it could mean trouble with our partners. We're in too deep to turn back now."

"I guess you're right, but it don't seem right. Not the girl."

"I ain't gonna tell you twice. Do it or face the consequences."

"This had all better be worth it." The Klansman's voice was petulant. "I've put a lot on the line for you and your big ideas. I'm expecting a big payoff in return."

"And you'll get the reward you deserve. Our Chicago friends will see to it."

"They better or you may just find yourself on the end of one of our ropes."

There was a hard thump against the stall boards and a howl of pain. "Don't threaten me. It could get you killed. Now get on with the job."

The sound of retreating footsteps followed by a truck door slamming and an engine catching fire told DeWitt that at least one of the suspects, probably Ike, was leaving the farm. He stayed hidden behind a hay bale, thinking about his next move. He could arrest the henchman on the spot, but he knew it wouldn't do any good in the long run. Meg and Zeke had to be his first priority. He could deal with criminals once the love of his life and the boy were safe.

Every nerve screamed at DeWitt to get out of the hayloft and run for his truck, but he was stuck until the henchman left the barn. He couldn't risk a gunfight or the man calling ahead for someone else to finish off Meg and Zeke.

Several minutes passed without any sound from the floor below. DeWitt silently rose up onto his haunches for a look. He still couldn't see what was happening and he couldn't move into position for a better view. Any movement overhead would risk drawing unwanted attention. He crouched frozen in place until his thigh muscles twitched with the effort. When he was sure he was about to jump out of his skin, the Model T's hand crank started grinding.

He let out a long, silent breath. The engine coughed into life. A door clicked open and shut. Within a couple of seconds, exhaust fumes filled the loft. As soon as the engine sounds died away, DeWitt scrambled from his hideout and dashed past the mule lot into the woods.

Isaiah Taylor had been lynched on Saturday. This was Monday. It was a miracle that Zeke and Meg had survived the weekend. The lynchings had all taken place on a Saturday, but it didn't look like Meg and Zeke were going to be killed in the same way. One man, not a mob, was after the person who was dearer to him than life itself. DeWitt guessed Ike thought even murderous Klansmen might balk at killing a young boy and a good, decent white girl. Carlton, however, wouldn't stop at murdering innocents. DeWitt had to get Zeke and Meg out of Columbia County, maybe even out of the state.

For once, his truck fired to life on the first try, as though it understood the urgency of his mission. DeWitt spun in reverse until he faced the road and then floored it. Sand and small stones spit up clouds behind him as he tore over the single track. The truck momentarily took flight when it bolted over a small log. Reaching the main highway, DeWitt yanked the wheel hard left. The truck made the turn with two tires spinning on nothing but thin air.

The distance to Preacher Jackson's house wasn't long, but it felt like time had suddenly slowed to a crawl. When he glanced at the speedometer, however, DeWitt was surprised to see the needle quivering as far right as it could go.

Visions of a small boy hanging from the limb of a tree danced before his eyes, making him pound the dashboard in frustration and anxiety. If Carlton had any sense, the Jackson farm would be the first place he would go. The preacher was the leader of the colored community in the south end of the county and knew everything about anyone of color in the area.

It occurred to DeWitt that it might be smarter to approach the Jackson home on foot with his truck again hidden in the nearby pine forest. It could be disastrous if he passed the yellow car on the way. On the other hand, this would make his journey longer and time was running out for Zeke and Meg.

After weighing his options, he abandoned the safer one for a head-on frontal attack. If he crossed paths with the other man, so be it. The cylinder of his sidearm was loaded and his deer rifle was behind the seat.

As he approached the turn leading to the preacher's

house, DeWitt saw in the distance ahead the battered yellow rear of Carlton's car barreling north towards town. He would never forgive himself if he were too late.

Forcing the truck to make the turn onto the sandy lane at maximum speed, he had to fight the wheel to maintain control as the vehicle fishtailed. Heart pounding, he righted the truck and pushed the accelerator to the floor once more. It felt like his teeth or parts of the truck, probably both, were being knocked loose as he roared over the road's washboard surface. When he came to the preacher's gate, he jerked the wheel and slid to a stop. The preacher met him at the front door.

Preacher Jackson's smile was tight, full of caution. He pushed the screen door open and said, "Good day, Deputy Williams. What brings you out to this end of the county? May I offer you a glass of tea?"

DeWitt ignored the attempt at casual hospitality. "Where's Zeke Taylor?"

The old man stepped back and let the screen door snap shut. "Zeke? What on earth could the law want with that child?"

"He's in danger. Where is he?"

Preacher Jackson's eyes narrowed. He looked DeWitt up and down before answering. "That child's been in danger since the day he was born, but not anymore than the rest of us colored folks. What makes you so concerned about him just now?"

"Look. You've got to trust me. I don't have time to explain, but we've got to get Zeke out of the county. Otherwise, the leader of the local klavern is going to try to kill him tonight. Now tell where he is."

"And how do I know you aren't Klan?"

"That's ridiculous. You know I'm not. They don't hold with race mixing and I'm part Seminole." If the situation hadn't been so dire, DeWitt would have laughed. This was the only time in his life that his mixed heritage had been an advantage.

"Doesn't make any difference whether you're Klan or not. I haven't seen or heard from Zeke since church service Sunday before last."

"That's not true and we both know it. Jack Blevins brought him here Saturday night. I'm engaged to Jack's sister. I thought you knew that."

At the mention of Jack's name, some of the preacher's caution eased a little. "I'm afraid I had forgotten. I must be getting old. I heard Jack's run away. Is it true?"

"Yeah. Meg says he took off in the early hours yesterday. Must not have been too long after he dropped Zeke off here. Seems Jack wasn't very happy at home."

"With Arnold Blevins for a father, I guess he had reason."

Frustration and anxiety put an edge in DeWitt's voice. "Look, this isn't getting us anywhere. For Pete's sake, tell me where Zeke is so I can get him away from here."

The old man stared into DeWitt's eyes like he was trying to see into his very soul. "I may not be able to do it, but God will punish you in an everlasting pit of fire if you harm that child."

"All I want is to protect him. Please, Preacher. You gotta see that. Where is he?"

The old man was silent for several beats. Finally, he let out a long, slow breath and answered, "When Zeke saw Mr. Carlton Smith's beat up old yellow car coming up the lane, he yelled like a banshee and hightailed it for the woods."

"Did Zeke tell you why he's afraid?"

A puzzled expression clouded the preacher's face, but DeWitt wasn't sure how genuine it was.

"Should there be another reason besides him being afraid of all white men right now?"

DeWitt wasn't about to tell the preacher what he now felt sure had happened at the sinkhole back in June. "None that I can think of. Did Carlton stop and talk to you?"

"He did. Said his best birddog's gone missing and somebody told him I had it. Searched all through the house and the outbuildings. Even crawled underneath them. Didn't find nothing, though. He left in a mighty temper. You white folks have strange ways and notions sometimes."

DeWitt studied the old man's face. The preacher was playing it close to the vest. It was clear he knew more than he was willing to say, but there was no good reason to waste more time trying to get him to tell all.

"Time's running out for Zeke. How long do you think he'll last being passed around the community here?"

Preacher Jackson shook his head. "Probably not too long, I'm afraid. I don't like giving him up, but I guess I'll have to trust you." The old man came out onto the porch. "Come on then. I suspect we'll find him hiding in a blackberry thicket."

As they made their way across the field toward the woods, it dawned on DeWitt that he knew very little about Zeke other than the basic facts. "Does Zeke have any family left?"

"The only family I know of is a great-aunt in Atlanta. We've been trying to figure a way to get him up there without raising the Klan's suspicions. We know they're watching the members of our congregation. We've seen too many strange cars and trucks passing where there's never been much traffic before."

Clearly, the hunt would only intensify with every hour that passed. The Klan leader must have called out the entire klavern before Ike's most recent orders for secrecy. They wouldn't stop until they found Zeke.

DeWitt couldn't locate the mountain of evidence he needed to convict the killers in a Florida court and take Zeke to Atlanta at the same time. But maybe there was another way. It was a long shot, but it was the best he had.

"Atlanta. That might work. Maybe I can kill two birds with one stone up there."

Chapter 32

Liz walked toward Hugh's office with the completed course proposals in her hand. As she tapped on his open door, she engaged in a little internal chastisement.

You really are turning into a coward, girl. Take a deep breath and calm down. Why do you have to read something sexual or romantic into every encounter? For crying out loud. He's your boss, not your new lover.

She should have brought the folder to him as soon as they returned from Christmas Break, but she hadn't been able to force herself to make the short walk down the hall to his office until today.

Every time she thought about it, she found an excuse to delay. The final draft needed one more review. An addition was made to the bibliography, dropped, and then added again. She had screwed around with the document as though it was her first freshman year term paper. It was ridiculous.

Hugh looked up at her and smiled, but the expression in his eyes was as neutral as she had ever seen in him. Disappointment, irritation, relief? She wasn't sure which emotion she actually felt. Since Thanksgiving Day, he had lurked beneath the surface of her thoughts like a problem that needed to be solved. She must have mentioned him a lot because her mother had asked if Hugh was the new man in her life. Her hot denial had been met with a cocked brow and a knowing look.

"How was Seattle?"

"Great. I saw almost all of my friends and family. By the

way, thanks again for Thanksgiving. I enjoyed meeting your family."

"You're welcome. They liked you too."

With the social pleasantries out of the way, they fell into an uncomfortable silence. It felt to Liz as though neither of them knew where their relationship stood. Were they colleagues who had experienced a pleasant holiday or were they headed for something more? Liz didn't want to think about the answer.

She placed the folder on his desk with a sense of relief. She had devoted a lot of the semester break to the work and her ideas were very good, if she did say so herself. Hugh might want the proposals tweaked some, but the tedious work was behind her. No more deadline hanging over her head and no more anxiety that she might disappoint Hugh.

"Here they are as promised."

He picked up the folder and put it in his inbox. "Thanks. I'll take a look and get any suggestions back to you by the end of the week. Will that work with your schedule?"

"It would. If there's nothing else . . ." She let the words trail away because she wasn't sure exactly what she wanted or expected from him. His casual notice of the proposals left her feeling surprisingly deflated, especially since she knew she had fiddled around until he was at his busiest to give him the folder. It felt as though the easy companionship of Thanksgiving Day might never have been. A fleeting sense of dissatisfaction curled through her.

Hugh shifted as though his chair had suddenly become uncomfortable. "No, there's nothing in particular." He looked at a point somewhere on the wall behind her, then his gaze met hers again. "I'm sure you have a lot you need to do. Maybe we could get together for dinner next week? To finalize the new courses. After you've had a chance to look over my notes. Whenever you have time."

"That would be good. I'll let you know as soon as I'm finished going over your notes."

His smile seemed strained. "Yes, please do."

She left Hugh's office confused and inexplicably miffed. The whole conversation had felt so awkward. Perhaps she had completely misread Hugh at Thanksgiving or maybe he had decided she wasn't his type after her display of temper by the lake. Maybe it didn't really matter.

The new semester, like the new year, had brought release and anticipation. The future looked washed clean. Jonathan's departure had left her shattered, but she no longer thought about him morning, noon, and night. When he did drift into her thoughts, it was with a mild melancholia, not the soul crushing pain she felt right after their breakup.

The thing that consumed her now wasn't a romantic relationship, but the fate of a young boy born around 1919. She twitched with impatience to get back to the search for Zeke. It was in him that she believed she would find . . . what? Her salvation? Where had that come from? The word salvation was a little intense. Actually, way over-the-top. Call it by any name. She instinctively knew she wouldn't be the same after this project was completed.

Traffic on I-75 was heavy as usual when she headed north on Thursday afternoon. Her second semester teaching schedule gave her a three and a half day weekend. A godsend for which she had forgotten to thank Hugh. With the newspaper archives at a dead end, Liz decided to turn to county records. Rites of passage—birth, marriage, death, taxes—left an informative trail.

The clerk in the county archives office was kind and helpful. Too bad the old handwritten record books gave up absolutely no information despite several hours spent cross-referencing anyone named Barnes or Taylor. If Isaiah Taylor had left behind other relatives or descendants, they had lived and died elsewhere. As to Silas Barnes, he and his wife married off two daughters who promptly disappeared from the county records after their weddings. Another dead end.

Almost as an afterthought, she asked for the crime reports and files for the sheriff's department. The sheriff and his department had been ineffectual to the point of gross negligence in pursuing the Klansmen responsible for the lynchings. Nothing unusual about that in the deep South of 1930, but there might be something of interest.

Those records yielded very little that she hadn't already gathered through the newspaper's crime reports. One file, however, peaked her interest. A deputy had suddenly dropped out of sight in August.

Surprisingly, his personnel file was attached to a single typed page, but it gave no reason for why he had failed to show for work or what had happened to him. She skimmed through the rest of the pages in the folder and found her answer. A note at the bottom of the last page dated October, 1930 sent a chill through Liz.

Deputy DeWitt Williams: missing, presumed dead.

Liz had read every line of the Columbia Tribune for the year 1930 and the first six months of 1931. There had been no mention of a missing deputy. Surely that would have been newsworthy. Liz wondered if it was possible that he had been a Klan victim for some reason she had yet to uncover. Suddenly she knew the answer was yes. She could feel it in her bones.

Liz lugged the last of the big books and file boxes back to the archivist's desk. Her hands and arms were smeared with grime. Her sinuses felt swollen. Hours of inhaling mold and dust usually ended in an infection. Liz would happily take the resulting postnasal drip and sore throat in stride if she had found answers instead of more questions.

"Is there anything else I can get for you, Hon?"

"No thanks. I've pretty much hit a wall."

"Do you mind telling me what you're looking for? I might be able to suggest something other than our files."

Liz briefly described her interest in the year 1930, beginning with Capone's stay at the Blanche. Her experience with Ethel at the 7 Lakes Café made her cautious about mentioning the full scope of her search, her grandmother's advice never far from her thoughts. She had been right about the insular nature of small towns. People didn't like their community's dirty laundry exposed, even if it was from another century. Especially not by outsiders.

"I can't tell you anymore about the Barnes and the Taylor families than you already know, but when the county bought the hotel to get more office space, we inherited all of the old registers and files. They're still stored over there. Would you like to take a look?"

"That would be wonderful." Liz sounded more polite than she felt. The hotel was nearly 110 years old. Boxes of old files were probably stacked to the ceiling with few labels and even less organization.

"Let me call over and tell them you're coming. Check in at the first office on the left."

A five-minute drive and a brief conversation with a receptionist led Liz to the accordion gate of an elevator that looked original to the 1902 building. The girl grinned when Liz stopped short of stepping into the car.

"Don't worry. It's serviced every six months. Nothing to be afraid of unless you object to a ghost or two riding along."

"The hotel's supposed to be haunted?"

"Yeah. If you believe in that sort of thing."

"Do you?"

The receptionist shrugged. "Some people say they've heard a woman pacing and crying on the third floor. I've never heard her, but a woman killed herself up there back in the day. There are no offices above the second floor. Who knows? I don't go up there myself." The girl held out a key with a tag labeled master. "Please lock the storeroom door before you come back down."

The elevator creaked and groaned its way upwards. When it reached the top floor, it bounced once and shuddered to a stop. Liz pulled the barrier back and stepped into a gloomy hall whose Edwardian style carpet runner looked like it hadn't been vacuumed in a decade, maybe two. Dust motes swirled in the shaft of bright sunshine pouring through the single window at the end of the hall. Liz sneezed loudly and headed to a door marked Presidential Suite.

After turning the key in the antique Yale lock, she entered a spacious area. In the hotel's heyday, the room must have been the height of elegance. It boasted a large fireplace complete with marble mantle and surround. Heavy velvet drapes hung at the edges of bay windows that formed a nicely sized alcove. She felt along the wall for the light switch.

Pushing the toggle upward created a warm glow from a gold leaf, many-armed chandelier hanging from an ornate ceiling medallion. Its light settled over a stack of cardboard boxes resting in the center of the wide blank wood floor.

Despite the layers of dust and the cobwebs decorating the crown molding, Liz could see that this room had once been reserved for only the most important guests. Perhaps Capone and his henchmen had stayed in this very suite. A shiver ran down her spine.

Liz chuckled. She usually wasn't subject to such flights of fancy. It must be the talk of hauntings that got her imagination churning. Ruefully eyeing the stack in the center of the room, she strode over and placed her hands on her hips.

As her gaze ran up and down the twenty or so boxes, she felt like whooping with joy. Each box bore a label with a detailed list of its contents. She tore down the stack and pulled two of them away from the others. One contained the guest register for 1930. The other contained personnel files for the early decades of the twentieth century.

Chapter 33

"Where you taking me, Deputy Williams?"

DeWitt looked down at Zeke's upturned face, still soft and rounded in the final days of childhood, and was awed by what he saw reflected in the dark eyes. After all this child had suffered and lost , he still possessed the ability to trust. A lump rose in DeWitt's throat. He reached over and patted the skinny knee protruding from the hole of Zeke's overalls.

"To your great-aunt in Atlanta. Preacher Jackson gave me the address and he's going to call to let your kin know we're coming."

Zeke turned and faced the passenger side window. DeWitt doubted it was the passing pine forests and tobacco fields that the boy was interested in or even saw. After a few miles of silence, Zeke spoke again, his voice soft and wistful.

"You think she'll take me to see the Atlanta Black Crackers? Granddaddy was gonna take me one day. We never got the chance to take that trip. I sure would like to see them play."

"Yeah. I think she'll take you to a game."

Another period of silence ensued followed by another question. "You think I'm gonna like Atlanta? I ain't hardly ever been out of Columbia County."

"You'll like Atlanta. It's a pretty place with a nice zoo. You like zoos, don't you?"

"I don't know. I never been to one. Do you think they have elephants?"

"I bet they do."

"Good. I've always thought I'd like to see me a elephant."

After a while, DeWitt felt the warmth of a bony little shoulder burrowing against his side. It didn't take long for Zeke's long curly lashes to begin drooping. When the child slumped in sleep, DeWitt gently shifted the small body so the child wouldn't topple over. Beyond thinking that having kids one day would be nice, he hadn't given much thought to what being a father would feel like.

If what he felt right now was even half of what a father felt, then being a good dad must be the best, the most important thing a man could ever do. No one had depended on him quite like this and his heart filled to overflowing with compassion and the desire to protect. At that point, he knew he would gladly kill anyone who tried to harm this child.

The sun was almost gone by the time DeWitt pulled the truck into the alley behind the hotel. When he got out of the vehicle, the air that enveloped him smelled of frying chicken. Nobody could fry up chicken like Flossie.

"Come on, Zeke. I'm not gonna leave you here in the truck."

"But they don't let colored folks in the hotel. Granddaddy told me to never go in there. That I'd get in trouble with the law."

"I'm the law and I say it's all right. Get on down and come with me."

Zeke stayed where he was. It seemed he doubted that even a sheriff's deputy could override generations of legalized discrimination. DeWitt put his hands on the seat on either side of Zeke and leaned into the cab.

"Zeke, I know you're scared, but you've got to do what I say. I'm not going to let anybody hurt you. The bad guys'll have to go through me first and I'm really tough. You believe that, don't you?"

He play punched Zeke's skinny arm, which must have been the right thing to do because a shy grin covered the boy's face.

"Yeah. I believe it."

Zeke jumped down, kicking up a little cloud of dust where he landed. Together they strode to the hotel's back door.

DeWitt removed his hat as he walked into the kitchen.

"DeWitt Williams! What do you think you're doing bringing that young'un into my kitchen? Look at his feet. They's covered in dust."

"Flossie, I need a favor. This is Isaiah Taylor's grandson, Zeke."

"Oh. I see." Flossie's voice dropped almost to a whisper. "What do you need?"

"Can you keep him with you and out of sight for a little while? I've got to talk to Meg. It's really important."

The cook cast a gentle, sad glance over the boy. "You like fried chicken, Zeke?"

"Yes, ma'am. I love it."

"Well, if you'll stay in the pantry and be real quiet, I'll bring you some fresh out of the pan. And if you're extra good, I just might be able to find some peach cobbler with ice cream. You think you can do that?"

"Yes, ma'am. I can be quiet as a mouse."

Flossie led Zeke across the kitchen, holding his small hand in her large flour covered one. She opened the pantry door and yanked the chain of the single bulb hanging from the ceiling on a long cord. Pulling a wooden crate from under the back shelf, she pointed to it and said, "You sit here and be a little mouse like you promised. In a few minutes that chicken'll be ready."

After she closed the pantry door, Flossie turned angry eyes on DeWitt. "Exactly what are you planning to do with that child? He's done had enough trouble to last a lifetime."

"The less you know, the less you can tell. Just believe that I'm doing everything I can to keep him safe."

"You best keep that promise or you'll have me to deal with."

"I'd never cross you, Flossie. I know you'd skin me alive."

"I would. And don't you think I cain't do it."

DeWitt found Meg sitting on the back hall steps drinking a Co'Cola. "Honey, I'm glad you're on your break. You gotta be brave. I've got something to tell you that's gonna be hard to hear." DeWitt sat down beside Meg and moved to put his arm around her.

"Don't. I've got something to say to you too. I've given it a lot of thought. I can't marry you now or ever."

Stunned, DeWitt could only stammer, "What . . . do . . . you mean? What's come over you?"

"The question is what's come over you, DeWitt? I know it's been hard waiting to get married, but how could you take up with another woman? And one of those kind of girls at that. Of course, I guess she was willing to give you what I wouldn't."

"What in hell are you talking about?"

"Don't you try to lie to me. Albert saw you with your arms around one of those prostitutes. Bold as brass standing on her front porch."

DeWitt figured he must look foolish because his mouth was hanging open. "I have absolutely no idea what you're talking about."

"You've already said that."

"Well, it's the truth. When did this supposed embrace happen?"

"A week or so ago. Albert and his wife saw you when they were coming back from visiting his cousin in Valdosta."

DeWitt didn't say anything while he combed his memory. "It must have been the day I interviewed Jesse Jardine's girls again. One of them ran out to the porch when I was leaving.

She was real young and scared to death. She threw her arms around me and begged me to give her money so she could get out of town."

"Did you? Did you give her money?"

"Yes I did. And don't try to tell me I did wrong. She was just a kid. She deserved a fresh start. If you don't believe me, then maybe you're right. Maybe we shouldn't get married," DeWitt hissed between clinched teeth.

He had never been so angry with Meg before—frustrated and disappointed, yes, but never angry enough not to care what she thought. He wanted to get up and walk away until he had a chance to cool off, but he loved her too much to leave her to face Ike and his henchman alone.

"We can sort this girl thing out later. Right now you've got to listen to me and do what I say. You, Zeke Taylor, and me are all in serious danger. This afternoon I discovered that the Klan means to kill us. I'm taking Zeke out of the state and you've got to come too. It's the only way to save any of us."

The color drained from Meg's face. "How do you know?"

"Because I overheard the plan. I'm not going to tell you everything until we're away from Columbia County, but we've got to go right now."

"DeWitt, we can't leave. What about our jobs? What about Mama?" Her voice was shrill.

DeWitt put his hand over her mouth. "Shhh! Not so loud. I'll take my hand away if you promise to talk quietly. Do you?"

Meg looked up at him, her eyes huge and desperate. It was an expression that he had hoped never to see. After a moment, she nodded and he let his hand drop to his side.

"We can't just walk away from jobs and family. How will we make it in this depression?"

Patience exhausted, he growled, "None of that's gonna matter if we're dead."

"I don't believe you. You're over reacting," Meg whispered on the verge of hysteria. "You've gotten so wound up about these lynchings that you see a bogey man behind every bush."

DeWitt realized that he had shocked Meg to the point that she wasn't thinking straight. Placing a hand on each shoulder, he turned her so that she had no choice but to look at him.

"Do you really think I'm so unreliable? I wouldn't be here saying these things if they weren't true."

"But Mama . . . She's already lost Jack."

"You can call your mother after we're away from here. You won't be gone forever. Just until the danger is over."

"But how long will that be?"

"I don't know. It all depends on who I can get to listen to me about what's really going on in this county." This time Meg didn't draw back when he reached for her. He leaned down and planted a kiss on top of her head. "Whether you love me enough to marry me or not, I'm not leaving you here to be murdered. Go pack a bag. Don't tell anybody you're leaving. I'll wait for you here."

Meg hesitated. She pulled back and stared at him, her head tilted to one side.

Without a word, she nodded and flew up the stairs.

"Hello, Deputy Williams. What brings you to hang around our back stairs?"

Albert's voice coming from behind made DeWitt jump. As he wheeled around, he hoped his face didn't betray the state of his nerves.

"I'm waiting for Meg to come down. She's gone up to get something for me. She's on her break, so she's not wasting time." Hearing the defensive note in his voice, DeWitt wanted to kick himself.

"I didn't say she was. I simply asked what you're doing here."

"Do you have a problem with me being here? I thought this was part of the public area."

"It is. I just wanted to know. I feel a responsibility for the girls I employ."

The gleam of amusement now dancing in the hotel manager's eyes made DeWitt feel like throttling him. "Albert, we're going to be married. I think you can trust us to meet in a public place."

"Maybe. Then again, maybe not."

DeWitt had no intention of encouraging the ridiculous conversation. He pulled his features into their hardest expression, the one he used when confronting a suspect, but he didn't utter another word.

Albert looked confused for a moment, then harrumphed and turned on his heel. "If you're going to get huffy, I guess I'll be on my way. Some people can't take a joke."

Soft footsteps sounded on the stairs behind DeWitt.

"Lord, I thought he was never going to leave. I'm ready if you are." Meg descended the last few steps two at a time.

As they entered the kitchen through a side door, a voice called out, "Girl, where you going with that bag?"

DeWitt's patience was wearing thin with all the female bossiness. "Flossie, all you need to know is that people are in danger and I'm taking them to safety. And if you know what's good for you, you won't talk to anybody about seeing Zeke, Meg, or me. Do you understand?"

Flossie must have been surprised by DeWitt's uncharacteristically aggressive tone. She bowed up and snapped, "Don't you worry about me, Deputy *De*-Witt Williams. I know when to keep my mouth shut."

Meg flung her arms around Flossie's ample middle and kissed her quickly on the cheek. "I'm going to miss you.

If Mama calls looking for me, tell her I can't come to the telephone right then. Okay?"

"Whatever you want, sweet girl. I hope you know what you're doing."

Chapter 34

Looking into the face staring up from the truck's floorboard, Meg could see the terror that clouded Zeke's eyes. Meg pushed her legs against the door and leaned down. "Hold my hand. We'll be out of the state before you know it."

Meg watched the dark shapes of trees and palmettos flying by. They passed the last house on this road several miles back and were traveling directly into the swamp. The state line couldn't be far now. DeWitt was pushing his truck as hard as it could go, but Meg still had to fight the urge to look through the back window every few seconds.

She believed him about Jesse Jardine's girl. She just didn't have the courage to talk about it right then. She was afraid her voice would tremble, something that might send the terrified child at her feet into a frenzy. The poor baby was so frightened he refused to sit on the seat between them.

DeWitt had told him he could put his head on one of their laps, but Zeke was afraid somebody in a taller truck would pass them and see him there, a colored child riding in the cab with two white people. It wouldn't look good. It would cause trouble. It might get them killed.

The simple wisdom of children could break your heart.

The heavy air whipping through the truck's open windows smelled of cypress, pine, and sawgrass—the fragrance of home. Meg wondered if she would ever breathe it in again. She sighed and stroked the silky forehead leaning against her knee. She'd thought there would be so much time to work, to build a life.

After all, she was only eighteen and DeWitt just twenty-five. They should be making wedding plans, not running for their lives. If they survived this night, Meg vowed to waste no more time worrying about stashing away money. She and DeWitt had something rare and she had foolishly come close to throwing it away.

Glancing at his handsome profile filled her with such deep emotion. He was a good man who only wanted to love her and make her happy. From now on, she planned to do the same for him. He must have felt her eyes on him because he turned slightly and grinned.

"We're going to be all right. The state line's only a couple of miles ahead. I'm not gonna let anybody hurt you, Baby. I love you too much." He grabbed her hand and brought it to his lips.

Meg's throat tightened with tenderness. "And I love you. When this is over, let's not wait for Christmas. Let's get married right away."

"You sure know how to make a bad situation better, my darlin'. If I didn't need to keep us on the road, you'd be covered with kisses right now."

After kissing her hand again, he released it and returned his attention to the road, a broad smile lighting his face.

After a few seconds, Zeke asked in a husky whisper, "How long it's gonna take to get to Atlanta?"

"I think we can make it there by day after tomorrow. We'll go to your great-aunt's house first thing. Preacher said he'd make sure she would give us a bed for a night or two."

"You don't care about staying in colored town?"

"No. We've got a lot more important stuff to worry about than being white or colored."

"What you gonna do once we're there?"

"I'll get some sleep, then go to the FBI district office. I don't know if they'll do anything about the lynchings. But

G-men are hard on moonshining and gangsters, especially when Capone's involved."

"Why not the lynchings?"

"Because that kind of murder isn't a federal crime. Strange, ain't it? The Declaration of Independence says life, liberty, and the pursuit of happiness, but for some people, those ideas got lost south of the Mason-Dixon Line."

Meg felt Zeke's body tremble. "I think that's enough talk about bad things. We haven't seen any other cars or trucks for miles now. Zeke, climb up here beside me and put your head in my lap. It's past your bedtime."

Weary didn't begin to describe how Meg felt. When Zeke's breathing evened out with the rhythm of sleep, she leaned her head against the seat and closed her eyes. At this point, she felt like she could sleep on a bed of nails if it was required. A dreamless sleep overtook her almost immediately.

A loud noise and a hand shoving her forward toward the floor woke Meg abruptly. She tried to lift her head to look at DeWitt, but he pushed her down even harder.

"Get down on the floor. Both of you. Now!"

Several pops sounded from behind the truck and then the back window shattered. Glass flew over Zeke and Meg where they were squeezed together half on the seat and half on the floor. Headlights from behind edged to the left.

"Hold on! They're trying to come around."

Meg's head slammed against the door as the truck jerked wildly to the left. A second jerk sent the truck flying across to the other side of the road. Meg's heart jumped to her throat as the scream of twisting metal rang through the night.

Chapter 35

"Hey, guys. Come over here. I've got the radio hooked up so everybody can listen."

Jack looked toward the edge of the orange orchard where the boss stood. This was what he had known was coming since they heard the news yesterday. It had been the only thing on anyone's mind. He strongly suspected when the broadcast was over, none of their lives would ever be the same.

Last night as they sat around after supper, the men had talked angrily of the day's events and some of the women had cried. For himself, Jack hoped for swift retribution, but dreaded it at the same time. He was only twenty-two. Plenty young enough to serve.

Crawling down from his ladder, he followed the other fruit pickers to where the boss stood by the open door of a field shack. They crowded around the little brown box where it sat atop a wobbly-legged stool and listened to voices thinned out and made tinny by their passage through the airwaves.

A soft murmur swirled among the gathering workers. Jack stood quietly at the edge of the group and listened. Some of the guys speculated on what they were about to hear. Others spoke angrily about what happened yesterday. The crackling from the radio ceased. The soft chatter among the migrant workers decreased as well.

When the broadcaster's voice resumed, a total hush fell over the small group of men, women, and children. It was as though even the wind and the birds understood that the next few minutes would change America forever.

Jack doubted there was any sound being uttered anywhere in the nation right then. The air around him crackled with tension in anticipation. From the radio, there was a scratchy scraping sound. Somebody must be adjusting the microphone. After another brief silence, the voice that had sustained the nation through the long years of depression rang from the Chamber of the United States House of Representatives.

Yesterday, December 7, 1941—a date that will live in infamy—the United States was suddenly and deliberately attacked by the naval and air forces of the Empire of Japan.

FDR only spoke for six and a half minutes. When he finished, the news commentator was nearly drowned out by the thunderous applause that filled the Chamber.

No one standing around the shack spoke. Husbands and wives hugged each other and their children. Some of the older men placed their hands on the shoulders of sons and young friends. Jack knew many of the old guys had seen service in the Great War. One had even served with the other Roosevelt, Teddy, in Cuba.

He looked at the faces of his fellow farm laborers and saw the same day-old shock, the same fear, and the same determination that roared through him. He didn't know exactly how soon Congress would declare war, but he was pretty sure it wouldn't take long. Probably only as much time as it took to organize the vote.

He turned to Mac and Bud, his brothers of the rails, and stuck out his hand. "Well, boys, it's been grand knowing you. Take care of each other and let me know where you are. I'll write when I have an address to send you."

"Where the hell you think you're going? We still got a day's picking to do before we get paid."

Jack could hear the anxiety in Mac's voice. He wasn't sure how old Mac was, but he was already moving with the beginnings of an old man's shuffle when they first met in that boxcar twelve years ago. He depended more each year on Jack and Bud to cover for him, to make up the difference in his tally when his arthritis kept him from meeting his quota. In many ways, Mac and Bud had replaced the family Jack lost when he ran away. He felt bad about leaving them, but he knew what he had to do.

Bud shook Jack's hand, but remained quiet. He surely knew what was coming. Jack had told him often enough what he planned to do with his life. He had only delayed this long because he couldn't face hurting the man who was like a father to him. Jack hated that the nation was entering the war, but he now had the reason he needed to make the break.

Jack placed his hand on Mac's shoulder. "I'm hopping a train for San Diego. There's a big navy recruiting office there. I'm going to sign up."

"But the government don't even know you exist. Why do you want to go and do that, son?"

"Sooner or later, everybody's gonna have to serve one way or another. I thought I'd get a jump on it while I can still choose which branch of the military I want."

Mac looked at Bud with frightened eyes. "You gonna desert me too?"

"I doubt they'd want me. I'm a little too old and I probably couldn't pass the physical. So I guess you're stuck with me, old man."

Mac looked at Jack and spat out his words. "You're gonna get yourself killed. You know that, don't you?"

Jack recognized the fear underlying Mac's anger. The old man really cared about him. He slipped his arm around Mac's sagging shoulders and hugged him close. "I'll be fine. You taught me how to be a survivor, didn't you? I'm too tough for any damned Jap or Nazi to get me."

"I hope so, son. I truly hope so."

Mac's trembling voice haunted Jack until he stopped at the end of the field. He turned back for one last glimpse of the two men who were like father and brother to him. Bud waved while Mac wiped his eyes with a bandana. Jack wondered how many families would go through the same motions and how many would experience tragedy before this war was over. He thought about Mac's words. Mac could be right. He might be making the biggest mistake of his life.

Chapter 36

Liz scanned the restaurant's small crowded dining room. Candles glowed in silver and glass hurricanes surrounded by fresh flowers. Starched linens covered the tables. Expensive art covered the walls. Everything he had promised save for one item. No Hugh. Irritated, she prepared herself to wait at the bar until he deigned to show up. She had begun to think he was different, however it seemed he might be just like all men—fickle and unreliable.

That was unfair and she knew it. It wasn't like Hugh to be derelict. She was already ten minutes late herself. Of course, she had an excuse. Finding this place had been a trick, especially in the dark. She should have taken him up on his offer to drive her here, but she hadn't wanted to make tonight seem like a date. Another misstep on the untraveled road of their non-relationship.

She was firmly convinced that she didn't want another lover so soon after Jonathan, yet she felt irrationally upset when Hugh hadn't been waiting for her. And irritation wasn't the only emotion that she identified curling through her. She found she was more than a little disappointed. It dawned on her that what she felt driving here was suspiciously like excitement at the thought of seeing him away from work. Lord, why did life have to be so damned complicated?

The hostess arrived and asked if Liz had a reservation, otherwise the wait might run up to an hour and a half. When Liz gave Hugh's name, the girl smiled and led Liz all the way to the back and through the kitchen service door.

"You must be a special lady. Hugh rarely begs the chef's table."

"Chef's table?" Surprise supplanted irritation and disappointment.

"Oh, didn't he tell you? Chef Tim only cooks like this for really good friends and only when they're trying to impress someone important."

Hugh smiled ruefully from behind a beautifully set table for two placed inside a glass walled alcove. "Thank you, Jeannie, for being the town crier as usual."

The girl laughed. "Nothing I said is untrue and you know it. Enjoy your dinner. Tim's been tweaking the menu since noon."

Liz sat in the chair Hugh pulled out for her. Sterling silver flatware, fine china, and etched crystal created an elegant table. "True or not, I'm very impressed. The reviews of this place are amazing. How do you know the chef?"

"Nothing terribly unique. We've been best friends since second grade. He'll be serving us himself so you'll get to meet him."

Liz felt a presence at her elbow. Looking up, she saw a short, husky guy with a boyish face that was cute in a "let me pinch your cheeks" way rather than handsome. He wore a tall toque and a chef's jacket embroidered with Chef Timothy.

"Welcome to The Alachua Grill, Liz. I've made Hugh's favorites tonight. I hope you'll love them as well." He turned to Hugh with a huge grin. "I'm still working on what I want in return. Maybe you could think of something, Liz? Hugh sure does seem to value your opinion."

"Thank you, Tim. I'm sure you'll think of something."

Tim bowed slightly from the waist and returned to his kitchen.

The tops of Hugh's ears flamed red. He raised his eyebrows and wiggled them.

A crooked smiled played across his lips as he said, "Restaurant people have strange senses of humor. I hope you won't let those little displays keep you from enjoying a good meal. Tim could make it as a chef anywhere. He's really fantastic."

Liz fought the urge to reach across the table and take his hand as she would a close friend who was embarrassed or upset. "Like I said. I'm truly impressed. Tim seems like a great guy. And I like his sense of humor. What keeps him in Gainesville?"

Over the chef's own take on traditional Southern dishes, Hugh became more animated than Liz had ever seen him. When Tim brought a third chair and joined them for the main course, the serious academician disappeared altogether replaced by an easygoing, laughing, and seemingly younger version of himself.

She decided this was what Hugh must have been like before all the pressures at work, before the gut wrenching divorce. Charming, exuberant, and boyishly handsome—hardly words she would have used to describe him in the past.

She rested her chin on her fist and tilted her head, amused as the two guys regaled her with wild tales of a childhood spent running barefoot through the forests and swimming in cold, clear spring fed rivers. It was really quite endearing to watch the interplay between them. Reptiles of all varieties figured large in the telling as well. It sounded like every boy's dream.

As the candle's flame lowered, Hugh seemed to transform before her eyes. Maybe it was the wine, maybe it was the excellent food, or maybe it was Liz herself. Whatever the reason, she felt that she was seeing him for the first time and she liked what she saw.

Tim cleared the dessert plates and opened a new wine selection. "This has been fun, but I've got kitchen cleanup to supervise and I know y'all have business to take care of. Stay 'til closing if you want to. I'll leave the bottle. You can serve yourselves."

When the chef left, Liz leaned toward Hugh and smiled. "That was everything you promised and more. Thank you for the best meal I think I've ever had. The company and conversation weren't bad either."

"Yeah, Tim really outdid himself tonight. I'm glad you've had a good time."

"Well, I really did."

Hugh's expression shifted as he leaned down beside his chair. Liz's spirits sank. The casual mood was broken and she feared the awkwardness between them might be rearing its head again.

"Well, I guess we've put off business long enough." Hugh placed her folder containing the proposals on the table.

Hoping to resuscitate the easy companionship, Liz tried to keep it light. "Well, don't keep me in suspense. What do you think? Will they work?"

"They're really quite good. I've made one or two notes that you can look over later. Nothing drastic."

"Thank you. I'm so glad you're pleased." For the life of her, Liz couldn't think of anything else to say. Maybe it was too much food and wine or maybe Hugh left her tongue-tied like a silly schoolgirl with a growing crush on her teacher.

"How's the research going?"

Grateful for the question, Liz replied, "I found the hotel registers in the Blanche's store room. The manager in 1930 was a man named Albert Menzies and there was a maid named Margaret Blevins who apparently lived at the hotel. I followed Albert to his obit. He died in his bed an old man. His daughters and grandchildren have disappeared from the county, so he's a dead end. The girl disappeared from all records around August of 1930. It's really weird too because a deputy disappeared at the same time. I'm wondering if there's a connection." Had she babbled? She hoped not. She was fixated on her research, but it could be that Hugh was simply being polite.

Relief curled through her when he made a bridge of his fingers and placed his chin on his thumbs. Liz had come to recognize this as a signal that one had his full attention and interest. "With all of the violence during that summer, it's a good bet. Do you have any other leads?"

Liz thought she detected a rewarding note of excitement in his voice. "Actually I do. You remember my telling you about the old lady at the café? Ethel?"

Hugh nodded.

"At first she was so eager to talk about county history and then she just shut down completely."

"Yes. You thought it really odd at the time."

"Well, this is the strangest of all. When I went back to the courthouse one more time to see if there was anything I'd missed, I asked for the sheriff department box again. I was bemoaning all the dead ends I'd run up against and the records clerk asked which sheriff I was interested in. When I said Ike Darnell, she asked if I'd talked to Ethel. It turns out Ethel is Sheriff Ike's granddaughter. Odd that Ethel failed to mention that little tidbit, don't you think?"

"Given how you've described her, yes I do. It seems there might be something about her grandfather she's ashamed of."

"Maybe it's that he didn't do anything to stop the violence?"

Hugh was quiet for a moment. "Perhaps, but I'm betting there's something more. An ancestor's incompetence or negligence rarely causes the kind of abrupt change you've described. I'd bet my next paycheck that Ethel has a darker secret. I take it you haven't talked to her about this?"

"No. I missed her last time. It was her day off, so I'm going up again. Probably the last Thursday of the month. I can't get free 'til then." She could have been mistaken, but Liz thought Hugh looked a little deflated, a shade disappointed even. Or it could be her overactive imagination at work.

"Will you be staying the whole weekend?"

"I really haven't decided. I guess it depends on what I find."

Hugh inhaled, but remained quiet. He looked into her eyes and reached across the table. His grip was warm and firm as he wrapped his fingers around hers.

"Liz, do you think you could come back by that Sunday afternoon? I have tickets for the symphony. It's an all Russian concert including Borodin. I remembered you humming along with his *Polovtsian Dances* when we were coming back from the first trip to Cross Creek. You know, the "Strangers in the Night" melody? I thought you might like to go."

At the mention of the song Jonathan once sang to her, emotion rose, but not the kind she might once have expected. Instead of a knife to the heart, pleasure that Hugh noticed and remembered such small details warmed her.

He really was a great guy. He was all of the things that any sane woman would want: kind, considerate, thoughtful, not self-centered. For the second time, Liz wondered why she'd wasted so much time on men who possessed none of those qualities.

Like Capone and Jonathan. The thought simply popped into her head, fanciful and unbidden.

But the comparison really wasn't so absurd when she thought about it. Capone and Jonathan hadn't cared who was hurt as long as their own desires were met. She titled her head as she gazed at Hugh across the candlelight. It was as though she was seeing him clearly for the first time, like a veil had been stripped from her eyes.

"I would love to go with you. I'll make a point of being back in plenty of time."

"In time for dinner before the concert?"

"It's a date, but my treat. I'm not Chef Tim, but I can stir up a pretty mean frozen lasagna. What do you say? Dinner at my place?"

Hugh's eyes lit up. "That would be terrific. And Liz, I really think you're on to something important and unique. Capone has been done to death, but not nearly enough has been written about the innocents who suffered through that period. You have a chance to tell their story through Zeke. I know you're going to find him. I can feel it in my bones."

Gentle warmth coursed through Liz, bringing a smile to her lips. Hugh used the exact words she whispered to herself the day she discovered that the deputy had gone missing.

Chapter 37

The last thing Jack remembered was a thud followed by a deafening roar. When he came to, he was flat on his back. As he sat up, a grimace spread across his face. His ears rang and he could taste blood trickling at the corner of his mouth. When the shuddering and screaming of falling metal eased, smoke and gas crept through the fire rooms deep in the bowels of the *USS Yorktown*.

Jack knew there was no time to waste. He grabbed a pipe running along the wall and hoisted himself to his feet. Dizziness sent him falling backward against the wall. Breathing deeply usually helped a swimming head, but now all he drew was smoke and gas. As a coughing fit took hold, he leaned over and put his hands on his knees. His head pounded in rhythm with the blood banging against his eardrums. He reached up and felt the place that burned. When he looked at his fingers, they were smeared red. He probably needed to report to sickbay, but there wasn't time to give in to pain or injury as long as he could walk.

Biting his lower lip for distraction, he dug in his hip pocket and dragged out a handkerchief that he tied over his mouth and nose. Picking his way through smoldering debris, he moved from boiler to boiler assessing the damage.

The engineering officer's grime streaked face greeted him at the door near boiler six.

"How bad is it, Petty Officer?"

Jack squinted through the circling smoke. "Boilers two and three are completely disabled. Fires are extinguished under two through six."

"Shit. What about one?"

"Still operational, but only on two burners. The men are working on it. How are things up top?"

"We'll know more when the damage to the uptakes has been assessed. Meanwhile, you and your crew do what you can to keep power coming."

Jack made his way back to boiler one. "Any luck?"

A sailor, face blackened with soot, looked up and frowned. "We got the throttle closed. Pressures up to 180 pounds, but I'm not sure how long it's going to hold."

"Who worked on the throttle?"

The sailor grinned broadly. "You know me, Jack, I don't leave the important stuff to the children."

Jack laughed and play punched the man's shoulder. They were considered the old men. They both had seven months experience on the eighteen and nineteen year olds who had come aboard recently.

"That should be enough to keep the auxiliaries going. Good job."

Unlike some non-coms, Jack thought it was important to acknowledge the work of men who put their lives in danger on a daily basis. Whether you worked on the flight deck or far below in the engine rooms, an aircraft carrier was one of the most dangerous places in the world.

He also knew the value of laboring along side them. Just because he had risen through the enlisted ranks at lightning speed didn't mean he'd forgotten what it felt like to be on the bottom rung of the ladder. Picking up a wrench, he went to see what could be done to get number four back on line.

An hour and a half of sweat and bone crushing work later, they were underway again at a speed of about twenty knots. Jack ran a rag over his face and sat down on a crate just outside fire room one. Although fires created by exploding Japanese bombs were under control, the air was still acrid with smoke and fumes that had no place to go. The overworked ventilation system kept ahead of the point where life was no longer possible, but just barely. Men coughed, sweated, and groaned as they went about keeping the power churning.

When this battle was over, Jack prayed that they would still be intact enough to limp back to Pearl for repairs. He took comfort from knowing they had recently refueled at Midway Island. At least the fighters could take off from the flight deck and give the Japs a taste of their own medicine.

Reports coming down to the engine room said that an air battle was well underway. Jack wondered how many American planes were in the air. Other carriers were taking part in the action, so chances were pretty good that the sides were equally matched. He prayed that enough American planes were up there to turn back the torpedo planes every sailor knew were part of the Japanese flotilla.

At about 1600 hours, Jack put his wrench down and cocked his head with an ear turned upward toward the decks above. Straining to hear over the roar of the number one boiler, he frowned at the soft thudding making its way down to the engine rooms. Up top, the *Yorktown*'s guns were booming away. It could only mean one thing. Enemy planes had gotten past the American fighters. He shouted to the men and they increased their already feverish pace. It would be fatal for the carrier to lose power now.

Without warning, Jack felt the floor shift from under his feet. Stumbling, he leaned against the wall to maintain his balance only to be tossed in the other direction. Evasive action to avoid torpedoes launched by Jap planes? Probably. He turned back to his work. When twenty minutes passed without further crisis, Jack breathed a sigh of relief. It was beginning to look like they had made it through the worst.

Without warning, the *Yorktown* convulsed heavily and

another deafening roar tore through the areas below decks followed by eerie silence. The gigantic screw that propelled the carrier through the water had stopped. They were dead in the water and rapidly listing to port. Jack peered around the pitch-black boiler room as rising water lapped around his ankles.

Chapter 38

Liz pushed on the front door of the 7 Lakes Café in some trepidation. She had waited until after the noon rush in the hope of finding Ethel with fewer customers. Looking around the dining area, she saw that her plan had worked. Only one other customer perused a menu. Liz chose a table on the opposite wall, as far away from the elderly man as possible. At best, she knew Ethel would be reluctant to talk. Having an audience would make everything more difficult.

As Liz sat down, the old gentleman looked her way and nodded politely. His deeply lined ebony face held kind eyes. His ramrod straight back suggested gentle dignity. He must have once been heavier because his shirt collar and tie stood out from his neck and his suit coat drooped at the shoulders. Liz smiled and returned his greeting. Liz decided she liked the old social customs of the South. People were friendlier, more hospitable than in other parts of the country, especially among the older generation.

Dampness formed in Liz's palms. Surprising considering it was late January, but then they were having an unusually warm winter. She wiped her hands with the napkin she unrolled from around the flatware on the table. Since the room was comfortably cool, Liz chalked up her sweaty palms to nerves. She was so close to the end of her journey that she could taste victory.

With no sound from the kitchen and no Ethel in sight, Liz began to wonder if the employees had taken the afternoon off and had forgotten to lock the front door. She was on the verge of asking the old gentleman if anybody was around when the kitchen service door swung open and Ethel bustled through carrying a cup of coffee.

"Sorry that took so long, Mr. Taylor. Cook forgot to put the pot on after the noon rush. Now what will you have?"

At the name Taylor, Liz's head snapped around as though yanked by a leash. She stared, taking in every inch, every feature of the man. It was clear that he was quite elderly, but was he old enough? Zeke Taylor must have been born around 1919 since he was eleven in 1930. Doing a quick calculation, Zeke, if he was still alive, would be ninety-two. This Mr. Taylor could be anywhere from eighty to one hundred. There was no real way to know without asking.

Ethel scribbled the old man's order on her pad and turned toward the kitchen. On her way to pass-through, she spoke to Liz without really looking at her.

"Be with you in a sec, Hon."

Liz looked from the old man to Ethel and back wondering if it could all really be this simple. A voice at her elbow made her jump.

"Oh, it's you. Do you want to see a menu or do you want one of those salads like you've had before?"

"Hello, Ethel. I was hoping to buy us both some pecan pie and coffee."

"I don't go on break for another hour."

"You aren't very busy and I promise not to take up too much of your time." The whine in her own voice disturbed Liz, but she was beginning to feel desperate. She was too close now to let go.

Ethel sighed heavily and said, "Okay. I guess I can spare you a minute or two. I got to get Mr. Taylor's order first."

In another five minutes, Ethel sat across from Liz. "Our pie and coffee are the best in town, but I'm suspecting you've got another reason for coming in today. You ain't been here since way back in the fall."

Liz felt the red creeping up from her throat onto her

cheeks. "I'm afraid you're right. I'm hoping you can tell me a little more about the past."

"And just what is it you want to know?"

Liz hadn't expected the conversation to move so quickly, but now that they were into it, she couldn't very well prevaricate. "I don't want you to think that I've been prying into your background or anything. I came across the information purely by accident."

"And what information would that be?"

"I know that you are Sheriff Ike Darnell's granddaughter. I can't help wondering why you didn't mention it before."

"Why should I? He died before I was born. I never knew him."

"I guess because you seemed so eager to talk about town history. People are usually ready to tell stories about family who were prominent members of the community."

"Well, I don't know no stories. He was sheriff for a while and then he moved on to other things. That's all I know. Now, if you'll excuse me, I got to get back to work."

Ethel rose from the table so abruptly that the motion shoved it against Liz's midsection. Ethel fled to the kitchen and didn't reappear.

So much for getting information from her. Liz's spirits plummeted. She had held out such hope for winning Ethel over again. Movement from across the room attracted Liz's attention. Mr. Taylor rose from his chair and placed money on the table. Clearly he was leaving. Liz opened her wallet and extracted a ten, the only bill she had. She tossed it on the table and scurried after Mr. Taylor's retreating form.

She caught up with him at the corner where he waited for the light to change.

"Excuse me, sir. Please forgive my rudeness, but could I ask you a question?"

Mr. Taylor turned and looked at Liz with the same mild expression she had seen in the restaurant. "I'm not sure that

I can answer it, but I'm happy to try. What is it you need?"

"This may sound strange, but I'm looking for an Ezekiel Taylor who would be about your age. By any chance are you he?"

The old man smiled. "No, I'm sorry to say that I'm not. My first name is Jasper." Liz must have looked terribly crestfallen, because he continued, "If you told me a little about him, maybe I could help you. There are several Taylor families of color in the county."

Liz told him what she knew about Zeke and his grandfather. When she finished, Mr. Taylor said, "Yes, those were terrible times. I didn't know the family you're speaking of, but I do know someone who might be able to help you."

With written directions on the seat beside her, Liz headed south out of town along old US 441. After about twenty-five minutes, she turned off the paved road onto a sandy lane. A tunnel of live oak canopies arched together over the road. Spanish moss dripped from the limbs and sword ferns grew in the crevasses formed where branches joined the massive trunks.

At the end of the lane, she stopped beside a white picket fence surrounding a white cottage with Charleston green shutters at the windows. In the center of the fence an arbor welcomed visitors. A climbing rose covered the arbor and graced all who passed underneath with a rich fragrance. Liz didn't know much about roses, but she thought it was surely unusual for a rose to be blooming at this time of year. She walked to the front door and knocked.

A youngish man in clerical collar, gray shirt, and black trousers answered her knock.

"Reverend Jackson?"

"Yes. How may I help you?"

"I'm hoping that you can tell me where I can locate someone who once lived quite nearby, I believe."

"Why don't you come in and tell me who you want to find."

In an effort at casual conversation, Liz commented, "That's a beautiful rose growing over your arbor gate. It must be a special variety to bloom at this time of year. Do you know its name?"

Rev. Jackson smiled and answered, "No, nobody knows anything about it except that my grandmother dug it up from a neighbor's place after their house burned to the ground. It was the strangest thing. The whole house and everything for yards around it was nothing but ash, but that rose's root was still alive. Grandma planted a cutting out there and at the neighbor's grave. It's bloomed its heart out ever since. Just let the temperature get above seventy and out it pops with buds. But roses aren't really what you came to discuss, are they?"

As Liz told him whom she sought and why, a surprised smile spread over Rev. Jackson's face. "Now that's a coincidence. The rose over the gate is from the Taylor place. Old Isaiah was a deacon in my grandfather's church, now my church, for most of his life. I know Grandpa missed him terribly after he was killed. Of course, I wasn't born until long after all of that happened."

"So you never met Isaiah's grandson, Zeke?"

"No. I've heard the name from my grandfather, of course, but I really know very little about him. Kids being what they are, I didn't pay as much attention to the old stories as I now wish I had."

Liz felt like she was in a deep cave and her candle had just been blown out. "Oh, no. I had such high hopes that you might know where I can find him or what happened to him."

"Well, I can't help, but I know someone who might be able to." Rev. Jackson wrote down a name and address. "It's not far. Just go back to 441 and turn south. You can't miss it. I'll call and let him know you're coming."

Chapter 39

After all of the months of searching and frustration, it had come down to this—an old man rocking on his front porch with a fat beagle snoozing at his feet. Liz watched the pair from the relative anonymity of her front seat, alternating between elation at the prospect of having her questions finally answered and the gnawing fear that this too would be a dead end.

The old man squinted expectantly in her direction, but didn't in any other way acknowledge the presence of an unfamiliar car in his driveway. The beagle, whose white muzzle indicated that in dog years he was nearly as old as his master, raised his head momentarily and then dropped back into his dreams, nose wiggling, soft yipping, paws paddling after some enemy that only he could see. The old man reached down and patted his companion, soothing him into more peaceful dreams. They made a good couple.

Liz couldn't decide if she wanted to get out of the car or not. It felt strange to think that her search might soon be at an end. Like many historians, she enjoyed the chase as much as she did knowing the answers.

The old man began to struggle up from his chair, so Liz jerked her door open and called, "Hello. Please don't get up. I think we have an appointment."

When she stood before him on the porch, the old man said, "We do, if you're the young lady who's asking about the time Al Capone stayed at the Blanche Hotel."

Liz smiled and nodded.

"And you're looking for Zeke Taylor."

"Yes I am, Mr. Blevins."

"Jack."

"I beg your pardon?"

"Jack or Master Chief. Mr. Blevins was my father. Why don't you sit down and tell me what you want to know."

The girl sitting opposite Jack couldn't be more than thirty, give or take a year or three. Too pretty and too young to be a university professor, but that's what Preacher Jackson's grandson said she was.

"I really hope you can tell me what happened to Zeke after his grandfather died. I'm gathering information about the summer of 1930 and what happened here."

"My goodness, that was all so long ago. Why would a young person like you be interested?"

"It's my job, Master Chief. I teach history and American crime is my special area of interest."

"I hope you don't mind me saying this, but it seems like a strange interest for a young girl."

She laughed and replied, "That's exactly what my own grandfather said. And thank you for calling me a girl, but I'm afraid I'm a lot older than that."

"So you really do want to talk about that time?"

"I do and I'd be very grateful for anything you're willing to tell me. When I read about Ezekiel and Isaiah Taylor, it touched me in a way that's hard to describe. The newspaper article wasn't more than a few lines. I guess reading between those lines was what really grabbed me. You see, I believe that Zeke must have watched his grandfather being lynched and either ran away or was killed as well. Reverend Jackson seemed to think that you might know the answer. I'm deeply committed to telling that child's story. He was surely the most innocent of all the victims."

Jack shifted his position to take the pressure off his arthritic hip and thought about what the girl was asking. It had been so long since he had spoken of that horrible summer. He didn't know if it would be a relief to finally talk about it or like tearing the scab off a wound. Probably both, but this girl seemed honest about wanting to do some good for Zeke. Jack knew it was long overdue. He looked at the girl for a few seconds and made up his mind.

"Zeke was my best friend. Did you know that?"

The girl shook her head. "No, I have very little information other than what happened to his grandfather. Do you know anything about that?"

Jack harrumphed. "Know about it! Young lady, I was there. Saw it all and hid Zeke at Preacher Jackson's until my brother-in-law could get him out of the state. Of course, he wasn't my brother-in-law until after they all got to Atlanta."

"Master Chief, I'm afraid you're losing me. Would you mind starting from the beginning?"

"Sorry. The story is so much a part of me that I guess I think everybody knows it."

Jack explained how he had gone to see Zeke that night. He told about them hiding in the woods and watching the lynching. He explained why he had taken Zeke to Preacher Jackson's and why he left Zeke there. Jack talked about riding the rails and joining the navy. Then he ran out of steam. Talking about the rest hurt too much.

"But where was Zeke all that time?"

"Maybe I should let you read Meg's letters."

"Meg? Would that be short for Margaret?"

"It is."

"Was she the Margaret Blevins who worked at the Blanche Hotel?"

"Yep. That's the one. She was my older sister. Thought you'd have figured that out by now. Wait here on the porch. I'll be back directly. Got some things you might like to see."

He struggled from his chair and went into the house, leaving the girl on the porch. It was a beautiful, warm day and he had no intention of being inside. He pulled junk from his desk drawer until he found a small packet of dog-eared envelopes tied up by a grubby old string. Loosening the string, he flipped through the stack withdrawing two of Meg's letters. He hesitated, and then took one from his mother as well. Back outside, he handed the envelopes to the girl.

"Go ahead. Read them. They tell the rest of the story much better than I can. Meg was there for most of it."

June, 1931

Dearest Jack,

It was so good to finally hear from you. Mama and I have been near out of our minds with worry. It sounds like Mac and Bud are good men who can be trusted. I feel a lot better knowing you have older companions to look out for you.

Mama sent me your letter to her. If you wrote to me, I'll probably never get it. I'm not at the hotel anymore. In fact, I'm not in Lake City anymore either. You may have noticed the return address on the envelope. It is Big Cypress down in the Everglades.

DeWitt and I are married and living with his mother's people until it's safe for us to return home. Of course, you don't know what happened after you left. DeWitt discovered that the KKK was after Zeke, him, and me. If he hadn't gotten us out of the state, I think we would not be alive today. Even though they chased us as we were trying to leave, DeWitt managed to force their car into a ditch even though they were shooting at us. I can't begin to describe how scared Zeke and I were.

After that, though, everything was smooth sailing. We took Zeke to his great-aunt in Atlanta. And then DeWitt went to the FBI. They were very interested in what he had to say about Sheriff Darnell, I can tell you. He is under investigation for moonshining as I write this. We don't know how long it will take for them to make their case, though.

Write to me soon at the address on the envelope.

All my love,

Meg

November 30, 1933

Dear Son,

I have some interesting news for you. You will remember that I wrote you last year when Sheriff Darnell and the Klansman named Carlton Smith were convicted on moonshining and racketeering charges. Well, they have been stabbed to death at the state pen. DeWitt says that he believes Capone's connections here in Florida arranged the deed. For myself, I always found it hard to believe that a sworn peace officer was involved in such, but then people will do many bad things in the name of filthy lucre. And I trust what DeWitt says. It's truly ironic that Prohibition will end in six days.

Your sister has news of her own, which I will not divulge. I don't want to ruin her surprise for you, but I must say that I am thrilled. Your father is less so, but I have learned not to let him and his foolish ideas influence me. He stays home and underfoot most of the time these days. Hardly ever leaves the farm now except to go to church and to the feed store. In some ways he is a changed man.

The girl only skimmed through the remainder of his mother's letter. Just as well, since it contained nothing of interest to anyone but him. She laid the letters in her lap and looked up.

"I get the impression that your sister may have been pregnant in 1933."

Jack laughed. "In 1933, 1934, 1935, and 1936. And again in 1938. Two nieces and three nephews. All lived to adulthood and have grandchildren of their own."

"How did you come to live here in High Springs?"

"I spent my life seeing the world courtesy of the United States Navy. When my father died, I inherited the farm, but I couldn't stand the thought of owning it. You see, my father and I didn't get along. Hell, fact is, I hated him for the mean, hardhearted SOB that he was. So I sold the farm to the state and split the money with my sister.

"When I retired, I bought this house with some of my share and put the rest in municipal bonds. Florida is the only real home I've ever had, so living here makes sense. My sister's family is mostly still here too. High Springs suits me."

"You talk like your sister and brother-in-law came back here to live as well."

"Oh, yes they came back in 1934. DeWitt ran for Columbia County sheriff. He won and kept winning until he retired. He ran on a promise to clean up the county so descent folks could have a safe place to raise their families. He kept that promise, too."

"He must have been so different from Sheriff Darnell. How did he manage to win when the other sheriff had been so crooked and yet kept being elected?"

Jack rubbed his chin and drew in a long breath. "You know, I've always believed that most people will do what's right, if they know what right is. The descent people in the county, and that was most of the people, didn't know what Darnell was up to. And they were too afraid of the Klan to cross them once people started being killed.

"The good people were willing to look the other way as long as it was just local folks breaking the law trying to make an extra dollar during a terrible depression, but they drew the line at organized crime. Ike's jury was out for only about twenty minutes before they brought back a guilty verdict."

"Did the FBI prove that Capone's organization was involved?"

"No, but it didn't matter. They had enough on Ike that he got a long sentence. Some say he was going to turn state's evidence against Capone and that's why he was killed. That's certainly what DeWitt thought."

"And what about Zeke?"

"Read that last letter. It'll tell you what happened to him."

Oct. 29, 1944

Dearest Jack,

I pray that this letter finds you safe and well. DeWitt, the children, and I are all well and send you our love. I am heart broken at the news that I must tell you, but there is nothing for it. You must be told. Mama has died of pneumonia. You know her health has been going down for a couple of years now and she just couldn't fight off this last illness. The church was full to overflowing last Sunday afternoon when we had her service. I have enclosed a snap of the flowers. Can you believe how many there were? Mama would have been so pleased. She loved flowers so much.

I'm afraid that isn't all of the bad news. You may have wondered why you haven't had a letter from Zeke Taylor in a while. I am so sad to tell you that he has been killed in Italy. His infantry unit came under heavy fire. His wife wrote that he was buried over there. She doesn't even know exactly where. His commanding officer wrote that he died a hero saving other men in his unit from sniper fire.

That's all for now. Please take comfort in knowing that both Mama and Zeke passed quickly and without pain. They are in a better place now. Stay safe and write when you can.

All our love,

Meg

The girl looked up at Jack with sad eyes. "Did you ever see him after the night of the lynching?"

"No, I never did."

"But you wrote to each other?"

"Yeah, all those years. Meg kept up with Zeke and his people in Atlanta and she sent me his address. I always thought we'd get together once we were grown men, but it never happened. California and Georgia were a lot farther apart in those days. Not like now when you can get on a plane and be there in three hours."

"These letters certainly explain a lot. Thank you so much for letting me read them."

"Glad somebody's interested after all these years. Preacher's grandson said you're gonna write about that time. Do you think you'll include Zeke?"

"Absolutely. In fact, he'll be one of the most important people I write about."

"That's good. He'd have liked that. He loved attention, you see. I always thought it was because he didn't have any folks. He was the sweetest little boy. He deserved so much better than he got."

"Was he happy in Atlanta?"

"I guess he was as happy as any child who'd lost every one of his close family. There were some cousins he liked to play with and the folks up there were good to him, but it could never be the same. After I heard about his death, I liked to think that he was finally home with his parents and his grandfather. I don't know. Maybe you're not religious, but it helped me get through it."

Jack noticed the girl's eyes grow unnaturally bright. She didn't say anything for a little while.

When the moment passed, she asked softly, "One thing I haven't been able to find out is if anyone was ever arrested for the lynchings. Do you know?"

Jack fairly gasped. The girl's question was a knife straight to his heart. He lowered his gaze and dropped a hand onto his slumbering beagle's head. The long ears, warm and silky, looked like molten gold as they passed through his fingers. It was a habit that soothed a troubled soul.

As much as they hated their father, he and Meg swore long ago to take the secret of his part in killing Mr. Taylor to their graves. They were determined to shield their mother regardless of the cost to justice. Telling what their father had done wouldn't bring Isaiah back from the dead or Zeke back home, and the truth would have killed their mother.

About a year after Atlanta, DeWitt wrote and begged Jack to return to Florida to make a statement, but Jack refused. He didn't know, never asked, if Meg told DeWitt the full story of their father's involvement. She could have done so after the old man and their mother were dead, when it was too late to hurt anybody.

Jack and Meg never talked about it, not after DeWitt passed away, not when Meg lay dying of congestive heart failure. They kept their secret for seventy years. DeWitt surely suspected, but he couldn't prove anything. And now the newest generation, Meg and DeWitt's great-grandchildren, would know only good things about the great-great-grandparents who died long ago in a time so different from their own.

What good was truth when it was too late to serve justice? Raising a hand to his eyes, Jack rubbed them as much to stop the tears as to relieve itching brought on by the drying effects of old age.

"Sad to say nobody ever paid for all those killings. I know he tried hard, but DeWitt could never get any of the

Klansmen to rat on the others."

Liz decided that the old man looked tired. It must have taken a lot out of him to relive the past as he had this afternoon. She gathered up her notes and rose from her chair. "Master Chief, thank you so much. You've been a tremendous help. I'm going to go now, but could I come again? I have a feeling that you have a lot more to tell me."

"I don't know what, but you're welcome anytime, young lady."

And so now she had her answer, maybe incomplete, but with enough substance to support a theory of the lynchings and to write the article about them. Although she was still unable to prove Capone's connection to the summer of violence in 1930, she had a fair idea that one day she would do so.

It made her blood boil to think of the suffering that Capone had inflicted on an innocent child through his never-ending quest for ill-gotten gains. And while she didn't condone murder, she couldn't help but feel some satisfaction at the grisly end that Sheriff Darnell and Carlton Smith met.

How she could ever have found such evil glamorous was now a mystery. When she thought about herself before Zeke, it was like looking back at a stranger, one of whom she wasn't sure she approved. Desperately pursuing bad boys as romantic partners and glamorizing the historical ones to the point of making them her professional passion were the actions of a very naïve and silly girl.

Experience is a mighty teacher. It had taught her the meaning of real love and the importance of seeing history through the eyes of the ordinary people who had lived it and suffered because of it. Perhaps most importantly, she had come to understand that history happens to all who live, not just the mighty and powerful. If she expanded her scope, a book wasn't out of the question. It would take months, maybe years, of additional research, but she was excited about what she believed she would someday have.

As soon as she was in her car, her hand scrambled in her purse for her cell phone. She waited impatiently while the number rang. She couldn't wait to tell Hugh.

A small smile played across Liz's lips.

Hugh. His bookishly handsome face floated before her mind's eye. He was the first person she wanted to tell what was happening in her work and in her life. After the dinner with Chef Tim, their relationship had taken a decidedly personal turn. Emotions that had never before been associated with her romantic relationships stirred and bubbled to the surface—contentment, tranquility, confidence.

Her need for the thrill that came with loving bad boys had vanished completely and it felt wonderful, like when she was a little girl and realized she was no longer afraid of the dark.

Her heart skipped a beat when Hugh's mellow baritone said, "Hello, Dr. Reams. Have I told you today that I love you?"

Biography

I have been in love with the past for as long as I can remember.

Anything with a history, whether shabby or majestic, recent or ancient, instantly draws me in. I suppose it comes from being part of a large extended family that spanned several generations. Long summer afternoons on my grandmother's porch or winter evenings gathered around her fireplace were filled with stories both entertaining and poignant. Of course being set in the South, those stories were also peopled by some very interesting characters, some of whom have found their way into my work.

As for my venture in writing, it has allowed me to reinvent myself. We humans are truly multifaceted creatures, but unfortunately we tend to sort and categorize each other into neat, easily understood packages that rarely reveal the whole person. Perhaps you, too, want to step out of the box in which you find yourself. I encourage you to look at the possibilities and imagine. Be filled with childlike wonder in your mental wanderings. Envision what might be, not simply what is. Let us never forget, all good fiction begins when someone says to herself or himself, "Let's pretend."

Favorite quote regarding my professional passion: "History is filled with the sound of silken slippers going downstairs and wooden shoes coming up." Voltaire

CPSIA information can be obtained at www.ICGtesting.com
Printed in the USA
LVOW04s1240200915

454936LV00018B/141/P